JAN IRVING

Dreamspinner Press

Published by
Dreamspinner Press
4760 Preston Road
Suite 244-149
Frisco, TX 75034
http://www.dreamspinnerpress.com/

Mask
Copyright © 2009 by Jan Irving

Cover Art by Anne Cain annecain.art@gmail.com
Cover Design by Mara McKennen

ISBN: 978-1-61581-047-5

Printed in the United States of America
First Edition
August, 2009

eBook edition available
eBook ISBN: 978-1-61581-048-2

Mask is dedicated with much appreciation to Carolyn Topol, Mickie B. Ashling, Laurie, Kim, Aschicca, Armandyouidiot, Camjakefan, Nish, Decembergurl, Habemus, Kata, Kitty, Missus Grace, Trintiff, Gabrielle and Lyn.

Perhaps all the dragons in our lives are princesses who are only waiting to see us act, just once, with beauty and courage. Perhaps everything that frightens us is, in its deepest essence, something helpless that wants our love.

—Rainer Maria Rilke

 CHAPTER 1

Obsidian: Let me guess, you got your nickname from a woman?

Moonbeam: How did you…?

Obsidian: I know a lot about you, Moonbeam. You should be more careful what you share about yourself on the 'Net. You're quite naive. But it's a useful quality to someone like me.

Moonbeam: Am not.

Obsidian: Are too.

Moonbeam: Prove it?

Obsidian: My favorite words. :smirk: You're nineteen—I saw you tell Steve a week ago when he wanted to know if you're going to dress up and cavort on Halloween—and you nicely avoided his fishing for a hook up, by the way. Very kind, aren't you? An interesting weakness. You said you were too old and he suggested certain venues where it's fun to wear a mask—year round. You are an art student. You enjoy working with oils, but you dislike water colors because they are… watery. So less control. And you like that, ingénue. You like control.

Moonbeam: So do you…

Obsidian: Of course. So you have to be a blond with your nickname...

Moonbeam: Yes, all right, I am blond.

Obsidian: A cute blond.

The curser blinked and Nick felt perspiration prickle his hairline. It was always like this in the chat room since the aloof and mysterious Obsidian had taken an interest in him, cutting him from the herd of other users.

He didn't know why he had let it happen, because Obsidian was... threatening.

And exciting.

Moonbeam: You said I reveal too much about myself, so maybe I'll leave that one.

Obsidian: Don't be fucking coy. I know you are cute.

Moonbeam: :sigh: I am cute.

Obsidian: I knew it. Your eyes are blue to go with that "moonbeam" hair?

Moonbeam: :squirms: Why this focus on what I look like?

Obsidian: Appearances are extremely important. Don't tell me you slob around in wrinkled cotton. :pained:

Moonbeam: I suppose you're some high-powered businessman who wears designer labels. I am just an ordinary guy. A poor, starving artist.

Obsidian: ...

Moonbeam: Obsidian?

Obsidian: Still here, Moonbeam. Tsk. We were talking about YOU. You also have a boyfriend. I'm not sure if he can't satisfy you sexually or you just haven't let him fuck you yet because I get a strong vibe that you are a virgin, aren't you?

Moonbeam: What? What the fuc-? You DON'T know me. YOU DO NOT.

Obsidian: Stop shouting! Excitable, aren't you? It's 2:22 A.M. If you were MINE, you wouldn't be in some fucking chat room; you'd be lying on a bed, coated with sweat, worn out with my arm lying over your body, pressing you to the bed. MY bed.

Nick heard the key in the lock.

Moonbeam: Right, because you're some kind of legendary lover. You're so infuriating sometimes! I have to go.

Obsidian: Don't.

Moonbeam: Good night.

Moonbeam: Has left the room.

Obsidian: Has left the room.

KAIN reached for a pack of cigarettes, lit one. At least he could still do this, and it wasn't like he could kill himself by smoking anymore. He got up and paced the halls of the big pile of a house he'd purchased on impulse. Mostly dust and wood floors, not decorated as his downtown penthouse had been. Maybe he should get that designer out here.

He shook his head, taking in faded wallpaper and the water stains on the ceiling. She'd probably run from this job.

His house was hopeless and he knew it, but it suited him now.

He picked up his Blackberry and hit a familiar number.

"Blond tonight. Not too tall. Blue eyes. And no talking. You know the drill," he directed his connection.

"We have someone new, Mr. Mitchell," Ernie's voice purred. "Young and he loves to be of service."

"Just be sure to tell him to follow instructions." Kain ended the call.

THE room for his "date" was set up. A bed, lube, condoms... and handcuffs.

"Put them on and face the wall," Kain ordered from the shadows.

"I can barely see anything. It's fucking dark in here!" Weak laughter. The young man looked over one bare shoulder, obviously trying to make out his client.

Kain ignored the curiosity. He needed this, a body under his control, purchased for his very specific needs.

Still burning with mingled resentment and stimulation, Kain sheathed himself and mounted his date from behind as soon as the trick was on the mattress. The metal of the handcuffs gleamed softly in the light from the hallway, clinking gently. Only stars lit the room.

His hired date let out a groan as he was penetrated by Kain's thick cock.

Kain wrapped a hand around his throat, feeling the pulse, the frailty of life.

4

Mask

He let out a long growl of relief. Against blond hair he whispered, "Moonbeam."

 CHAPTER 2

"SO IS your secret admirer on?"

"He's just…." Nick shrugged, tucking some of his silver-blond hair behind one ear, uncomfortable. He spent a lot of time on his own since Miguel spent nights at a Laundromat, but they'd worked that out, deciding that it was… best. Or maybe he'd let Miguel go because he knew it was easier for him. He shifted his feet, feeling the ground between them a little off. He missed him. Missed how they used to be.

Nick knew he was a romantic. He was the one who liked to cook a meal, light some candles, buy the best wine he could afford and spoil his boyfriend. Even though he was lost in his art half the time, talking, touching, making contact, was important to him.

But for the past year whenever he reached out to Miguel, there was nothing solid. Just a feeling of things unsaid.

"Yeah." Miguel lifted Nick's hand, entwining their fingers. His lips parted, the ones Nick had once drawn over and over in a sketchbook, along with his heavily lashed sherry eyes and the springy black hair he'd inherited from his Chilean-American mother. "Seems like you spend a lot of time with this guy online lately. Should I be jealous?"

"He's not real," Nick said pragmatically, reminding himself of that again. And reminding himself that the mysterious Obsidian served a purpose. "So spending time with him is really killing time." He got up from the worn wood of his desk chair and went to settle on Miguel's lap, curling his arms around his boyfriend's sturdy neck. He didn't treat him as delicate or untouchable. He knew that was important from their counseling sessions. Miguel had had a bad relationship with his first boyfriend, who could be violent, and still shied away from Nick because of it. "Just the requisite fantasy, which helps my art, Mr. Darcy in the chat room. Is that all right?"

Miguel scratched his eyebrow. "I'm not sure I like it, you having a fantasy man who is not me."

"He could be you," Nick couldn't keep from saying. He bit his lip a second later, knowing what was coming.

"Nicky, we've been through this before; it's not like I don't want to! I just... I can't."

Nick felt immediate guilt. It was just sex, for Christ's sake! He needed to get over it. Everything else between them was comfortable, so why couldn't he just leave it alone like Miguel asked? "I know. I'm sorry. Really."

"If you know, why do you bring it up all the fucking time?" Miguel glared.

Nick swallowed. "Because we've been together a long time. Because I get scared, I guess," Nick confessed, "that you and I...." Miguel had been his first crush. The first guy he'd kissed. "I barely see you."

He didn't want to admit it, that it hurt sometimes that Miguel spent more time with his musician friends than with his loyal boyfriend. But Miguel was talented and ambitious. They were both just starting out, taking classes, hoping for a break. He understood that. He needed to express himself so fucking badly. Some nights his muse woke him up and he was dabbing oils while half-asleep, rubbing his eyes, sipping cold coffee.

Miguel was the same, often leaving the shower with shampoo bubbles clinging to his half-washed hair so he could scribble some musical notes on a free piece of paper.

"He inspires my art. You know what that's like." Nick knew that Miguel would understand. That was within the boundaries of their unconventional arrangement, which had deteriorated into one of buddies, of being in a comfortable rut. But Nick didn't know how to change it. The more he tried, the more Miguel pulled away, leaving him alone.

"Oh." Miguel shrugged since Nick had plenty of experience sketching male models in school and he had never been jealous of them—until recently. "Well then, I guess he's no threat."

"He can't give me what I need," Nick said honestly. "Because he's just a fantasy so he can never touch me."

Miguel studied him, lips tightening. "Neither can I, remember?"

Obsidian: Moonbeam? Stop fucking lurking.

Moonbeam: What if I am?

Obsidian: Moody. Maybe you should take some evening primrose.

Moonbeam: Is there some reason you are riding me tonight?

Obsidian: Maybe I only wish I was. Are you still there? I was waiting for you for… some time.

Moonbeam: …

Obsidian: I may have been a tad abrasive. I'm… sorry.

Moonbeam: You think?

Obsidian: So tell me more about the boyfriend. Is he tall, dark and handsome? Does he make your heart beat faster and your cock hard?

Moonbeam: As if I'll share more about him with you.

Obsidian: I know you help support him. Must be hard since you barely scrape by.

Moonbeam: How do you know that? I've never talked about that with you.

Obsidian: I may have had you investigated.

Moonbeam:

Obsidian: I was curious. It was not stalking. Not the way I define it anyway.

Moonbeam:

Obsidian: I obtained a picture. You are cute. I like to look at you.

Moonbeam: I'm leaving now!

Obsidian: Don't. Don't do that. Nick—! Moonbeam.

Moonbeam: You admit you— Fuck; I don't even have words...! I just met you online two weeks ago. Okay, we've talked every night, and it's been good for my art, but—

Obsidian: Talked for hours. You've told me things you've never told anyone, haven't you? Not even the boyfriend. And don't tell me the climaxes I've given you have been just for your art.

Moonbeam: How do you know I—? That doesn't give you the right. And can we get off the topic of my boyfriend, please?

Obsidian: You could have been anyone. I needed to know. I wanted to own your face.

Moonbeam: "Own my face?" Obsidian! I'm me. I am not comfortable with a fake persona so I'm just... me.

Obsidian: You drew me and I admit it made me feel a little vulnerable. I'm not accustomed to that. And... I wanted to see what you looked like.

Moonbeam: That is both creepy and—

Obsidian: What?

Moonbeam: Oddly touching.

Obsidian: Don't go. Don't be pissed. You should be flattered. I think of you every night I wrap a hand around my cock. I spill with your name on my lips.

Moonbeam: Shit! Will you behave? Now, I want an even playing field. You tell me about you. Or I leave.

Obsidian: ...

Moonbeam: I fucking knew it! Fine, continue playing the dark mystery man, but I'm leaving.

Obsidian: I was... am thirty-five years old.

Moonbeam: Was? Strange choice of word.

Obsidian: Do you want to hear this or not, you little pest? I have dark brown hair. Green eyes. I'm taller than you— Over six feet.

Moonbeam: Why have you been spending all this time with me? I'm alone a lot at night, working on my paintings, but you...?

Obsidian: ...

Moonbeam: Obsidian? Talk to me.

Obsidian: I have some time on my hands. Just lately. And I live at night.

Moonbeam: To stalk someone?

Obsidian: Very funny. I don't need to do that. I can— I did—

Moonbeam: What?

Obsidian: Nothing. What are you working on?

Mask

Moonbeam: The seascape. I think that I've overcome the problem I had with perspective. And I like that it's set in winter since the clouds are heavy with rain, but drifting fast. It's really wonderful to try to capture that. You know, there were many great landscape artists in the last century who just painted clouds, changing weather patterns. I imagine that sometimes. Everything just stopping long enough so you can paint clouds every day. It was another world.

Obsidian: You were frustrated.

Moonbeam: You told me to go jerk off and then look at it again. :amused:

Obsidian: It worked, didn't it?

Moonbeam: Sex is not the answer to everything.

Obsidian: Says someone not getting what they need.

Moonbeam: About that...!

Obsidian: Yeah, yeah. Your boyfriend is a saint. I take back all the ~~true things you can't handle~~.

Moonbeam: ...

Obsidian: Don't be pissy.

Moonbeam: I did mention "infuriating," right?

Obsidian: I make your heart rate pick up. Admit it.

Moonbeam: Obsidian, I'm poking back. Tell me one true thing about you from the past few days that you would normally not share.

Obsidian: That's unwise.

Moonbeam: Be unwise.

Obsidian: I hired a hustler who looks like you.

Moonbeam: You what!

Obsidian: You asked.

Moonbeam: I have a boyfriend!

Obsidian: So tell me when you jerked off for your "art," you didn't imagine my hand on you, gripping your cock, my voice in your ear, urging you on. Come for me, boy, so fucking beautiful, shoot all over my hand!

Moonbeam: No!

Obsidian: Little liar. We are engaged in real flirtation, Moonbeam. What do you think this is? It's not fucking Victorian pen pals. I'm closer to you. I touch you; put my hands all over you whenever we meet.

Moonbeam: No, this is just fantasy. It has to be fantasy!

Obsidian: Fantasy is a powerful thing. It's where dreams and goals bud.

Moonbeam: I'm signing off!

Obsidian: You'll be back... Right? Probably.

Moonbeam: Has left the room.

Obsidian: That went well.

Obsidian: Has left the room.

OBSIDIAN pressed his hand against the glass of the Pancake House window, looking in.

Nick was working tonight, serving customers, sharing his smile freely.

Mask

His hair really was the color of his nickname, Moonbeam. Soft silver shafts in his eyes, dimples, beautiful pale skin that would feel like silk against the back of Obsidian's hand. Skin that would bruise so easily.

He shifted back and forth down the aisle between tables, talking to customers, sharing his conversation so easily, sharing himself so that Obsidian wished he could lock his Moonbeam away where only he could touch, see, enjoy that smile, that fresh skin, like Hades stealing away Persephone.

He thought of his home, of the vines strangling it, of the quiet so the dull tick of the grandfather clock kept him awake for hours.

It was on an endless night like that one, when he could hear nothing but his own heartbeat, when no one wanted to know him, that he had met Moonbeam in a chat room.

Radiance.

He wanted him under his roof, locked in a room with a big silver key. Watched by Obsidian alone, only for Obsidian's pleasure, so he could spill his desire on him, taste him, his come, maybe steal a droplet of blood. He'd be so careful—

Obsidian watched, hands on the cool glass, on the outside, until a drop of rain spattered his cheek, falling from the awning that circled the storefront. Wiping the wetness from his skin, he was reminded.

He couldn't touch Nick. He couldn't risk hurting him.

Aching, he almost turned away.

OBSIDIAN was so focused on Nick, watching him, that he was oblivious to a man sitting on a shaded park bench across the street, watching him.

His observer folded his newspaper when Obsidian hesitated, then finally headed into the restaurant.

"Feeling a little lonely, are we?" the stranger whispered, satisfied. This would fit very well with the larger game in play.

"YOU'VE been distracted lately." Miguel reached for the syrup when Nick placed a plate of waffles in front of him in Charlie's Pancake House where he worked part-time.

"Just working on a piece." Nick shrugged, rubbing his hands on his apron. Oh shit, the things he'd exchanged with Obsidian! He knew it wasn't real, but he felt a little guilty. How much of what belonged rightfully to Miguel alone had he given away? Worse, *wanted* to give away.

Touch me.

Nick ground his teeth, reining in his feeling. He was using Obsidian, his virile genie in a bottle. He had to stopper him up again and live his life.

"I thought you finished that," Miguel continued, seemingly oblivious to Nick's confusion.

Nick blinked. "You knew I was having trouble?"

Miguel stroked Nick's arm, making a silent apology for his harsh words previously. "Of course. Aren't you just like me? Whenever I can't master something on the cello it puts me in a pissy mood until I get it. Even knowing better, knowing I'm tired or played out, I keep going. But not to play, not to create, would be like living death. You're the same; that's why we belong together."

"Yeah." Nick kissed Miguel, smiling. It would be okay again. They would be okay. They understood each other. He'd push Obsidian aside again. His sexual allure. His… loneliness.

But when he pulled away from Miguel, his gaze collided with the cat-green eyes of a customer. Staring at him. Examining his face, his body.

Slouching in a booth across from Miguel's table, wearing a hat pulled low. Insolent eyes. Eyes that claimed what didn't belong to anyone but Miguel.

Nick's heartbeat picked up and he looked away, flushing.

"Hey, Nick?"

"Sorry." Nick shrugged, self-conscious for some reason. "I promise to give you my full attention tonight!"

"Don't go online," Miguel urged. "I hear from my friends there are a lot of predators in chat rooms and you're pretty open about yourself. Innocent."

"I'm not exactly Little Red Riding Hood." Nick gave his boyfriend an indulgent look. "But tonight... I stay safe."

"Safe." Miguel stabbed some waffle with his fork. "Interesting choice of words, don't you think?"

Feeling eyes on him, Nick glanced again in the direction of the booth and he pulled out his pad, ready to take an order, forcing himself to face that probing gaze again.

But the stranger with the beautiful green eyes was gone.

CHAPTER 3

KAIN MITCHELL lit another cigarette, ignoring the pile in an ashtray by his laptop. Couldn't sleep. Couldn't block out the memories, the pain, the fear at what he'd become.

He rubbed his eyes, which were so sensitive now. Closed them and thought about Nick: the blond hair, the cool skin, the quick smile. Soothing. When was Kain going to bring him closer, under his hand?

He stirred, restless. The nights were for staring at the ceiling, seeing to his abominable need, and occasionally getting quick, nasty relief in an alley or crouched in a shadowy room.

The only thing that provided any light, any ease, were his conversations with Moonbeam.

He stared at the flashing cursor in thei—*the* chat room. Moonbeam hadn't shown for three nights and Kain was restless.

Unstimulated. Needy. He hated that it came down to that.

Rubbing his eyes, he glanced at the book of Greek myths he'd been rereading. No wonder Hades had dragged Persephone into his dark world, if this was how he felt.

"Fine, that the way you want it?" Kain muttered, narrowing his eyes. Kain had been sifting through Nick's life. His employment records. His tuition payments. What he threw out in the fucking trash. Kain's fingerprints were all over Nick's life, like his hand pressed against the cool glass looking into the Pancake House. Looking into Nick's life.

He picked up his phone and speed dialed Cassandra. "A fine arts student named Nick Anders."

"Kain? I do have a personal life, you know." Her normally smooth whiskey voice was burred with annoyance. "It's three-thirty in the goddamned morning! Uh, boss."

But she had worked for him for years, taking a chance on a new guy who had barely unpacked his desk when he had a flash on how to fix the Problem of the Week in a manufacturing firm. She'd been an assistant to a VP, but she'd helped him out and eventually wound up working for him—which had paid off.

"And you're already sleeping? Not very promising. Who is he? Maybe I've had him before."

Cassandra sighed and then, as if knowing better than to argue with him, asked, "Who is this student again?"

Kain spelled out Nick's first and last name, imagining Cassandra shoving back her sleek blond hair and writing on the notepad she kept by the bed. He knew her habits. He'd even slept at her apartment a few nights after the accident, trusting her to keep him safe until he hired Finn and bought his house.

"And what did the unfortunate Mr. Anders do to piss you off?"

"Something," Kain said, frowning at the blinking cursor. "He works at the Pancake House on campus. Get him fired from his job."

"Kain, have a heart! He's just some kid."

"I know what he is." Kain swallowed. "He interests me, Cass." *She couldn't doubt him. Not like the others. Not like himself.*

"You're not yourself. I've been worried about you. You're barely interested in making the board meetings lately."

"I doubt I'll ever be 'myself' again, not after…." He took a deep drag and confessed something he'd only share with someone he'd known a very long time. "Cass, he *touches* me." And no one had. Not in months. Not since the fire.

"Oh, shit. I hate it when you use that husky voice," Cass murmured and Kain knew that if he'd been another kind of man, she'd have allowed herself to love him, maybe. But she was smart enough to remain a good friend.

He smiled now, sensing victory. *Nick. I won't give you a choice.*

"We fund interns at the university sometimes so hire him to work in the library at Telemachus House. That way he won't really be out of work."

"Oh, sure, you're doing him a favor," she agreed wryly. "Are you sure he can *find* the library? Your house is a fucking scary ruin."

NICK paced, arms crossed, chewing on the end of a paintbrush. He had a pan with some almond oil simmering in the kitchen and the scent relaxed him even as it stimulated his senses. To paint, he needed two things: to be alert and to *feel*.

If his work lacked passion, then it was flat canvas coated with blobs of oil paint, but if he could nail it, channel it, bring it up and make it live, then he made something that moved people.

And at this point, it helped a little to pay the rent, as well as give him the grades he needed for his degree.

Finding a touchstone of passion lately wasn't a problem; he'd filled canvas after canvas. His time offline had been fruitful.

Obsidian.... The name teased him and he frowned.

He scrubbed his jaw, thinking that even when he chose to avoid his connection to his mystery man, Obsidian lit him up. His imagination... his fantasies.

And more than that, he could sense how lonely Obsidian was. As alone as Nick felt?

Mask

He was reluctant to share the crimsons, the bulbous shapes, and the frankly sexual works with Miguel. They were new growth in Nick's art that his boyfriend hadn't been a part of, by choice.

Now he leaned his head against the window and looked from the dusty attic to the rainy asphalt below. Fall leaves blew in spirals, going nowhere. He saw a figure on the street below, and for a moment it looked like the man was looking up at Nick's window, but then he continued walking and Nick shook off the impression.

He could return to his single bed now, to the room next to Miguel's, be a good boy and lie awake, staring at the ceiling, wondering if somewhere Obsidian was doing the same thing. If he was thinking of Nick.

Abruptly he returned to his computer, his heart rate picking up, his hands a little shaky and his throat dry.

He sat there, staring at the blank screen, chewing his lip.

Obsidian was the forbidden. Bad for him, he just knew it, but Nick felt so isolated and he felt a match for his loneliness in Obsidian.

He turned on his computer.

Obsidian: Where the fuck have you been?

Moonbeam: ...

Obsidian: Nick? Don't you fucking sign off!

Moonbeam: Don't call me that. You shouldn't call me that! Here, I'm Moonbeam. I told you this has to be fantasy.

Obsidian: Fine, although one day I will know why you are so insistent. Here in cyberspace, Moonbeam belongs to me.

Moonbeam: ...

Obsidian: Moonbeam?

Moonbeam: You missed me; that's why you're so pissy. I... missed you too. I couldn't stop thinking about you.

Obsidian: You're an interesting distraction. If you were in my house right now, this second, do you want to know what I'd do to you?

Moonbeam: No, please.

Obsidian: Liar.

Moonbeam: What would you do? Tell me!

Obsidian: I'd handcuff you to the towel rail in my bathroom. I've got this big fucking palace of a spa, kind of seventies retro since it hasn't been redone, but as large as some living rooms today, as long as you like yellow and orange... I'd kiss a path down your spine and your head would fall back, silver-blond hair gleaming dully like metal in the light from the hallway.... By the time I reached your backbone, just above your full ass, your legs would be spread. I'd open your cheeks and put my tongue inside you.

Moonbeam: Jesus!

Obsidian: I want to eat your ass.

Moonbeam: Obsidian, stop!

Obsidian: But you're excited, admit it. I excited you. You'd let me do anything to you, wouldn't you?

Moonbeam: You're angry with me. But I have a life, I have a boyfriend, and this thing with you.... I need to kick you like a bad habit. I keep trying...

Obsidian: This is me doing you.

Moonbeam: Yes, I know it is. I should go.

Obsidian: Don't.

Mask

Moonbeam: This is wrong. I'm a loyal boyfriend.

Obsidian: It's not wrong. I touch you, he doesn't, and from what you've told me, it's his choice. Do you even share the same bed? I've... imagined you together and I'm sure you're "affectionate" or whatever you want to call it, but he might as well be your best friend.

Moonbeam: Can we talk about something else?

Obsidian: Don't leave.

Moonbeam: I can't stay long. I have to get my transcripts together.

Obsidian: Why?

Moonbeam: I, uh, lost my job.

Obsidian: Does the boyfriend know?

Moonbeam: No, I didn't tell him, didn't want to worry him. Turns out I got a call from the dean's office and they found another gig for me since the waiting job fell through. The Pancake House where I wait tables is on campus. I think this new job probably would suit me better, but—

Obsidian: Pays the same?

Moonbeam: Way better! But... I liked the people I worked with, you know? And there was a lot of time to just space out, think about a piece I'm working on. Plus my manager was really good to me and I was helping her organize her collection of gothic novels. She has arthritis, so—

Obsidian: Good news then.

Moonbeam: Except I have to commute to some creepy house just outside the city. And I'll miss Marilyn; she was very accommodating if I was trashed from working late on my paintings. She even lets me hang them in the Pancake House sometimes to try to make a little extra money.

Obsidian: I'm sure you'll make out all right. She's just someone you worked for, after all.

Moonbeam: I guess I'll have to, but she's a friend and I'll miss her.

Obsidian: But you'll have more money.

Moonbeam: That's not all that matters to me! I liked my little rut of a job, can't you see that?

Obsidian: Sounds like rut is a good way to characterize it. Maybe doing something unexpected will stimulate you.

Moonbeam: How do you mean?

Obsidian: Your muse, of course. You better get your rest if you have a big day tomorrow.

Moonbeam: You're letting me go so early? And... How did you know I start tomorrow?

Obsidian: Apparently, I'm psychic as well as indulgent. You will come back because you can't stay away and we both know it, don't we, Moonbeam?

Moonbeam: :sigh: You didn't answer my question, you evasive bastard. And yes, master, I will return.

Obsidian: Good.

Moonbeam: I read your tone as purring.

Obsidian: You artists are so imaginative!

Moonbeam: Uh-huh.

Obsidian: I want you to use that imagination.

Moonbeam: Ummm?

Obsidian: Indulge me.

Moonbeam: Depends.

Obsidian: Close your eyes and imagine my lips against your backbone. My tongue—

Moonbeam: God!

Obsidian: Sweet dreams, Nick.

Obsidian: Has left the room.

Moonbeam: :Squirms:

Moonbeam: Has left the room.

NICK climbed out of the Lexus, staring at Telemachus House, the place he'd been assigned to work—what he could see of it. Ivy and jasmine draped over the portico, covering the windows with tenacious green tendrils. It looked like the vegetation had the house in a death grip, slowly crushing the life from graceful columns and wedding cake architecture.

He shivered, reaching back in the car for his transcripts, muttering his annoyance over this necessity. He didn't *want* to work all the way out here, miles from the university. As he'd told Obsidian, he liked his little rut of a job because his mind could range free while he was on autopilot, and now—

Something told him he would be marked by being in this house. Gripped like the pallid timbers and Corinthian facade.

A heartbeat after he closed the passenger door, pebbles struck his shoes.

The Lexus pulling away!

"Hey, what the fuck? How do I get home!" Nick yelled, slamming a hand against the retreating trunk of the car. But the driver only continued down the road at a serene pace, ignoring Nick.

"Dandy!" Nick put his hands on his hips and stood there, a little shaken.

He chewed his lip, but then turned reluctantly to face the house. The light hitting the windows at an oblique angle made them shine like secretive eyes, watching him.

Nick shook his head at his own imagination and took a deep breath, again wishing he was back at Charlie's Pancake House. His rut of a job. His rut of a life.

But he was here now and he had to stay and meet with the mysterious Mr. Mitchell, his new boss. He needed this job. Without it, he couldn't afford his share of the rent or to keep taking classes. This was life or death for him.

He trudged over sodden piles of damp leaves to the double front door which sported curled white paint, like the scales of some abandoned creature. There wasn't a bell that he could find at first glance, only a quaint door knocker in the shape of a lady's closed fist.

Heart thudding in his ears, Nick reached for it, feeling a bit like Jane Eyre as he struck the door and the sound echoed ominously.

 CHAPTER 4

"MMMMMM, very Jane Eyre," Nick muttered to himself, surrounded by the scattered chocolate truffles he'd been feasting on while lying on his luxurious silk-draped bed. "So I guess all I need is a white nightgown, according to Marilyn."

He typed in his password—*a rolling stone crushes toes*—before logging into the chat room. "Come on, Obsidian," he whispered, desperately needing to connect. "I need to talk about *him*. My mystery boss."

Moonbeam: So what do you think?

Obsidian: I think it sounds like the plot from Northanger Abbey. So your new employer is an eccentric?

Moonbeam: Very!

Obsidian: What did you think of him?

Moonbeam: :sigh: I didn't actually get a good look at him, for one thing.

THE explosive sound of the bolt giving sounded overly loud to Nick. He squeaked, covered his mouth, looking around to see if anyone had seen his embarrassing moment of fright. Shit! Obviously the atmosphere of the house and overgrown garden was working him.

You artists are so imaginative; he could hear Obsidian mocking him.

Yeah, yeah, he snarked back.

Cheeks flushed, pulse thudding in his throat, he paused, waiting to see who had opened the door.

And waited.

Frowning, he rubbed a hand through his hair, thinking of all the work he had to do for class. Somehow he also had to meet with his new employer and then find his way back into town. Plus, it was cold out here, the damp chill of fall cutting through his thin jacket.

Finally, when no one appeared, he twisted the knob and entered a dimly lit hallway.

"Hello?" Who had unlocked the door? Nick felt a chilly feather stroke down his spine.

"Second floor, Mr. Anders. Third door on your left," a soft, disembodied voice ordered crisply. "And I'm glad to see you brought your portfolio; although you will be working primarily with my book collection, I want to see your work."

"Um, yeah, all prepared. Hello?" Nick looked around until he spotted the intercom and surveillance camera. He let out a slightly shaky sigh. Okay, so Mr. Mitchell wasn't some kind of psychic, even if his house gave off the vibe of being possessed.

Despite what he'd heard when he'd dropped by the man's workplace, the whispers and uneasy speculation brought on by Mr. Mitchell very seldom being seen by his staff, he was obviously merely an eccentric.

"Happy soon-to-be Halloween, Nick," Nick chided himself before heading toward the stairs.

Mask

Soft music was playing as he climbed worn wooden stairs past bare walls dressed in yellowed William Morris wallpaper, the hall lit by a sconce with a flickering bulb. He could make out the brighter rectangles where artwork had hung. The water-splotched ceiling above had a few tendrils of ivy poking through the roof.

The house smelled damp, like a giant sleeping creature that lived deep under the earth. A cool finger of a draft poked through Nick's clothes and brushed the back of his neck.

"Nice," Nick muttered, shaking his head. His boss *had* to be an eccentric for wanting to live here!

He shivered in his thin coat, catching the rising crescendo of violins and cellos. The music was classical, somber in tone.

The third door on the left opened into a library, walled with black walnut bookcases with Doric molding. Nick frowned on seeing them since the cases were only a quarter full. If there were so few books, why had he been hired to work here?

The room was lit by a single candle on a massive mahogany desk. Nick hesitated, heart pounding.

"Mr. Mitchell?" he breathed, strangely loath to break the mood of the music. He felt like an interloper here, as if the man and his house were both waking up, watching him.

Movement caught Nick's attention, a hand replacing a golden snifter of alcohol on a wooden table. Someone was seated in a leather club chair, facing a fire reduced to yellow and orange embers, his back to Nick.

"Sit down on the chair in front of the desk," he was ordered.

"Uh." Nick scratched his eyebrow. He wouldn't be able to see his future employer if he did that. He shrugged. Whatever. He wasn't sure he wanted the job even though he needed it.

"Did you bring the requested transcripts as well as your portfolio?"

"Yes."

"Leave them on the desk."

"Hopefully you can read them without straining your eyes," Nick cracked, referring to the candlelight.

"We'll discuss your employment in the morning. I'm... weary now."

"Tomorrow? But—"

"I had your room made up for you. Two doors down."

Nick shook his head, feeling like he'd fallen down the rabbit hole big time. "My *room?* You can't be serious! I can't stay here!"

"Of course you can. I saw through the camera at the front door that you'd brought your knapsack. It has your sketchbook, yes? I'm sure there is plenty of inspiration on the estate for an imaginative mind— though I should warn you the grounds aren't safe, since there's a half-buried wine cellar with a rotting deck over top. But as long as you stay indoors you should be comfortable. You'll find food and drink in the mini fridge in your room. Not alcoholic, of course, since technically you are here on business."

"Mr. Mitchell, you are not listening. Staying here with you is...!"

Amused, the man said, "Eccentric?"

"Yes!" Nick tried to get a closer look but a languid hand waved him back. He couldn't even tell the age of his infuriating new employer.

"But if you don't take this position you might have to leave school," the voice pointed out silkily. "What a shame since you are such a promising young student."

Obsidian: Seems he has you at a disadvantage.

Moonbeam: Yes!

Mask

Nick ate another truffle, considering. He was picking up a weird vibe of satisfaction emanating from Obsidian. Feeling shouldn't transmit without expression, without voice, but somehow, when chatting with Obsidian, he'd found he could often read both from his odd companion, as if the wires, the electricity, transmitted more than mere flat text. It somehow allowed them to touch.

Allowed the intimacy Nick craved.

He swallowed the candy, deciding not to examine that thought too closely.

> **Obsidian:** What about the "boyfriend"? Or are you going to call him after talking to me first?
>
> **Moonbeam:** Stop smirking! And don't use that tone when you refer to Miguel.
>
> **Obsidian:** :Lifts eyebrow: How do you know I have a "tone" when we are online?

Nick shook his head ruefully.

> **Moonbeam:** I just do.
>
> **Obsidian:** Fine. So what about Miguel, your saintly minstrel?
>
> **Moonbeam:** Uh, seems that Mr. Mitchell even arranged something for him—dinner out at a nice restaurant with a companion of his choice. And I'm not sure how I feel about that any more than spending the night in this creepy house!
>
> **Obsidian:** :indulgent: Calm down and tell your good "friend" Obsidian all about it...

AFTER his odd meeting with his new employer, Nick wasted no time in protesting by phone to Cassandra Moore, Mr. Mitchell's personal assistant, "I promised my boyfriend I'd celebrate with him tonight. Uh, if I got the job. So you see, I can't possibly stay here in this house."

"Yes, fortunately you mentioned your plans to one of my staff so I was able to have a car sent to your apartment and your friend is on his way even now for an evening on the house at Manticore."

"Manticore?" Nick's fists balled at hearing the name of the exclusive club that had opened recently in town. From what he'd heard, it possessed fine dining as well as a club for dancing. "But Miguel isn't into a place like that. He never goes to clubs except to perform his music."

"Apparently tonight he does," Cassandra retorted calmly. "All thanks to Mr. Mitchell."

Nick took a deep breath, gritting his teeth. "Peachy! He seems to have me at a disadvantage."

"You have no idea."

Obsidian: It doesn't sound that bad. How's the food?

Moonbeam: :munching: How do you know I'm eating?

Obsidian: Please. You plus a well-stocked mini fridge? It sounds like your employer has done some research.

Moonbeam: I guess. There are these chocolate truffles? I have this thing for fine chocolate but I can never afford the good shit so I don't eat it very often.

Mask

Obsidian: :purrs: Do you want to know what you can do with chocolates?

Moonbeam: :groans: Please stop tormenting me!

Obsidian: You torment yourself. If you do what I say, I'll take care of you, pleasure you, give you release.

Moonbeam: ...

Obsidian: Nick? Moonbeam.

Moonbeam: I'm here. You're not a very good person, are you? I mean... You know I'm with someone else.

Obsidian: I'm not the good guy, no. I am the villain.

Moonbeam: Are you really? Then maybe you can tell me why Miguel would go to that club? I've heard some strange things about the place. We've always disapproved of clubbing anyway.

Obsidian: :rolls eyes:

Moonbeam: Don't tell me you go there?

Obsidian: I used to.

Moonbeam: Primitive hunting grounds.

Obsidian: Mmmmmm. Sweet prey.

Moonbeam: :rolls eyes:

Obsidian: Let's not analyze your little boyfriend and if he's enjoying what a place like Manticore offers.

Moonbeam: Obsidian!

Obsidian: Like you aren't wondering. Be honest, Moonbeam; it wouldn't be your "feelings" he'd bruise, but your ego. Don't you ever wonder why he doesn't fight harder to keep you away from me? Maybe he is looking for what he needs elsewhere, just like you.

Moonbeam: I told you—!

Obsidian: I know nothing about real relationships. Blah blah. So, chocolate? Or do you want to log off and pout? I... can't stay long tonight.

Moonbeam: One of your headaches? Chocolate.

Obsidian: I'd remove whatever cheap cotton T-shirt you are wearing and bare your flesh. The pale lines of your chest, your pink nipples, the line of your neck when you arch it... Then I'd take one of those truffles and run it gently down the center of your body. Back...forth... before teasing your nipples. The chocolate would warm and melt against your skin so I'd have to put my mouth on you, taste you. Taste the chocolate, taste your skin, taste all of you.

Moonbeam: Jesus! Obsidian.

Obsidian: Are you touching yourself, you naughty boy? Come on, tell me you're not.

Moonbeam: ...

Obsidian: Tell me.

Moonbeam: Yes.

Obsidian: I want you to buy a dildo soon. I've been thinking about just what model. Something ribbed with a nice bulbous head to nudge you with maximum effectiveness deep inside.

Moonbeam: :blinks: Say what?

Obsidian: A dildo. I want you to lube yourself and the toy and put me in. Metaphorically speaking, of course.

Moonbeam: This isn't real! Oh, Christ, I have to—

Obsidian: I'll feel pretty fucking "real" gripped in your hand. Shove me in and out, can't get enough, legs spread, feet flat on the mattress, head turning back and forth, my name on your lips as you come.

Moonbeam: I've never...!

Obsidian: I will be your first. Does that excite you?

Moonbeam: You know it does.

Obsidian: Never be ashamed, my beautiful slut. You know you want to be that way for someone. You're ready for this. Ready to belong to me. To lie under me.

Moonbeam: Obsidian...! Please.

Obsidian: Are you close? Don't come until I say. I want you to ONLY come when I say.

Moonbeam: I... Please? Please let me come!

Obsidian: Come for me, Nick. I can see you on the center of that king-sized bed, legs sprawled, wanton, lit by candlelight, chocolates all over the yellow silk duvet... So fucking beautiful, my sleepy, naughty boy. All mine.

Moonbeam: Yours!

Obsidian: :wistful: I wish I could lick your skin right now. Taste the salt of your excitement, your come, the melted chocolate; bite down so I could almost drink you...

Moonbeam: :panting: I wish... I know this is wrong.

Obsidian: :lulls: Go to sleep now, Moonbeam.

Moonbeam: 'K. You'll take something for your headache, right? I worry about those migraines you get. And...You really think I'm safe here, in this house?

Obsidian: I told you I researched Mr. Kain Mitchell thoroughly. Seems he's a...recluse but he doesn't have a habit of chopping up little blond boys and serving them as an hors d'œuvre. Sleep now, angel.

Moonbeam: Mmmmm.

Obsidian: Has left the room.

Moonbeam: :Sitting up, blinking: Obsidian? Wait, how did you know what color the duvet was?

CHAPTER 5

KAIN didn't need much light, not anymore. Still, he closed his sensitive eyes, trying to block out the pounding in his skull.

One thing could answer his pain. Soothe it. Distract him as always. And at last he was under Kain's roof, where he should be.

Nick.

Kain got up from his chair and drifted through the library, taking in the books covered in dust bunnies. What must Nick think of his excuse for hiring him? Still, there were some older volumes here and a large collection of art books in the alcove.

He should know since he'd scoured some book dealers to collect them specially.

He closed his eyes as he drifted into the hallway, fingertips brushing the wall. He could almost sense the warm trail left by Nick as he walked through the drafty space. Catch his scent almost, which he hadn't been able to detect in the crowded and over-warm Pancake House the first time he'd been close to him.

Nick was under his roof.

A savage satisfaction gripped Kain as he unlocked Nick's bedroom door with his special key.

Nick was sprawled over the large bed, face mashed into the pillow, arms out, hands curled like the abandoned fall leaves outdoors.

Kain stared at him, knowing he should probably feel some qualms about what he'd done to bring this young man under his roof. Cassandra had certainly scolded him.

You are not yourself. How can you be so cruel and manipulative, Kain? She'd pressed him.

But he'd been willing to do anything from that first night when Nick had dared to debate with him over something trivial in the chat room. His passion, his innocence, had come through the wires, touching Kain. Fixing his attention so that he'd shoved aside the boyfriend, brought Nick here at last.

Even drugged a couple of the chocolate truffles he knew Nick couldn't resist because he'd certainly observed him eating chocolate pancakes with chocolate syrup and raspberries on his break.

Nothing too heavy in the candy, just something to relax Nick so Kain could be close to him the way he needed.

"I don't want to hurt you," he whispered. "Nick...."

A gloved hand reached out, stroked the pale back, from the knob of the slender, fragile neck and down the slope that led to a rounded ass.

Kain cupped it, closing his eyes. Squeezing gently.

Shit! He wanted—

Nick snuffled into his pillow, shifting his legs and then turning over onto his back, baring his body to Kain's hungry gaze.

Seeing Nick so vulnerable hurt Kain. He had the urge to protect him as much as to take him.

He closed his eyes now, reliving watching Nick perform through one of the cameras. How he'd lost himself, doing everything Obsidian asked, giving himself completely.

Kain had burned with lust and frustration, locked in his study, locked in his other persona, and unable to go to Nick, to truly make contact.

But how would Nick react if he saw Kain, his true face?

Mask

Kain took a deep breath, flashing back to shortly after the fire, hiring someone and not taking enough care in hiding himself.

His gut twisted.

Nick couldn't turn him away like that, could he?

In the chat room he desired Obsidian, responded to him eagerly, wanting his domination, his care.

Unable to resist, Kain pushed Nick's legs open a little wider. When he didn't stir, he pressed his face against the young man's soft bush, inhaling his scent of innocence, chocolate, and come.

Nick.

MIGUEL passed through the colored beads which led into the club portion of Manticore. He squinted as sudden light struck his eyes, the color working over the walls in warm washes of scarlets, sunflower yellows.

Colors he knew Nick would love.

He shook his head, shoving aside thoughts of his boyfriend. It wasn't working out and they both knew it, but he knew that Nick didn't want to hurt him by breaking it off.

Maybe tonight Miguel would be the one to take that step?

He looked around at the tiny tables with couples, gay and straight, the male and female serving staff wearing thongs only over muscled and oiled bodies, so a customer had the feeling they could reach out and touch. A stage act was in progress, looking like some kind of erotic magic act given the nudity of the people on stage, dominated by a man in leather.

Miguel's eyes were caught by a compelling blue gaze. The entertainer gestured him closer to the half-moon stage. The man wasn't much taller than Miguel and had swept-back black hair with a dramatic white streak. His tanned face had creases by his eyes, signaling he was much older than Miguel's early twenties. Yet there was something compelling about that face, a knowing sensuality stamped into the prominent bones and heavy-lidded eyes.

Normally Miguel would head for the shadows at being so exposed. Only his music mattered, and his memory of how he'd felt with Nick once upon a time, when they'd first met.

"Don't be shy," the man coaxed, talking into his mike, yet his eyes holding Miguel's startled gaze created intimacy, as if they were totally alone. "Come closer. I've been waiting for *you*, Miguel. I'm Siren, your host for the evening."

NICK felt oddly languid when he woke up. Even though his head was fucking pounding!

He blinked, sitting up in the luxurious bed, taking in scattered wrappers from the candy he'd eaten, the afghan he didn't remember wrapping around himself, the warmth in the room when he didn't remember turning up the heat.

Something felt off. His thoughts, body.

Scratching his inner thigh, Nick discovered the skin was pink, as if it had been chafed by something.

Beard burn?

He remembered being sleepy, despite eating the chocolate, which usually left him wired.

He closed his eyes and seemed to feel again the brush of sensitive and possessive fingers, touching his skin, exploring him.

Mask

Moonbeam: You're Kain Mitchell, aren't you?

Obsidian: ...

Moonbeam: I know you're there, reading this, watching me! I found a camera in my room this morning while I was shaving. You...watched me last night, maybe even came in my room and—

Obsidian: Yes, I watched you. Why not? You were only feeling what I made you feel, after all.

Moonbeam: Fuck! My job on campus, my coming here... It was all your doing, wasn't it? You're stalking me for real.

Obsidian: Your new job pays better and you can't say you don't already have a unique form of rapport with your employer.

Moonbeam: Lucky me! I can't believe the extent of your manipulations. I just met you in a chat room and you've invaded my life, watched me, interfered with my long running relationship; in short, played with me as if I'm a toy!

Obsidian: You'd like being my toy. There's some Tylenol in the drawer by the bed.

Moonbeam: And how did you know I had a headache?

Obsidian: I know you. I know your default is to be kind even at the expense of your own feelings. I know you hide from yourself unless you are painting, or talking to me.

Moonbeam: You don't know me at all! Now I want you to unlock this door—which I only now discovered was locked—and let me out of your house.

Jan Irving

Obsidian: Of course. You'll need to bail out your friend, anyway.

Moonbeam: What?

Obsidian: Miguel, the one you refer to as your "boyfriend". He got himself into some kind of trouble last night outside the club Manticore. He's at the station house downtown.

Moonbeam: This is your doing, isn't it? You did something, tricked him!

Obsidian: Hardly. But I'm sure I could be of help. If you make it worth my while.

Moonbeam: I won't listen to this.

Obsidian: Fine. The door is now open. Walk out and never mind helping poor Miguel.

Moonbeam: Obsidian— Mr. Mitchell— Whathefuckever! You took an unhealthy interest in me and fucked up my life! I knew as soon as I woke up that I was dealing with the same mystery man.

Obsidian: You are exceptionally bright, yes. You felt me.

Moonbeam: Wait. You wanted me to know? A trail of bread crumbs, describing my bed when you talked to me? You wanted me to know you're Kain Mitchell!

Obsidian: Let's not forget that I also brought you to climax. Left you smiling and satisfied. As I have for weeks now, if you were honest with yourself, with me.

Moonbeam: Your ends do not justify the means.

Obsidian: Unless you get your end away.

Moonbeam: Why do this? Why did you want me to know the truth of who you are? You had to know I'd be pissed!

Mask

Obsidian: I wish to touch you. Careful packing up your art supplies. Must you slop everything together in that pathetic knapsack? Ha! Nice giving me the finger. Feisty. Should I put that on your personnel file?

Moonbeam: You have no fucking idea!

Obsidian: Nick, I thought it would be easier.

Moonbeam: Easier for whom?

Obsidian: Me, of course.

Moonbeam: Of course! Well, goodbye, Obs— Mr. Mitchell.

Obsidian: Wait. I meant what I said. I can help your friend.

Moonbeam: For a price.

Obsidian: Nothing is free in this world. And since I'm already a villain in your eyes, why not?

Moonbeam: Forget it! I don't want to ever hear from you again! This ends now.

Obsidian: Nick, I know you're a trusting person and... I regret if I hurt you.

Nick shivered, hearing a whisper: *I don't want to hurt you.* Feeling hands on him. Hands he wanted, if he were honest with himself.

Moonbeam: Setting me up like a fool? Why would that hurt me? I LIKED you.

Obsidian: I...like you too.

AT THE police station, Nick finally managed to see Miguel, who was unshaven, wearing wrinkled clothing that smelled of alcohol.

"Nick!" Miguel hugged Nick, pressing his face against his neck and closing his eyes.

"Are you aware of what they have you in here for?" Nick rasped, pulling away.

Eyes on fire, Miguel growled, "I was drunk. I never should have gone to that place, but I can't deny that something happened last night, Nick."

"You can't blame the venue for your actions!" Nick exclaimed. "My God, Miguel, sex in a public place just to start!"

Miguel rubbed the back of his neck. "I'm sorry. I don't... I don't remember much after I watched a stage act. But I did take part somehow. Nick, look at me, please! I'm sorry. I love you enough to want to be honest with you, and on the bright side, I think I found what I was looking for to get over my hang-ups."

Nick turned away, taking a deep breath.

"You got what you needed from someone else. *Not* me."

"Yes, same as you, if you're honest."

Nick swallowed and confessed, "I've just been so lonely."

"I know you're angry, disappointed."

Nick shook his head. "I don't know what is real anymore. What I can believe in." Had he wasted all that time with Miguel, settling when he could have been truly touched, taken? No wonder he'd been such an easy mark for Obsidian, his vulnerability exposed through their chat.

"It's all a blur, like a dream, but I think I did make a choice. What matters now is... I don't want to lose you as a friend."

Nick frowned, wondering if someone had slipped his boyfriend a mickey in his drink. But it didn't matter. "I need some time. I, uh, know someone who offered to help you out." He swallowed thickly, taking another step away from Miguel. But why not? His boyfriend had apparently found what he needed elsewhere, after years of Nick patiently trying to reawaken him sexually. It burned him, and he was ashamed to realize that if he hadn't met Obsidian, flirted with him, he would have been more devastated when Miguel moved away.

"I'll do what I can for you and I'll be moving in with Marilyn." Nick's lips twisted. "Still have to finish sorting out her gothic novels anyway."

Miguel nodded jerkily. "Maybe we can talk sometime. I never meant to hurt you, Nick."

Nick sighed, not sure if he was precisely happy that he wasn't hurting more. Like Obsidian had predicted, it was more his pride that was damaged. "I believe you never meant to hurt me, which is why I'll help you now." What he'd had with Miguel had broken like a brittle fall branch, leaving Nick with… what?

He tried to shove aside the name that came to mind.

"POOR Nick," Marilyn said as Nick pushed up his protective goggles and shut off his welder. "You're wiped. And you won't find your answers driving yourself with your art."

"Yeah." Nick's T-shirt was soaked with sweat, sticking clammily to his body. He'd been working for hours at the free studio for students to create an armature as the base for his soon-to-be plaster relief of a 78-year-old drag queen's face—sans makeup.

"So you and Miguel? I just can't believe it. Listen, Nick, I know that maybe the romance was an illusion for a long time, and you grew apart, but the friendship?"

"Over." Nick slumped on one of the stools. "At least for now. I know he's going through some shit now but I just can't—"

"So don't push yourself," the older woman, his former boss at the Pancake House, recommended. "But you don't have to help Miguel by making some kind of reckless bargain with the devil."

"Obsidian—Mr. Mitchell isn't the devil. Um, not quite."

"Some think he is! I Googled him at the library just now." She smiled at Nick's surprised look. "Hey, I can Google with the best of them, despite my hands being a mess. There was a fire a little over a year ago in Mr. Mitchell's penthouse apartment. Someone died there, Nick, some friend of his...."

Nick picked at the wire he'd been soldering. "I want to help Miguel and I can let it go for now, just... leave him in a place where I don't worry about him. And as for Mr. Mitchell, it's not like I'm willing to do anything."

Marilyn sipped her herb tea in a paper cup, sober eyes on Nick. "Aren't you? I've never seen you like this, unless it was over your art. It's like you're under his spell."

Moonbeam: I was reading just now about your chosen nickname. Obsidian is created by lava flows and then cools into something hard and brittle which may be used as a weapon.

Obsidian: So?

Moonbeam: :tired: What do you want? And it better not be sexual favors.

Obsidian: I want you to live in my house.

Moonbeam: That's...it? Why, for fuck's sake?

Obsidian: You've been to my house, seen it. It's...very quiet. I only have one servant. I told you I find you very diverting.

Mask

Moonbeam: You manipulated me!

Obsidian: I'd do it again to get what I want—you. And anyway, you wanted to be manipulated. Then you could tell yourself, he did that to me, that's not who I am, what I want.

Moonbeam: :Deep breath: You'll help Miguel.

Obsidian: Done. And I hope you're done with him. Done with holding onto something out of habit and misguided friendship.

Moonbeam: So what now? When do I see you?

Obsidian: You don't. A car will arrive in the morning to pick you up at your friend Marilyn's place. Bring the bare minimum of clothing; I will provide the rest.

Moonbeam: :curious: The hell...? Why would you want to do that?

Obsidian: Because I want you wearing clothing against your skin that I chose, I touched.

CHAPTER 6

"WHAT are you going to do with this?" Finn asked, showing off his inquisitive mind as he lifted some scrap metal from Nick's work table.

Nick shut off his old welder and pushed back his goggles, his face shiny with sweat from a combination of proximity with the flame and intense concentration. "I've gotten into three dimensional in a big way lately. I thought… wings forever stuck to the wall. How we want to fly but can't allow ourselves."

"Expressive." Finn raised a brow, pushing some of his curly red hair out of his golden eyes as he studied Nick's face. He cocked his head. "I can see a little of what his lordship sees in you, why you are suddenly his big obsession. You're different from his, um, usual companions."

"So you're Kain's…?" Nick sat on another one of the long tables in the atrium-turned-studio attached to Kain Mitchell's house. The sky was nearly blocked out by reddened ivy over the glass dome, so light came into the room with a greenish tinge, as if Nick and Finn were in some special watery world.

He'd met Finn O'Connell when he'd arrived at Telemachus House the second time and an actual person had opened the door instead of the disembodied hand of his employer.

"Manservant, cook, whatever needs doing, Nick. I'd be here more often, but Kain has taken to liking lots of time on his own. A… recluse."

"Uh, his whatever?" Nick flushed when Finn looked amused.

"Not that! He doesn't let anyone close except—" Finn chewed his lip and shrugged. "I probably shouldn't say."

"Who?" Nick pressed.

"Paid prostitutes," Finn said succinctly. "Lately slim little blonds."

Nick colored further, playing restlessly with his goggles and welder. But he wasn't above pumping Finn for more information about his mysterious employer; it seemed that Obsidian wasn't the only obsessed one. "I guess it must be interesting working for him since he owns his own company and…. Well, this house is pretty unusual. What's he like?"

"Cranky since you had a tiff," Finn said ruefully. "Keeps to himself, but he's pretty restless at night. He used to get me to play cards with him until he found you online."

Nick shrugged. "I'm only here because we made a bargain. He promised to help a friend who got into some trouble. But I didn't expect him to give me my own studio space or anything."

"I was sure he'd done something to get you here," Finn grunted. "He's alone too much and this is a big house in need of a major renovation, if you ask me. But he never asks."

"His choice, I guess, but all the vegetation and the decay make you wonder why he'd want to live like this. I, uh, heard he had a penthouse at one time."

"Yes, he did. Slick, Italian, an elaborate showpiece, a fuck pad. Nothing like this house," Finn said, reflecting. "Well, I have to go order in dinner, so I'll leave you here. I'm sure his lordship will be curious what you think of the gift of studio space, even in the old atrium." Finn pointedly looked over at the open laptop, cursor blinking softly.

Nick shifted, frowning. "I don't feel like talking to him. He invaded my privacy, manipulated me into working here, and… I feel raw about something else right now. Something I was holding onto." Nick didn't say more, not wanting to bring up his failed relationship with Miguel.

Finn smirked. "Then don't talk to him, even though it'll put him in a bitch of a mood."

NICK lost himself, enjoying the slanting sun through glass despite the autumn chill. He'd put on a sweatshirt over a sweatshirt though the metalwork warmed him up. He found himself thinking that here he'd have light, even in the winter months. Real light, unsparing of his creations, and like most artists, he worshiped light.

Obsidian had given him this. Manipulated him, yes, but given him this glass house.

He sipped some of the herbal tea Marilyn had insisted sending him off with—this one was rose petals and chocolate—and looked around his work space.

The atrium had a roof of white metal spines, some of them rusting a little and blotched where they leaked. Tendrils of ivy had managed to penetrate one side of the folly and take over a corner, almost swallowing a statue of Apollo, frowning sternly, as if slightly put out over his green mantel. A dry fountain surrounded by stone benches was in the center of the space and there was a little feeder and water put out for the wild, and so far shy, canaries that lived among the overgrown orchids and tufts of horn plants and palms.

Majolica masks peered out from each column. Fall, a smiling empty-eyed face wearing a wreath of corn and grapes; spring, bearing a crown of soft pink porcelain petals; summer, lush with shiny green leaves and yellow-centered daisies. And yet, each smile, benign at first glance to the drifting eye, had an edge. Pagan. Secretive.

Very like Kain Mitchell and his unusual and atmospheric house.

Contemplative, Nick molded the plaster he planned to use for the face of his drag queen, thinking of what it had been like to talk to her, Ms. Appleby. She'd worked as a secretary for a high-powered businessman for years and many people hadn't known she was a man at first glance. "It's the Adam's apple that gives it away," she'd told Nick almost mournfully. "I took to wearing attractive chiffon scarves. I was even asked out by quite a few attractive 'straight' men."

The laptop gave a sudden squawk, disrupting the mood.

Apparently Obsidian's patience was at an end.

NICK deliberately looked straight up at the camera staring back in his direction. Raised a brow. And spotted his cold soup and bread on the corner of the table. When had Finn left his supper? He couldn't believe he'd been so lost that he'd missed that, but he had been, very happily lost in this space provided by Obsidian, in his art.

The mood broken, he munched on peasant bread and put out a few pieces for the birds. They flew out to steal his leavings when he stepped back to the chair by his computer.

Obsidian: Is the studio to your liking?

Moonbeam: You must know it is. You've been watching me, haven't you? Shit, I just...lost myself for hours. Not that I forgive you but... It looks like you were gathering supplies for weeks. And cleaning out the atrium to create more room for me to spread out a work space. The light, Obsidian... Uh, I mean, Mr. Mitchell—

Obsidian: Call me Kain or Obsidian. You like it, that's all that fucking matters.

Moonbeam: :shrugs: I do. And...thank you. By the way, I can fix the fountain if you like. I was even thinking since the sculpture was missing from the top that I could make a little something, maybe out of beaten copper so it would green naturally.

Obsidian: Do whatever you want. Is there a fountain in there? I never noticed. When you lose yourself in your work you're so fucking intense. It's arousing, wondering if—

Moonbeam: I know I'm going to regret asking, but wondering what?

Obsidian: If you bring that same intensity to fucking; if I'll see that same dreamy, lips parted, out of focus look in your eyes when I have you.

Moonbeam: Shit!

Obsidian: You asked.

Moonbeam: :firmly: And you ambushed. We need to talk.

Obsidian: What about?

Moonbeam: You're watching me in here.

Obsidian: Yes.

Moonbeam: We need some rules for the cameras.

Obsidian: I only follow my rules under my roof.

Moonbeam: Your roof is just about to fucking collapse from the ivy alone. So, wrong. You used to only follow your rules when you lived alone with the obliging Finn, but now you share this house with me.

Nick waited, chewing his lip. Perspiration stung his hairline and the skin above his upper lip. His heart was beating, very fast.

Obsidian: Why do you need rules?

Moonbeam: Because I lived with someone for years and I thought... It didn't work out.

Obsidian: Fine, what do you want to suggest? Obviously I'm a barbarian.

Moonbeam: There's a camera in my bathroom.

Obsidian: I like to watch you take a shower, but I can have it set up so you can activate that one if you choose, otherwise the picture will remain black.

Moonbeam: Why would I ever turn it on...?

Obsidian: You don't imagine you'll ever want to tease me, knowing I watch, by taking a slow shower? Think how you can punish me, seeing all that pale skin, that untouched mouth made to suck my cock and I can only watch. And I notice you didn't mention the camera in the bedroom. You want to display yourself for me.

Moonbeam: :Rubs forehead: This is fucked up!

Obsidian: Then it must be a relationship. Of sorts. If there is anything else you require in the studio, let Finn know. And if the fountain needs plumbing work, he can bring someone in. Stick to the creative shit. By the way, I noticed you started sorting through the books in my library. Not bad work.

Moonbeam: :sigh: I know the studio is you offering me another bite of the apple. As much as things you say, the way you make me feel.

Obsidian: How do I make you feel? Tell me.

Moonbeam: Why should I share myself if you won't?

Obsidian: Because you are better at it. Because you want to spread your legs for me, but this is easier. For the moment.

Moonbeam: That's not acceptable in the long run. You'll have to compromise if I'm to live here. I need... I need contact, Obsidian. After what happened with Miguel, my confidence is at an all time low. Can you understand that?

Obsidian: ...

Moonbeam: The word "compromise" takes you aback, I can feel it, but you need to deal. Mr. Mitch— Obsidian, I want to see you.

Obsidian: No.

Moonbeam: Why not?

Obsidian: Never. You are never to see me.

Moonbeam: You apparently see prostitutes, so why not me?

Obsidian: ...

Moonbeam: Don't you want to be in the same room and...truly make contact? I want to know you.

Obsidian: Do you know the story of Cupid and Psyche? Beware what you wish for, little one. Finn will come for you when I'm ready. Do as he says.

Moonbeam: Obsidian?

Obsidian: Has left the room.

"THERE! Blonds look so hot in black or charcoal. Actually blonds look great in anything," Finn sighed, looking rueful.

Nick looked down at the Kanji figure Finn had drawn on the pale flesh just above his left hip. "What does it mean?" he asked, still bemused at the attentions. It felt good to be touched, by a brush, by fingers, the focus of pampering. It soothed the raw wound that Miguel had made, however inadvertently. Nick felt oddly languid, like a boy being prepared for his pasha's pleasure.

"Luck," Finn said, looking up with a smile. "If you like it, I know someone in Japan Town who could make it permanent. Thanks for letting me play; Kain doesn't offer many outlets for that."

Nick reached for the heavy brocade gold and charcoal kimono and swung it over his shoulders, leaving it open so he didn't smear the line of dark paint on his body, just above his low-slung black silk pajama bottoms.

"Very Asian." Finn nodded approval. He stood directly behind Nick. "And you like the eyeliner; admit it."

Nick swallowed, seeing a sensual stranger in the mirror. Finn had even reddened his lips, so he looked like he'd been doing something Obsidian often said he was made for, sucking cock. Shit! "I feel like I'm looking at a stranger."

"A stranger you like or not?" Finn probed.

Nick looked at him. "I don't know, but it's almost like I'm donning some kind of mask."

"Masks are aspects of our psyche."

"Psyche." Nick grimaced. "Obsidian—I mean, Mr. Mitchell—mentioned the Greek myth of Cupid and Psyche."

"Appropriate. A beauty is married to someone she has never seen." Finn stroked Nick's hair, almost as if he wanted to offer a silent kind of reassurance. "But other people interfere and make her doubt her mysterious husband, so she lights a lamp to see him and… loses him." Finn suddenly gripped Nick's slim wrist, swallowing. "Are you sure you want to go to him tonight? Being caught up in a fairy tale is not easy."

"You act like he's some kind of monster! Melodramatic, Finn."

Finn held Nick's gaze in the mirror. "More things in Heaven and Earth. Oh, and you're to put this on." He handed Nick a black silk scarf.

"What is that for?"

"Blindfold. His rule."

"But you've seen him, so why…?"

"He doesn't want *you* to see him. I'm afraid he's adamant about it, Nick."

"I don't see why," Nick grumbled as Finn tied the blindfold on.

"Don't you? He's afraid. No one can reject you like a lover can." For a moment Finn looked despondent, memories living in his golden eyes. Then he took Nick's hand and led him from the bathroom where he'd insisted on changing because he'd switched off the camera. He'd wanted some time to talk to Finn unobserved.

"I'll take you to him."

NICK'S head was cocked, as he felt the breath of heated air from a fire touch his face. He had the sense he was in the same room where he'd first met the mysterious Mr. Mitchell. Except this time he was guided closer to the warmth, seated carefully in a leather club chair. Lacking vision, he stroked the leather, lips parting.

"I know you're here," he whispered. "Finally here within touching distance."

Kain grunted.

Amused Nick said, "Well, this is promising."

"I don't know what you want. I am not going to entertain you."

Nick leaned his cheek against his chair, head raised to stretch his senses, experiencing Kain differently because he couldn't see him. "I'll just sit here then."

"Fine," Kain said.

Mask

HE must have fallen asleep, lulled by the fire, the sound of Kain's fingers tapping on keys, no doubt working his high-octane business. He was tired from setting up his studio, from early classes that morning.

He woke when someone lifted him.

He clutched a shoulder and felt hard muscle through silk. "What time?" he mumbled, groggy.

"It's after three. Finn has gone to bed."

"Hummm." Nick licked his lips, his body swaying, his pulse throbbing so he was aware of it in his inner thighs, his throat, his stiffening sex as Kain carried him easily, obviously much larger-bodied than Nick, which turned him on.

He stroked Kain's arm as they traversed the hallway, the now familiar draft giving away the location, and then the key rattling so he knew they'd reached his room.

He was shortly lowered to his bed. He clutched Kain's forearms. "It wasn't so bad, being in the same room with me, was it?" He reached up, blind, his fingers stumbling over Kain's collar to his neck, feeling the rasp of new beard under his touch.

Kain pulled sharply away.

Heart thudding, Nick sat up and tried again, his hand moving over Kain's back, gripping. "I want you. You made me want you...."

He strained up, grazing Kain's lips with his own. Prodding them, coaxing. *Please.*

He heard the sound of uneven breathing, felt Kain's pulse pounding in his neck, under his fingers.

The larger man was actually trembling.

"Be careful what you invite! Christ!" Kain shoved him away.

Nick reached for his blindfold as the door slammed, the lock turned.

Aroused, hurting, he put his head on his knees.

# CHAPTER 7

"CAN I help you?"

"Detective Lisa Manners. Is Mr. Mitchell at home?" A hard-faced woman in her early forties with blunt-cut auburn hair sprinkled with white flashed her badge.

Nick rubbed his eyes, still waking up. *A detective? What the hell? Something to do with Miguel?* "I, uh, haven't seen him." *Wasn't that the truth!*

In fact, he'd still be sleeping since he'd had a restless night, tormented by his embarrassing desire for Kain, but he'd been jolted awake by the dull sound of the bolt in his bedroom door unlocking at dawn.

Apparently the master didn't want him wandering the house at night, maybe finding him, forcing things between them.

It seemed Kain knew him very well, knew that sooner or later, despite what he feared he might find in the shadows, Nick *would* go looking.

But fine and dandy. Nick would save his snooping for the daylight hours. He did a lot of his painting at night anyway, spilling out his feelings and confusion and slightly pissed-off longing for Obsidian.

"I would like to speak with him," Manners repeated, mouth firm.

"I'm afraid that's impossible," Finn called, interrupting Nick's uncomfortable standoff with the cop. Finn was wearing a green silk robe;

his mussed red hair and his sharp, elfin features made him look sexy and secretive, like the love slave of a fey king.

Manners, though, only gave Finn a derisive glance, as if judging him for his choice of clothing only. "Why is that? And you are?"

"Finn!" Finn gave her a sunny smile. "Mr. Mitchell is… indisposed this morning since he had one of his migraines last night. But you are very welcome to come inside and enjoy a latte with us. I was just whipping one up for Nick."

"Uh-huh." Manners' eyes went from Nick to Finn, as if she was wondering if they were up to something.

But whatever it was, Nick was out of the game. He took the opportunity to probe, wondering what the hell a detective wanted with his boss. "Why are you here?"

"Hustler murdered last night. Found in a ditch not too far from this…" Manners' eyebrows rose as she took in the vegetation-covered entranceway of Telemachus, "house."

Nick swallowed sickly and looked to Finn, whose mouth only tightened in reaction.

"Oh," Nick said, drawing a blank.

Manners cocked her head, studying Nick. "Slim little blond, like you."

Nick ran a hand over his unshaven jaw. "I'm sorry to hear that. Do you know who he was?"

"His wrist was stamped last night at the club Manticore, which I understand Mr. Mitchell owns."

"He does?" Nick blinked. Shit! The same club where Miguel had run into trouble…. Coincidence? "Is that why you wish to speak to him?"

"Yes, but he doesn't go clubbing there anymore, kitten," Finn said, waving a hand dismissively. "That was Kain's… we'll call it a past life. So he wasn't there last night, Detective."

Mask

Manners raised a brow. "Mitchell may not frequent his club, but there are other places for a man of his... tastes. Other connections a powerful man can utilize."

Finn gave the detective a bland look. "Whatever do you mean? But I'll be sure and pass on your message."

"You do that," she growled. "And tell him I want to see him."

Nodding, Finn closed the door and then looked at Nick. "So, ready for that latte?"

Moonbeam: Why can't you just understand? I don't feel like talking to you.

Obsidian: Um hum. I understand you are working on a piece for the charity drive hosted at the university.

Moonbeam: So?

Obsidian: I happen to also own a share in a gallery downtown which is auctioning works by the most promising young talent.

Moonbeam: Why am I not surprised? You seem to have your tentacles everywhere, Obsidian.

Obsidian: I'm saying that I have a connection.

Moonbeam: :sputters: Not interested!

Obsidian: Nick. You are talented, but finding recognition for your work means grasping opportunity.

Moonbeam: :primly: It's "Moonbeam" here, remember?

Obsidian: Funny, but you don't exactly put me in mind of a ray of light today. And now we are living under the same roof, I will call you Nick when it pleases me. Now tell me what's wrong? Something's upset you.

Moonbeam: ...

Obsidian: Your "offer" last night, perhaps?

Moonbeam: You pushed me away.

Obsidian: Nick, I was trying to do the right thing. You don't know...

Moonbeam: All right, fine, we'll start with that. You were afraid, I think.

Obsidian: ...

Moonbeam: You left bruises on my shoulders. Did I imagine that? Did I imagine you were trembling?

Obsidian: You made a clumsy pass.

Moonbeam: Don't try to shake my confidence because you don't want to face what happened between us last night. You know I can have just about anyone I want.

Obsidian: I'm sure you can, Nick.

Moonbeam: Grrrrr. And I don't need you to play the patron for my art. I prefer to make my own connections, thank you. I'm not blind to opportunities—I just prefer to make them on my own.

Obsidian: You telling me off is oddly arousing.

Moonbeam: Right now, do you know what I feel? Like biting your bare shoulder. Feeling your skin under my teeth. Marking you so you feel me, hear me!

Obsidian: Christ! Don't say shit like that! Didn't I warn you?

Moonbeam: All night I felt the air against my skin, almost like a touch. I ached for your hand on me. On me, Kain.

You woke this sleeping beauty. Like I said last night, you made me want, so deal with it!

Obsidian: ...

Moonbeam: So don't tell me I don't know what I want, you patronizing son of a bitch. By the way, we have a guest coming, so you better stick to your lair since you seem to have an aversion to being seen.

Obsidian: :Eyes narrowing: I don't remember saying you could have your little friends over.

Moonbeam: Probably because I didn't ask. We're going to work together on a collaborative metal sculpture for the event you mentioned.

Obsidian: Oh, good. I'll tell Finn to break out the milk and cookies.

Moonbeam: :lightly: Be sure to watch, Kain, since that's all you do.

Obsidian: I told you to be fucking careful what you invite! You don't know what could happen if I—

Moonbeam: Moonbeam has left the room.

Obsidian: FUCK!

NICK massaged his sore shoulder, since he hadn't been kidding about the bruises Kain had left on his body, while studying the metal that his companion, Mark, had begun welding since Nick had run out of steam for the moment. The brass was stained from the chemicals they'd rinsed it in so blotches of greens and azures covered the blade, reminiscent of the shades of a peacock feather.

Mark shoved his goggles up, huffing from the heat of welding. "Fantastic!" he said, face glowing. "This is going to be the top piece in the show. You know that, right?"

Nick gave him a sideways look, forcing himself to take in the way Mark's T-shirt was sticking to his chest. Nick was single now and he was determined not to be too vulnerable to Kain, as he had been with Miguel, not be shoved away because he desired more than Kain was ready to give. This time, he was keeping his options open, as much as he could.

Finn interrupted his brooding by placing a heaped plate of cookies on the table. "Here you go, fellas. Mr. Mitchell thought you'd like some cookies and, er…. What would you like to drink?"

Nick raised an eyebrow and Finn shrugged, looking rueful, as if he was fully aware he was playing the pawn in the game between Nick and Kain.

"Soda for me," Mark said. "I need steady hands, especially with Nick here directing the action." Mark's eyes slid over Nick.

And Finn gave Nick a very sober look, as if asking him if he knew what he was doing.

Nick's lips quirked and he eyed the camera as he bit into a cookie. *Are you watching me now, Kain? See what you pushed away?*

"So how long have you two known each other?" Finn asked, folding his arms and lingering.

Mark munched on a cookie, happily oblivious to the undercurrents, like the chill breeze that worked through Telemachus House. "I helped Nick and Miguel move a couple times. We, uh, are all friends."

"Uh-huh." Finn settled on the long table and Nick wondered if Kain had ordered him to play chaperone. "I don't think I've seen you around before at the clubs."

"Students are too poor to afford the scene," Mark said. "In fact, I have to fucking move again. I managed to get my stuff in storage when my lease ran out, but I don't have a place to crash for a few days." He looked rather pointedly at Nick. "I may have to sleep rough."

Mask

"Shit, Mark, you didn't say! That sucks," Nick commiserated.

"Yeah." Mark lifted his T-shirt, scrubbing his face.

Finn and Nick couldn't help but examine his softly muscled torso since he'd put himself on display.

"I can help you," Nick offered quietly. "I'm pretty experienced with moving. And maybe you could stay here until you find a place."

Finn cleared his throat and hopped off the table. "Nicky, help me get Mark's soda?"

Nick rolled his eyes at that excuse, but followed Finn just out of earshot, while Mark ate another cookie, studying the budding sculpture.

Face suddenly looking weary and much older, like an aged elf, Finn said, "You're playing with fire when you play with Kain. He's not like other men, Nick."

Nick tugged his T-shirt down at the neck, showing off a finger-shaped bruise. "I know. But it can't be all the way he wants it."

"He wants you, kitten. Don't doubt it. He wants you, but he's...." Finn sighed. "He just wants you safe."

"He shoved me away last night! He seduced me for weeks, woke me up, and then he fucking pushed me away like he couldn't stand my touch!" Nick's throat tightened as he remembered. Innocent need. Crushed. The slam of a door. Shaky, uncertain.

Rejected.

"He wants inside you as much as you want him there," Finn repeated, shaking his head. "Okay, work with your friend—who is delicious, by the way, and so obviously available—and after you're done, come to my room in the north wing. I'll give you a massage for those sore shoulders."

"I should ask Kain if Mark can stay the night."

Finn chewed his lip. "Nuh-uh. You let me do that. And to be on the safe side, I'll ask his lordship if Mark can be *my* guest."

SO THAT was how Nick found himself later on Finn's massage table, relaxing against the heating pad that warmed the skin of his stomach. It was covered with fresh white towels and a linen pillow, smelling faintly of freshly crushed rosemary.

Finn obviously took massage seriously.

Acting on a hunch, Nick probed, "You do this for him, don't you?"

"Sometimes he can't sleep because he's hurting, yes," Finn sighed. "Did you ask him about the cop this morning?"

Nick shook his head. "Not yet, and since you told the detective Kain was with you after… after he was with me, he couldn't know anything about that hustler, right?" Nick raised his brows at Finn.

"Um. I've warmed some river rocks. I'm going to put them on the center of your back."

Nick turned his head to watch since this kind of exotic pampering was new to him. The stones felt smooth and oddly comforting as Finn carefully placed them.

"All right, just lie there and relax for a while. I'll go find Mark and see if he wants to stay here and then prepare him a room."

Nick's eyes were closing, as he hadn't had much sleep. "'K…."

"OBSIDIAN…?"

Nick blinked, malleable from the combination of warm oil, hands digging into his shoulders, his back. He'd be embarrassed at his hardness but some time during the massage he'd recognized it wasn't Finn ministering to him.

A single candle lit the space. He saw a shadow through the curtain that surrounded the cot and sat up.

"I felt one of your hands so I know it's you. Why is it gloved?"

"I didn't reject you, Nick. Christ!"

A black silk scarf was held out in silent invitation, fluttering to Nick's lap.

Heart pounding, Nick took the olive branch, covering his eyes.

He felt the breath of sudden movement against his face. Kain pushed him down on the massage bed, took hold of his wrists. Ruthless, gentle, totally in control.

Kain fastened them above Nick's head, with what felt like another silk scarf, leaving Nick totally helpless. He'd obviously come prepared.

Nick held his breath, waiting....

A gloved finger ran down the center of his chest, circled one nipple.

"Please! Please don't pull away from me this time!" Nick begged, exposing his hurt, his need.

The towel was yanked aside and Nick could feel Kain looking at him. A gloved hand bracketed his sex, possessive over his thigh.

Lips brushed the tip of his needy erection. A tongue. Tasting him....

Nick shuddered, whimpering, open.

"This is mine," Kain said, very firmly.

"Yes," Nick whispered.

 CHAPTER 8

"I MEAN… um," Nick backpedaled, blushing.

"You can't take it back." But Kain was smiling against Nick's thigh. Nick could feel it, his senses hypersensitive to every sensation since he was blindfolded. No, more than that, it was like his body, heart and mind tuned up to another level when Kain was around. Like Kain unlocked something inside Nick and unleashed it so they could both enjoy his effect on Nick.

"Can too," Nick rasped, his body tight as wire, eager slave to Kain's breath, lips, tongue, touch. "I feel a bit like one of those Victorian maidens I've read about. If a man took down her hair, it meant—"

"She belonged to him now. It meant sex." Kain stroked Nick's hair. "I'd like it if you grew it longer. Maybe down your back so I could wrap it around my wrists." Kain bent closer to Nick and whispered, "You won't be deprived or guilty or stifled the way you were with your boyfriend. I'll give you everything you crave."

"Uh-huh…." Nick closed his eyes tightly under the blindfold. "In the meantime, I have the idea we are going to argue a lot."

"You're just naturally contrary, kitten. If I said 'white,' you'd say—"

"'Vermilion,' seeing as I'm an artist. I wouldn't want to be clichéd. Kain…." His hands knotted into fists in his silk bond. He needed—but it was completely up to Kain when he would be touched. He had submitted himself when he gave Kain his sight and now trusted him with his vulnerable body.

"I shouldn't get so close to you." Kain's fingers brushed the bruises on Nick's shoulders, as if he was aware of the direction of Nick's thoughts.

Nick frowned, not liking that at all. "What if I want you close?"

"You don't know what you want. You were pulled away from a long-term relationship, from your regular workplace, from your home, even. And I'm the bastard who shoved you from your safe rut, so I should know."

"Brought me under your roof. Regrets? It's too late, Kain."

"Aren't you afraid of me? A detective came by this morning, wanting to speak to me. You *should* be afraid."

Nick brushed Kain's fingers. "You feel like shit because you left bruises on my shoulders. It doesn't strike me as the behavior of a killer of prostitutes."

"Then I guess I'll just have to reward your belief in me."

Kain swallowed Nick's cock, smooth.

"*Oh!* Oh, shit! Oh, Obsidian!"

"Like me, Nick? Like me taking you, owning you?"

"I want to come, come inside your mouth," Nick begged, embarrassed by the sound of his voice, begging, but needing it even as he flushed at his own bald admission. Yet how often had he thought about this after a sizzling back and forth with Obsidian? His come on Kain's lips.

Kain asked, "Can you hold on? It will be better if you can, little one."

"Tease me. Kain, please tease me, use me…."

Kain's gloved hand slid up to cover Nick's. "You're mine to use."

Nick gripped it, hanging on, both anchored and aroused. He felt like the only solid thing was Kain, like his own body was a feast to be eaten, to be enjoyed. Only for Kain. Archaic thoughts, but deeply sexy to Nick.

"I bet you're a wonderful little cocksucker, aren't you? I can't wait to have you on your knees, hands cuffed behind your back, maybe with your ass red from my hand, while I feed it to you, fuck your mouth, use my little cocksucking whore."

Nick's opening contracted as a finger circled it....

His lips parted. Kain would penetrate him. Fuck him. Spend on his skin at some future time when Nick's hair was longer, so Kain could fist it in his hands as he rode Nick.

Wait.

Dazed, he frowned, wondering what it was about Kain's finger that had caught his attention, but then Kain devoured him, humming, ruthless, demanding Nick's absolute seduction, absolute release.

Panting, Nick spread his legs wider, raising his heels so they dug into the padded surface, so they shifted, restless, as he pushed up, his body an arc of need, suspended, toyed with at Kain's will.

When he came—a starburst kindled in their chat room, teased by Obsidian, so now he wanted nothing more than to be Kain's slut, to be what Kain said he needed to be, a hot little whore—when he came, his balls tightened, Kain greedily sucking him. His nipples, his fingertips, up his arched throat and through his ragged cry of submission.

"Kain! Take me!"

PANTING, he felt lips on the chilly trail on his cheek, touching the single tear. Kain nuzzled him, his heavier stubble marking Nick's skin, as his touch had marked Nick's feelings.

"Nick, it's just sex. Come down, kitten."

"I gave myself! I've never done that so completely before. I just….
Fuck, I feel like I shed a layer of skin or something, kind of raw now."

"Unwise to give yourself so completely, but I knew you'd be like
this." Kain's voice vibrated with suppressed feeling. Satisfaction, buried
need. "I knew all I had to do was touch you and you'd let me have you,
let me tease you, hurt you."

Struggling to shove down feeling, Nick sat up. His body was
trembling, singing; his emotions felt rasped by sandpaper. "Hurt?"

"I like to do that sometimes, just a little. It's what the detective was
referring to when she said my 'tastes'."

"Oh." Nick chewed his lip. "You were monitoring her this
morning."

Kain chose to focus on their intimacy. "I want to cane your ass, get
you to a place beyond tears. You'll kiss the hand that hurt you and beg
me to spend all over your open legs."

Nick's breathing picked up. He reached out and groped for Kain's
face.

Kain immediately stiffened, pulled away.

Did Kain… fear him? Why?

"Just a kiss," he breathed, shifting closer by slow inches until his
searching mouth glanced against Kain's lips. "Please, I was good. And
maybe one day I'll let you cane me. I want to wear your come."

His lips stuttered against the side of Kain's face, persuasive,
asking….

"*No.*" Kain gripped Nick's wrists, holding him away. "Oh, God,
no. You have to be safe. It has to be on my terms, or I'll lose control."

"Didn't you ever kiss any of those prostitutes?"

Flatly, he said, "No, I never do that."

"What…," Nick licked his lips, "what do you do with them?"

He heard Kain's quickened breathing, felt the warmth of the
proximity of his big, muscled body.

"Kain, it's all right. For some reason I find the idea of you being with men who look like me weirdly erotic. As long as you won't do it anymore, of course! Talk to me, take me deeper."

"Sometimes I like to watch them," Kain admitted. "I make them perform for me, hump my leg or slut themselves for me while we're observed in some club."

"So you do go to clubs?"

"I always wear a black mask." Kain tugged Nick's black silk blindfold. "And I blindfold them as I do you. There is nothing like caning a slim blond boy, making him cry out, lick my leather boot, and then jerking off and coming over his upraised ass. And sometimes...."

Nick was barely breathing, spellbound as he had been in their intimate chat discussions. Kain took him forbidden places. Pushed him. Turned him on.

"Sometimes I don't let the boy come. We might reach an agreement that I can turn him over to a couple of men I select so I can watch him get gang banged. Does that scare you?"

"I don't know," Nick admitted, rawly honest. He swallowed thickly, heart hammering in his throat. He wished he could tell himself he was turned off, but at least in fantasy, he wanted to play that role for Kain. "Did you know the boy who was killed last night?"

Nick's wrists sagged, abandoned by Kain's grip.

"Kain, no, I was just—!"

But he knew he was alone before the soft sound of the door closing.

MARK fell away from the door when Finn opened it.

"Oh, uh, I could have sworn it was bolted," Mark said, flushing under Finn's arched brows.

"It was. The master of the house didn't care for the idea of a house guest stealing the silver."

"If you mean that stuff we ate with at dinner, it was black and spotted. Almost as dingy as the lace tablecloth."

Finn shrugged. "I like to call it the 'ruined Gothic' look."

Mark leaned against the door, crossing his muscular arms and smiling, reluctantly caught by Finn. "You invented it?"

"I work with what I have." Finn spread his hands. "Are you going to continue to hit on Nick?"

"I don't see how that's any of your business," Mark said coolly.

"None at all. Only I wouldn't mind sleeping in here with you, all locked up." Finn's eyes warmed when Mark took a deep breath... and came up with nothing to say. "It's what I told Mr. Mitchell, and the only reason he allowed you to stay here."

"So it was a ruse."

Finn leaned close and brushed Mark's lips with his own smiling ones. "Oh, no, it wasn't. I'm always very honest with my boss and even more honest when I'm fucking or being fucked."

Breathless, Mark sputtered, "Jesus!"

Finn kicked the door shut.

MARK was yawning later that morning, rubbing his wild peaks of brown hair as he walked into Nick's studio. He studied the colors his friend was mixing.

"Red and yellow ochre, lamp black, burnt sienna, raw umber...." Mark took note. "All you need is some crushed lapis lazuli for Van Eyck's pure blue."

"I'm feeling primal." Nick shrugged, studying the canvases he'd previously prepared for one that felt the right size, shape.

"Man trouble," Mark said abruptly. He sat on the bench and watched Nick claim his choice. "While you burned the midnight oil, I slept with Finn," he added baldly. "Well, we didn't exactly sleep. And we were never quite horizontal either."

Nick's eyes widened and his brush lowered. "Oh, wow."

EMPHATIC charcoal stuttered over pristine surface. Nick closed his eyes, fading in and out of his conversation with Mark, the thoughts that had driven him, pushed him all night until he'd exhausted himself on innocent canvas.

Kain's left hand. Bare skin. His right hand had been gloved, but not the left. Why?

"He doesn't want me to see him," Nick muttered darkly. "But I *need* to see him, and I will see him."

"The monarch butterfly's pigmentation warns predators—" Mark began.

"...that it is poisonous," Nick finished, remembering the recent lecture they'd both attended about the role of color in nature. "Why don't the men who crush our hearts wear tattoos or something?"

"Oh, Nick." Mark slid off the table and went to Nick, waiting until the blond looked up at him.

Nick bit his lip.

Mark hugged him. "So soon after Miguel? Nick, I'm sure that's all this is, just a need to fill the void. A need to be swept away, and from what you've told me about Mitchell, he sounds the type to do that to a fella. All mysterious Alpha male."

"Is that what happened with you and Finn? He swept you away?"

Mask

Mark smiled, shaking his head ruefully. "Finn just…. You can't say no to him, turns out! I actually came out here with the nefarious plan of getting closer to you, now that you and Miguel are done."

Nick played with Mark's Claddagh ring, worn on his right hand with the design facing outward, letting prospective men know Mark was single but open to a relationship.

"I'm so fucking tired. Kain and I…. Another disagreement."

Mark pressed his lips to the corner of Nick's mouth. "If you can't forget him then maybe I can help you get his attention. And if you need a rebound guy…." Another kiss. And it felt so good to be kissed. So good to be out in the open, in the light of the morning sun. Not confused and aching and left in the dark by the man he truly wanted.

Nick turned his head, accepting momentary comfort, his hands buried in Mark's bed hair now.

 CHAPTER 9

"WHERE the fuck is Kain?"

Nick and Mark sprang apart at the harsh voice interrupting their near miss with intimacy. Nick instinctively moved in front of Mark, suddenly feeling protective of his friend in Telemachus House, though he wasn't sure why except he felt the brush of angry eyes.

Kain?

I like to watch.

He raised his brows at the newcomer, a short, curly-haired brunet who was glaring at him and Mark while holding a bouquet of crushed long-stemmed red roses, some dripping as if they'd been yanked from water. "Who the fuck are you?" the invader demanded.

"I was about to ask you the same question, albeit more politely," Nick retorted, crossing his arms. "I'm Nick, a new employee of Kain Mitchell's. Did Finn let you in the house?"

"I walked in. The door was unlocked."

Nick frowned. That carelessness seemed unlike Kain and Finn, unless for some reason Kain had allowed this angry stranger to invade his home. But why?

"I'm Ross Green. I'm here to see that cowardly son of a—"

"I'm sure he's *aware* you are here, but Mr. Mitchell is something of a recluse. He doesn't just see people. And... he's not a coward," Nick gritted, forgetting his annoyance with Kain. He felt protective of him now, the way he'd felt moments ago about Mark. Oh no, his life wasn't confusing at all!

"He's ashamed," Ross sneered. "And so he should be after what he did!"

Finn suddenly appeared, hair pulled back with a bright pink and yellow bandanna, golden eyes hard. "Ross. I was making pastry in the kitchen when I saw you come in. *I* wouldn't have let you in, of course."

"He sent these to my mom!" Ross growled, shaking the flowers at Finn. "How dare he? Doesn't he see it's over between us, after what he did?"

"He's not a monster, Ross." Finn put his hands on his hips. "Even if you want to make him into some kind of villain over your loss. It's not that simple. He's not entirely black."

Ross took a deep breath and tears suddenly glittered in his eyes. "He killed Aaron. You know it and I know it. And I can take care of my mom. It's just appendicitis. I can handle the hospital bills. You tell him we aren't best friends anymore and I don't need his help!"

Finn glared. "I think he heard you. And on the friend front, maybe one day you'll get your head out of your ass and realize that losing you was the last thing he wanted."

Ross threw the roses to the stone floor. "But he did lose me. It's too bad he didn't just die in that fire!" He ignored Finn's angry growl and strode from the room, leaving Mark and Nick staring at Finn, wide-eyed.

"Go back to work, gentlemen," Finn barked, very unlike his usual serene self. "Show's over."

Instinctively, Nick looked up at the camera and thought about Kain watching. Ross had said they'd been close. How did it feel to have your former best friend hate your guts?

Lonely, the thought came through, almost as if Kain had whispered it for his ears alone.

Moonbeam: Will you talk to me?

Moonbeam: Kain, talk to me.

Obsidian: Did you enjoy it, his touch? Putting on a display for my eyes? Because I found I wanted to kill him for touching what is mine.

Moonbeam: It wasn't anything. Didn't you hear? He'd...slept with Finn.

Obsidian: I heard. I don't believe sleeping entered their encounter from what Finn described. I'm sure you're pleased with yourself, getting back at me with Mark. You knew I would be watching.

Moonbeam: Yes, but you know it's more complicated than that. Mine field. I'm just doing my best to walk through it to the other side.

Obsidian: The other side of what? You wanted to show me up. Does it make you feel better to know you can do that, even though I sign your paychecks?

Moonbeam: I... When we're together, I lose myself in you, like love against my skin. I need to get beyond the mask. Make it real. You didn't like being hurt, and turns out you are not the only one afraid of that.

Obsidian: Nick, don't touch him again. I won't be responsible if you do.

Moonbeam: What do you mean by that? It almost seems like a threat.

Obsidian: There is so much you don't know. I try never to harm you.

Moonbeam: Why is Ross Green so angry with you? Why does he believe you're a bad person?

Obsidian: He can think what he likes. He doesn't matter anymore.

Moonbeam: Somehow, I don't believe you. I think he hurt you. He said you killed someone called Aaron, but that can't be true.

Obsidian: I might have. Aaron...burned.

Moonbeam: Kain, I don't believe you meant anything to happen to Ross's friend.

Obsidian: Obsidian, call me Obsidian. You said I was a weapon, that I was brittle. You should be afraid of me.

Moonbeam: I was angry that you forced my hand into staying here but the truth is... I was drawn to come. I couldn't stay away from you. And you aren't like that. When we get close, I can feel your gentleness. You are careful with me.

Obsidian: What if I tell you I don't want to be?

Moonbeam: You are not a monster. I would feel it if you were. It would come out in the way I paint you.

Obsidian: I'm not what you think I am. I wish I was...safe.

Moonbeam: I'm not sure if I'd be so drawn to you if you were. So okay, what are you then?

Obsidian: Buried.

Moonbeam: That's why this choice of house? Buried in vegetation? But if you're so horrible, did you kill that boy, that hustler?

Obsidian: I don't know.

Moonbeam: How can you not know? Finn said he was with you.

Obsidian: I hope he was. I don't remember. And Finn... He's difficult to know. He says and does things for his own reasons.

Moonbeam: So your servant is as much shades of gray as you are. But I think Finn is loyal, whatever his reasons for doing things. And as for you, you can't just say something like that to me and not expect me to— What do you expect me to feel? Are you trying to drive me away?

Obsidian: I expect you to leave, of course. I will honor our bargain about Miguel, but you and Mark should leave this house. Especially Mark!

Moonbeam: Is Mark in danger?

Obsidian: I...don't know. He touched you. And now I want—

Moonbeam: Kain, I know this isn't easy for you, but I need you to talk to me! Please don't shut me out. It hurts...

Obsidian: Has left the room.

Moonbeam: It hurts. Goddamn you!

"NICK, you can't. You have to leave him alone, especially now!" Finn grabbed Nick's arm, glaring at him. "You don't know. You haven't.... Shit! You probably have led a very mundane life."

Standing outside the double doors that led to Kain's wing of the house, Nick yanked his arm free. "I am at a disadvantage but I'm not a fool and I'm not a child, Finn. And why is it that he trusts you, when he holds the rest of us away?"

Finn leaned against the paneled wall. "Some things I experienced growing up, probably. I understand him and I don't push him."

"And I do? But someone has to. Do you think he's happy, locked away like that? He's... frightened, Finn. As powerful as he is, as dangerous as he wants me to believe he is, I can feel him bleeding. I can't leave him alone like that."

Finn sighed. "He wants you to be his lover."

"So?"

"So that complicates things, I know. I once met someone... extraordinary. But it probably would have been better for both of us if I'd stayed away."

"But you didn't."

Finn's eyes were heavy with the weight of memory. "No, but we couldn't mate, not the way we needed to, so we finally broke apart. It was like ripping away skin. For him, and for me. Now... I don't even know if he's alive."

"Finn." Nick squeezed the other man's shoulder.

"So I know how you feel!" Finn stepped out of Nick's path. "But there are some doors you walk through and there is no going back to who you were."

Nick said, "I think we're already past that, Kain and I. I think the first night he singled me out... scared me, turned me on; he became my obsession as much as I am his. He seemed to know me. Know the side of myself I was hiding from, except in my art. And I need to be naked with someone. I need to be revealed, opened like a mystery."

Finn gave him a wry glance. "Very poetic, my passionate young artist friend. And speaking of mystery...." He nodded at the closed door.

Nick drew in a deep breath and moved toward it, knowing it was more than a simple threshold he was about to pass.

He was walking into Kain's world.

HE OPENED the door, surprised at first to find it unlocked, but then he remembered how nothing happened in Telemachus House that Kain was unaware of so he must want Nick here, the open door a silent invitation—if Nick was only brave enough to accept it.

Taking another deep, steadying breath, he entered a sitting room paneled with cherry, the thin wiry vines of ivy and wild jasmine piercing the cracks in the wood from the stained ceiling to open fronds and live inside the house.

The master's room was simply furnished with a wing chair, fireplace, cobwebs, and a pile of dusty, neglected books.

The floor creaked under his feet, another warning to Kain, if he was listening, that he was not alone.

Nick paused, his heart thudding in his ears, his palms damp. Should he invade deeper? The room was silent, just the disinterested tick of a grandfather clock, dust shifting in the faint light in lazy streams. And Nick, hesitating....

He pressed one of his hands against the door to Kain's bedroom. It swung open easily.

Kain, I have to know you. You woke sleeping beauty, made me want you.

A large canopy bed with stiff ivory lace curtains stood in the center of the room, dimly lit by a single candle. Nick frowned. Why did Kain have such a liking for primitive candlelight?

The tall windows were covered in swags of heavy bronze fabric, blocking out the morning light, but Nick could feel the residue of cool October air breathing from the bones of the room, hinting that the windows had been open recently, letting in the chilly, damp night.

Mask

Nick went to the bed, put a knee on it, nestled next to the long curled form.

He paused when he spotted the items on the bedside table, recognizing bruised red roses. Ross's roses. In a vase now, close to Kain.

Like hell you don't care.

He reached out and clasped a gloved hand.

"Hey," he whispered.

Kain turned his head, and jungle-green eyes caught Nick, burning, taking his breath.

Nick tugged Kain's glove off, closing his eyes. Words, wild feelings, blocked up in his throat, his chest.

He touched the roughened skin he'd exposed with his lips.

And Kain growled, *"Kitten."*

 CHAPTER 10

RED OCHRE.

Nick's brush hesitated like a caught breath, the moment before he put color to canvas. And that moment translated into remembering Kain's kiss.

He squeezed his eyes tight, the moment rippling through him like standing in the path of a bonfire pushed by the wind.

Kain's possessive kiss, taking him, reshaping him.

How could he even begin to channel through art the singing blood, the perspiration dampening his hairline, that moment of perfect anticipation before their kiss?

Staring into Kain's feral eyes, and then dropping his own because he was overwhelmed. Because he felt untouched, until now.

Hearing him whisper, "Kitten," and cup Nick's cheek, comforting him even as he took control. "It's just a kiss. Isn't that what you came for?"

The light touch of Kain's caress down his side, pulling him closer into an almost embrace. Hesitating, reading him.

His gaze moved back up, caught by the patience in Kain's green eyes. Patient as a predator waiting by a watering hole, watching Nick, watching his reflected emotions, his body language.

Mask

Waiting for the moment Nick's body wilted, shifted, awkward, falling like a leaf detaching itself from a tree.

BURNT SIENNA, RAW UMBER.

Music. He thought he'd almost heard it when they touched at last, fanciful as that was, as they made contact, building a bridge of flesh. How often had he shared things with this man that no one else knew?

Something passionate and unnameable tightened his throat, adding percussion to the beat of his pulse from his racing heart and stiffening sex.

It wasn't music. It was panting breath, wide eyes; it was suspense, like a wave readying itself to crash on the beach.

Kain rubbed his arm, almost seeming to need to reassure as Nick's body stuttered closer to his, to the moment when—

Kain leaned down and took him.

Nick gasped, "Oh, shit!"

His arms tentatively curled around Kain's shoulders, drowsy eyes meeting narrowed green ones.

Kain took his time, thoroughly kissing him. Slow, gripping him now, Nick's head falling back, released so he could take a breath, while Kain cupped his face, licking his parted lips.

But then Nick had to return, to demand, as he'd pushed things by coming to Kain's bedroom and offering himself in the first place. His lips prodding, joining Kain's, more broken breath, back again, hand moving higher, into Kain's silken hair, tugging. Take me. Crazy dance of blood.

LAMP BLACK.

Trembling now, shaking with the force of his arousal as Kain hefted Nick above him, their cocks rubbing together through their clothing. Gripping Kain's hair, restlessly moving.

Panting. Hurting.

Kain?

Kain gentling him… pulling away when Nick rooted for his mouth, answered with a slow lick that made Nick shudder.

"Oh, God, I want…!" Nick groaned.

Kain smiled. "That good?"

"You woke me up," Nick said, each word emphatic, billboard-sized.

The ache eased in intensity but went unanswered.

And Nick stared at the candle flame on Kain's bedside table, guttering from the chill that haunted Telemachus House like a moving spirit.

YELLOW OCHRE.

Now he leaned his forehead against the canvas, oblivious to the dampened pigment.

Show me. Be a mirror. Let me see him. What is he hiding from me? You have always been there, muse, and when I can't see someone, when I don't understand why I might feel lost or uneasy, you show me why.

Show me Kain.

FINN looked in on Nick and saw he was lost in his art. More, he looked like he needed to be.

Mask

Dinner was hot mushroom soup with peasant bread oozing melted butter and dark, foamy beer.

He sighed. He'd reheat it.

One thing was certain: Kain had met his match, someone as ethereal as himself, as driven.

"Finn?"

He spotted Mark by the entranceway and frowned as he watched him putting on a coat. It looked like one of Nick's.

"I need to walk and Nick needs it quiet, so…." Mark shrugged.

"So no metalworking."

"Not after his last encounter with the mysterious Mr. Mitchell, apparently. Now he needs oil and canvas far more than my humble presence." Mark grimaced and raised a brow when Finn's expression remained carefully bland. "Oh, come *on*, they definitely hooked up. But Kain left Nicky wanting. Treacherous bastard."

"You only say that because you wanted Nick for yourself."

Mark's head dropped back and he sighed. "I'm no match for Mr. Darcy, or whoever the fuck haunts this dump." He looked at Finn. "Care to go walking?"

"I'll just get my coat. I was going to come with you anyway," Finn said. "It's not safe walking around the estate after dark."

"Why is that?"

"The gardens are a mess. Fallen statuary, rotten porches. Like the house, it dates back to the Victorian period."

"Mitchell should clean this place up." Mark shook his head, lit up with irritation for the master of the house.

Finn smirked. "Kain would only do that if he actually welcomed visitors, but he wouldn't be much of a recluse if he liked people."

"I heard at one time he was the life of any party."

"Um."

"But now he prefers to be alone. Strange. Makes you wonder what could change a life so drastically, hmmm?"

"It's best not to get too curious about Kain."

"Nick being the exception."

Coat on, Finn put his arm through Mark's. "I really like you," he said as Mark opened the door. "And it's good I'm going walking with you. You never know who you might meet on a damp fall evening."

Moonbeam: I can't believe I fell asleep in your bed. When I woke up again, I was conveniently back in my own room.

Obsidian: Too much melodrama, poor Nick. But you're obviously giving that excess of emotion a workout in your art.

Moonbeam: I saw your hand but your face was shadowed. I could only really make out your eyes—which are extremely distinctive, by the way.

Obsidian: I don't want to talk about my appearance.

Moonbeam: Okay, so why the candles?

Obsidian: They don't hurt my eyes.

Moonbeam: Hmmm. Kain, I can't believe you didn't... I couldn't have stopped you.

Obsidian: I stopped me.

Moonbeam: I fell asleep and you kept me safe.

Obsidian: Not safe. I can't—you don't know.

Moonbeam: I still feel the energy of being with you. It flows out of my body and onto canvas but I can't find any relief.

Obsidian: Relief, hmmm? Something I know a little about offering you. If I'd hired you tonight, do you know what I'd do with you?

Moonbeam: You said you like to watch. Would you like to watch me?

Obsidian: Yes. Finn would take you down to my dungeon.

Moonbeam: You've got to be kidding! You have an actual dungeon in this house?

Obsidian: Not a real one. More like a playroom. It's in the basement.

Moonbeam: I imagine it smells earthy and there are vines covering the walls. Oh, a playroom. I've heard of those. So you like using toys on someone?

Obsidian: Yes. I have collected some, handled them with you in mind. Some are leather, some are cane...and some are blown glass, threaded with a blue filament which reminds me of your eyes.

Moonbeam: Blown glass? Sounds very...artistic.

Obsidian: I am an artist in my own fashion.

Moonbeam: So what would you do with me if I'd been hired as your companion for the night?

Obsidian: There would be wine at the table. I'd order you to strip, turn around so I could examine you from where I was sitting, paying particular attention to your high, round ass. I'd order you to open yourself for me and stand there, exposed, for as long as I wanted.

For you, it might seem like forever, your heart pounding, wondering just what I am going to do to you. Hurt you? Spank you? Whatever it is, you know I'll take you completely, mark you as mine.

Moonbeam: Oh, shit, Obsidian! Where would you be watching me? Describe your dungeon. I want to see it.

Obsidian: I have a wing chair. Books. A fireplace. It is set up for my comfort as I examine the merchandise I have purchased. Decide if I want to cane a boy, or tie him up, or have him suck me.

Moonbeam: Master of your own very cozy dungeon.

Obsidian: I'd finally allow you to sit down and sip your red wine. Your legs would be spread wide, of course, so I could admire your stiff prick. Your lips would be parted and there would be color in your face. I would take my time and I'd decide what I wanted to do with you.

Moonbeam: Wouldn't I be nervous? It would be my first time. I would be untouched...I mean, I am untouched.

Obsidian: I know you're a virgin, Nick. I like that, I like that sooner or later, I'll take your virginity. Feeling nervous is good, natural—it adds to the potent cocktail. I want you to fear your master, kitten, just a little. But something in your wine would settle you. I've used it before, the first night you slept under my roof...

Moonbeam: Shit, I wondered!

Obsidian: Does it make you angry? But alone with me, you can't smell of...fear.

Moonbeam: I am not afraid of you, even if sometimes I feel like you want me to be.

Obsidian: Nick...

Moonbeam: What next?

Obsidian: :deep breath: If you were really there, I'd choose between the spanking horse and the fucking machine.

Moonbeam: Fucking machine?

Obsidian: Finn custom designed it for me. A man of interesting and eclectic talents, Finn.

Moonbeam: How does it work?

Obsidian: I have to watch you; with you, it's only safe if I watch. But to see you come, to control it completely.

Moonbeam: How would it play out?

Obsidian: You wouldn't be afraid now, but so aroused. I'd get up from the chair and lead you to it. Before you climb on the table, I'd convince you to put on nipple clamps. Have you ever worn them?

Moonbeam: No, never. Do they hurt?

Obsidian: A little. I'd suck your nipples till they puckered and then I'd put them on. You'd gasp from the sudden hurt, but I'd stroke your hair and talk you through it. I'd promise you they'd add to the experience and your cock would be hard when I touched it, so I know you'll let me do what I want. You'd climb on the table and mount the long bench. I'd buckle you in. Your ankles...wrists...your neck, even a band across your lower back.

Moonbeam: I'm so hard now.

Obsidian: Fixed in place and ready for my toy. I'd coat my fingers and invade your ass, rubbing.

Moonbeam: :Squirms:

Obsidian: :Smirks: When you were loose enough, I'd place the blown glass dildo inside, warmed so it feels intense as it broaches you.

Moonbeam: And then?

Obsidian: I'd return to my chair to watch. I love the expression on your face as it slides in firmly for the first time. I have the remote control in my hand. You can see me holding it and know I totally control your experience.

Moonbeam: What does it feel like inside me?

Obsidian: Thick. It's me, Nick. It's an extension of me. You're moaning now as it slides in and out, your erection slick with your excitement but you're utterly helpless.

Moonbeam: What do you do?

Obsidian: After watching you take it, watching the machine fucking you, I get up and unzip myself. I feed you my cock and you want it. Licking my taste, desperate to come. My slutty little glory hole.

Moonbeam: Fuck!

Obsidian: When I'm close, I pull out of your hot little mouth and I come over your face. I want to see that. My come on your face.

Moonbeam: Kain!

Obsidian: You want to come?

Moonbeam: Yes!

Obsidian: Good boy. While you lick my cock clean, I reach underneath you and gently remove the nipple clamps, giving them a tug just as I pull them free.

Moonbeam: Uhhhh! Kain!

Obsidian: I can see you through the camera. Lick the come from your fingers. Let me see you. That's mine, the relief I gave you.

Moonbeam: :meekly: Yes, Kain.

Obsidian: So beautifully slutty. I think I'll hire you again for another night.

Moonbeam: :Whimpers:

Obsidian: Nick, go to sleep. There's a blanket on the couch I had Finn leave for you.

Moonbeam: Did you...feel so... drug me?

Obsidian: Your cocoa. Sleep, little one.

Moonbeam: I'll be pissed...s'in morning.

Obsidian: But now you're smiling. I pleasured you and now it's time to be safe.

Moonbeam: Safe?

Obsidian: From me.

Moonbeam: I don't want to be kept safe from you!

CHAPTER 11

"IS THIS your friend?"

Shaking, Nick swung away from the steel slab and the white sheet-draped body.

He crossed his arms, shoulders hunched.

Oh, no. Not him.

Tears pricked his eyes.

"Mr. Anders?"

"Yes." He looked at the doctor, avoiding Detective Manners' narrowed gaze. "Did I do this somehow?"

"Excuse me?" the detective butted in.

Hoarse, Nick said, "I feel... responsible."

"Could be you are." Manners nodded.

Oh fuck, he was going to.... He choked, streaming tears, barreling from the room. Trash can, shaking hands, bent over—

Finn was there, his eyes also reddened from crying. He reached over and rubbed Nick's back. "You knew him a long time?" he asked softly.

"Y-yes," Nick rasped. "Long time." He squeezed his eyes shut, but a tear escaped, rolling a chilly path down his cheek.

Mask

The doctor had followed him from the morgue along with the detective. He reached out and cupped Nick's shoulder. "A lot of people feel responsible, but unless you murdered him, you're really not."

Nick shook his head. *This can't be happening!*

Finn passed him a handkerchief he'd dampened in the nearby water fountain.

Detective Manners crossed her arms, waiting.

"I won't apologize for my reaction," Nick whispered, still shaking. He couldn't get warm. "Mark was a close friend for a long time. We worked together on many art projects, which takes a special kind of trust. Oh, shit, Why him?"

Manners looked unmoved. "Was he a boyfriend of yours?"

Nick closed his eyes, remembering the single kiss, and then Obsidian's veiled threat, but Obsidian would never— "No, we... I'd just broken up with someone so we were just friends."

"Yet he was staying in your employer's house. Kind of out of the ordinary."

"He, uh." Nick rubbed his smarting eyes. "He needed a safe place to crash for a while."

"Didn't turn out to be so safe, did it?" she asked silkily.

Hoarsely, he said, "No."

"Is this really necessary, Detective Manners, grilling Nick this way? Mark was a close friend."

"Then he'll want to know what happened to him, won't he? Do you know why he went walking alone on the roads near the house?"

Nick shook his head. "I was consumed with my art last night." He swallowed thickly. "I wanted him *gone*, all right? I wanted him to leave me alone so I could concentrate because my painting was so damned important!"

Finn rubbed Nick's back. "You didn't mean for anything bad to happen to him, kitten."

"And what about you, Mr. O'Connell? When did you see him last?"

"I made dinner and he didn't show. I assumed he was working on one of his own projects or taking it easy in his room."

"You didn't see him leave the house?"

Finn blinked. "No. If I had, I would have gone with him; the estate has all kinds of broken statuary and unsafe wooden structures."

Manners looked up from writing on a pad. "So the last time someone saw him alive was at lunchtime, is that right?"

"Yes, at the time he told me he was going to look for a place of his own." Finn chewed his lip. "Because Nick was obviously with... he is spending time with Mr. Mitchell."

Manners raised a brow at Nick, obviously mulling. "If there was nothing between you and the victim, why would he leave if you and Mitchell got cozy?"

"I don't know. I didn't speak to Mark, but it wasn't like that. Not from my side, anyway. Though one time...." Nick cut himself off.

"One time what?"

"I think what Nick is reluctant to say is that Kain was a little jealous of Mark," Finn interceded. "Of course, that eased when he understood that Mark and I had spent some time together."

Manners shook her head. "Nice arrangement, living under Kain Mitchell's roof. Apparently you can get everything you need—on hand," she looked pointedly at Nick, who flushed, "or order in."

Finn pressed his lips together primly but didn't take her bait.

Manners held up a plastic bag which contained drawing paper, from what Nick could make out, the curled edges stained brown. He stared at it, wondering what its significance was, and then he realized it must be the remains of Mark's sketch pad.

The brown wasn't *ink* but Mark's dried blood, and under that watery imprint he could still make out the fine sepia lines of a sketch. A familiar figure in the nude.

Nick took a deep breath, rubbing his own upper arms. Oh, Mark.

"He seemed to have some pretty strong feelings about *you,* Nick. This is just one of the sketches we found near the body, most of which were shredded, either by the victim… or his killer, we figure."

Nick shook his head. "I didn't know he was doing that, sketching me," he offered, bewildered. "I do the same thing, work out my feelings in my art. Some I don't choose to share with anyone."

"Well, maybe someone did know he was sketching you. You had a breakup recently?"

"Yes, but it wasn't…. Miguel wouldn't hurt anyone."

"He was arrested recently." She smirked at Nick's surprised look. "Oh, I've been looking into your life very closely, Mr. Anders. You and anyone else who lives under Kain Mitchell's roof."

"That had nothing to do with hurting someone!"

"And what about Kain Mitchell? Finn already said he was jealous of your relationship with the victim."

Nick shook his head. "I can't believe he'd hurt anyone. He's not what you think, Detective. I think he's actually a very lonely man."

"And also a possible killer." Manners looked at Finn and raised a cool brow. "You be sure to let your boss know I'll be out to see him. Soon." Then she leaned close to Nick. "Three little blonds dead, who look just like you, and now a close friend of yours who had a thing for you. If you're protecting him, remember, you might be next."

IT WAS still dark when Ross wheeled into the back alley to his bicycle shop. He shoved back his brown curly hair and wiped the sweat the long ride had given him. But it had felt good, clean. Helped him to forget about Kain and the ache of everything he'd lost; his best friend, and his lover, Aaron, both in one night.

He shook off his gloves and dug in his jeans pocket for his keys, thinking he wanted to get organized today, spiff the place up since a certain hot medical doctor would be dropping by, someone very much into mountain bike riding, which Ross admired but personally found too reckless for his more conservative tastes. But he sold a lot of beautifully modified bikes to enthusiasts. Dr. Armand Leyland had suffered an accident only a few days ago but already he wanted to talk to Ross about replacing his wrecked bike with the newest model—specially made for him, of course.

Thinking of the gorgeous doctor made him eager to enter his shop, and so he nearly stepped on the latest offering.

A black rose, wrapped in cellophane.

Breath hitching, he looked up and down the street, deserted at this hour.

He forced himself to pick it up. The creepy gifts had stopped coming a few weeks back. Up until the incident with sending his mother flowers at the hospital and offering to pay for her care, he'd been sure Kain had been responsible.

And now after storming Kain's house, here was another one.

It couldn't be a coincidence.

IN THE long black car sent to return them back to Kain's house, Finn reached out and squeezed Nick's hand.

Hoarsely, Nick whispered, "Do you really think Kain...?"

Finn chewed his lip. "I think maybe you should consider moving out, kitten."

Unshed tears brimmed in Nick's eyes. "Oh, my God! It wasn't a coincidence, like Manners said. Somehow it's my fault!"

"No, Nicky, no, no." Finn rubbed his back. "It's not *anyone's* fault, not even... not even *his*."

"How can you say that?" Nick was so knotted up and confused he was afraid he'd have to ask the driver to stop so he could get out and walk around. Just breathe....

"It's not his fault because of what he is," Finn said, very simply, sending a chill down Nick's spine. He'd wondered... sensed something. What was the truth about Kain?

Nick wilted against Finn, one white hand clenched in his coat. "What is Kain?"

"Whatever did that to Mark, it was a monster," Finn said, not answering Nick's question. Or possibly he was.

IN THE foyer, Nick stared up the long curved stairs that led to Kain's wing.

"You need to stay away from him," Finn scolded again, taking off his coat and then the one he'd lent Nick, since Nick couldn't find his.

Nick stood wooden, wanting to shut Finn out. Just... think for a moment.

Finn repeated, "You need to leave this house."

Nick's gut and throat ached. Yet underneath that, making him feel guilty, was a familiar prickle of excitement because he was close to Kain.

He put a hand on the banister, looking up at the shadowed hallway.

"Nick, listen to me!" Finn urged. "He doesn't know what he wants from you. But I do, and it's not... not a safe thing. You can't stay here! He's trying so hard but—"

Nick's jaw tightened. He glared at Finn. "What happened to my jacket?"

Finn answered, "Mark took it."

"How do you know that? Manners told me he was found wearing it but you weren't in the room when she did."

"It was only logical. Most of his possessions were in storage." Finn frowned, elfin features sharpening under Nick's steady gaze.

"Ummm." Nick stared at Finn, mulling. "About my moving out to get away from Kain. Come take a look at something with me," he directed, heading for his studio.

FINN stared at the slashes of primal color on canvas. The clenched white hand. The blood on sensual, cruel lips.

"Oh my," he said, hand on his throat. "How is it you see him?"

"My muse," Nick said. "Kain and I connect. It's as if I was waiting for him. As if I was always meant to be touched, burnt, by his need." He shrugged. "So I'm not sure leaving him would change anything between us."

Finn grimaced and then nodded to another panel, buried behind the shadowed portrait of Kain.

"No." Nick shook his head. "I don't want to share that one."

Finn studied him, much as he had Nick's painting.

"It was a dream I had," Nick breathed.

A little at a time, Finn pulled away cloth, unveiling the unfinished triptych.

Nick flushed, still finding it hard to accept what his painting had exposed.

Kneeling at a leather-clad Kain's feet, kissing the hand that held a cane. On a nearby spanking horse, another young man was tied, his body marked by Kain, and now Nick wanted... asked....

"I'm sorry," Finn whispered. "I shouldn't have—some stuff is meant to be private."

"I can't believe I'd have such dreams," Nick admitted painfully. "It's like I don't know myself. But this is how I see him, us, at some future time."

Finn shook his head, looking at Nick almost wistfully. "How you feel about him is all here, as if you'd painted your body with the shades of your desire."

Nick rubbed his eyebrow tiredly, going to the window and the dawning light, leaning against it and seeing the barren October wild garden, tall grass laced with frost. "If he hurt Mark," he whispered. "Why can't I hate him?"

Finn went to Nick, put an arm around him. "You ache to have him inside you. I understand, little one. It was the same for me once, with—" But Finn closed his mouth.

Nick's eyes widened. "When you said you understood him...?"

"I... knew someone like him once. I belonged to him."

"Belonged?" Nick stared into Finn's eyes, looking for answers to the mystery that had caught him, that was cutting into him.

"Yes," Finn admitted hoarsely. "Nick, he doesn't know what he's asking of you, only that he needs you."

AS BEFORE, the door into Kain's rooms was unlocked. Nick took a deep breath, hesitating at the threshold.

Grief wanted to spill for Mark yet, strangely, he felt like he could only find surcease with Kain. Kain, who he didn't know, wasn't sure could be trusted.

His mysterious employer was lying on his bed, an open book beside him. He looked up when Nick entered the room, an uncertain expression in his shadowed green eyes.

Finally, he held out his hand.

Nick didn't fight fresh tears now. Not now he felt he'd come home to some place where he could relax, truly be himself.

He was alone with Kain, open, vulnerable, and it was right he feel this way.

Burn me.

But if Kain had hurt Mark...?

Kain's hand dropped.

Nick crossed the room, crossing more than just the physical space between them. He went to Kain, knelt by the bed. He took the scarred hand, pressed his lips against ruined, melted flesh.

 CHAPTER 12

NICK reached out, as tentatively as if he were about to pet a black jaguar through the bars of a cage. Green eyes burned his, holding him in place.

Kain jerked away from Nick's fingers.

"I can't—!" Kain pulled his knees up, his clenched hands gleaming taut white in the candlelight. Turning his back partially to Nick, as if needing to shut him out. Still Nick could barely make out his features in the semi-darkness, which he knew must be a deliberate choice on Kain's part. "I always think I can, but when you're here it's so much more." Softer, he asked, "Do you feel that?"

Nick nodded, licking his lips. "This thing between us… growing stronger. Kain, it hurts. I can't sleep. If I didn't have my canvas to project these feelings on…." Nick scrubbed his hair, restless.

"I know."

Nick ached to ask him what was going on. He could feel the other man's pain radiating like a red hot wound.

Let me help you, let me touch you. Kain, you're only alone if you want to be.

"I'm afraid for you, afraid of what you make me feel," Kain whispered.

Nick tried to keep it light, teasing. "I thought you were in control."

Kain gave a weak laugh in response but Nick clearly heard the desperation, the hint of almost tears threaded through it like dark strands. "Not when it comes to you. I was numb." He looked at Nick, sharp green eyes almost accusing. "You woke me up too."

"Hey, you're the great manipulator who brought me here, remember?" Kain so unsure of himself ripped into Nick. He didn't like it. He wanted to right the balance between them, and that meant somehow helping Kain find his equilibrium. But he had no idea how to do that.

Kain would only let him so close.

Finally, Nick leaned his head against Kain's back.

Kain allowed it, although Nick could feel him trembling. He allowed Nick to play with his fingers, trace the scars on one hand until it was as if he could take no more, and he got up silently and went to the window, staring at the trees made ratty by the cold fall winds.

"I'M SORRY about Mark," Kain said, ages later, as Nick watched him, a pencil moving over a pad he'd found by Kain's phone, sketching Kain's back, trying to capture the occasional flash of his eyes. He was hungry for any glimpse.

"Did you hurt him?" Nick asked quietly.

Kain's body tensed and Nick hated that he needed to ask.

"I can't believe you did," he added. "Maybe it's because I don't want to, but when I think of how afraid you are to get closer and hurt me…. But even with all those things you like to do in clubs, the caning and watching and maybe participating in those staged gang bangs, the young men you hire always agree, don't they?"

"Yes, of course they do, even if I pay," Kain said. His head fell forward. Weary, he continued, "I don't know about the rest. Finn says I

102

go out sometimes at night. He's even found me places and driven me home. But I don't remember."

"Finn's a very handy man," Nick said lightly.

Kain looked over his shoulder at Nick, as if alerted by his tone. "I thought you liked him?"

"Very much." Nick sighed, reluctant to say more. "And I...." He swallowed. "I have feelings for you. You know it."

Kain gave a curt nod. "You wouldn't paint me if you didn't. You wouldn't come to my room."

"But I don't know if I'm ready for the world I paint," Nick admitted, feeling raw when he remembered the triptych Finn had glimpsed. "For the things I want you to do to me."

"COCOA?" Kain offered later.

"Is it drugged?" Outrage was threaded through Nick's question. He wasn't going to put up with this much control on Kain's part, not anymore.

Kain sighed. "I know it seems extreme but I really only do it for your safety. Finn thought—" He closed his mouth.

"Finn? So the drugged cocoa was *his* idea? Interesting. But I don't understand you, why you're so afraid you feel you have to resort to this. It always seems as if when I get closer, you find some way to shove me away."

"I know you don't understand. How could you?"

"Kain, don't do it again."

"Nick, it's not *you* I don't trust."

Nick could see how tired his maybe lover was. See it in the slumped long lines of his body, even though Kain was careful, as always, to keep his face in shadow.

Still hiding.

"Then trust me! If you need a time out, just let me know and I'll give you space."

There was a long pause as Kain considered.

Nick felt suspense that seemed far out of scale with the simple request, but instinctively he knew this was a building block, an agreement for a relationship.

Equal partners.

Would Kain agree, offer Nick that respect, or was this another wrong turn that Nick would have to put behind him?

"Let me help you protect me, if you are so sure I need protection," Nick said, finally unable to wait on Kain's response. He knew he was pushing again, but even their temperaments were different; Kain, crafty and a planner, a watcher, spinning a web in silence while Nick exploded like a firecracker if he didn't get the touch, the reassurance, the grounding he needed.

"I won't do it again," Kain finally agreed, green eyes burning a promise from the shadows.

IT WAS entirely natural later, even though they still shared the same room filled with pendulous jasmine and ivy swaying in the invisible chill breeze of Telemachus House, that Kain went to his armchair and after paging through a book listlessly, reached for his laptop.

As if it were the signal he was waiting for, Nick returned briefly to his own room and retrieved his, but brought it back to Kain's room because he wanted both kinds of intimacy: physical and the familiar cyberspace confessional he shared with Kain, and only Kain.

For Nick, the best of both worlds, until they were closer, until they mated.

FINN stood in the entranceway of Telemachus House, staring at the coats hanging in the massive old-fashioned wardrobe. His fingers reached out and traced the carved black walnut.

As he did, he heard the floorboards creak above as Nick left Kain's rooms and then returned moments later. No matter how he tried to caution Nick, it seemed he was determined to believe the best of his employer.

Finn knew he hadn't been the last one to see Mark alive. He hadn't seen him here, borrowing Nick's coat for an ill-advised walk alone.

Had he?

Moonbeam: Why do you always pull away?

Obsidian: I can't be around you for very long without wanting to—

Moonbeam: What?

Obsidian: Hurt you. Possess you in pain and in ecstasy. Both are ways you would surrender to me completely, ways I could move you.

Moonbeam: Okay. :deep breath: We are going to talk. We need to talk. This thing, it feels like a bonfire we've started on a beach. One gust of wind and it could burn out of control.

Obsidian: Nothing will change just because we talk! This is primal, predator and prey. You know I see you that way. It excites me.

Moonbeam: Calm down. And…it excites me too.

Obsidian: :grits teeth: You should be afraid. Why aren't you ever afraid?

Moonbeam: You want me close to you, otherwise why do you leave your door unlocked? You know I'll come here, that I can't help but come here.

Obsidian: Maybe.

Moonbeam: You tease me sexually, making me want you inside me. It's like you are luring me closer, readying me for your hand.

Obsidian: …

Moonbeam: You are a very frustrating beast sometimes.

Obsidian: :ironic: I suppose you see yourself as Beauty.

Moonbeam: Why, yes, thank you. And you make me feel the role, make me live it.

Obsidian: Brat.

Moonbeam: I bet I made you smile.

Obsidian: Maybe. You also make me want to spank you and not entirely for pleasure.

Moonbeam: :Radiant: Thank you. :wistful: Will you ever do that to me? Your palm on my bare ass…

Obsidian: I didn't say it was a good thing, the way you make me feel. If I thought I could control myself I would spank you, warm your ass under my palm, control you.

I'd love to have you walk in my bedroom one night and on my orders, push your jeans down before you spread yourself over my lap. You'd take your spanking like a man and then beg me to let you come.

Moonbeam: Okay, enough with the sexy or I won't be able to talk to you! I need to understand some things. Clear answers, please.

Obsidian: Yes, sir, Mr. Anders!

Moonbeam: :serenely rises above sarcasm: Tell me what happened to your hand, your face?

Obsidian: A fire.

Moonbeam: The fire at your penthouse apartment?

Obsidian: Yes.

Moonbeam: How did the fire start?

Obsidian: I was told that I set it. Are you sure you want to enter this castle? There are thorns, hungry thorns to make you bleed.

Moonbeam: Funny you say that; when I painted you, I painted blood on your lips.

Obsidian: You see me.

Moonbeam: That was my subconscious, but I need to understand in the daylight world. I don't always understand the fragments. Disturbing...

Obsidian: This is hopeless! I brought you here because I thought you'd be under my thumb, my total control. Handcuffed when I needed to spend myself on you. Blindfolded. My perfect slave. But you push for more. You demand to see me.

Moonbeam: Why is that wrong? I believe you are not a bad person. It's why I am not truly afraid of you, even though this house...the things Finn implies sometimes... And what happened to Mark—I know something dark is going on.

Obsidian: ...

Moonbeam: Okay, let's start with the fire since I think it's key. Why would you set it?

Obsidian: Because...because he was dead. I thought I tried to help him. Keep them off him, but—

Moonbeam: You mean Aaron, Ross's boyfriend?

Obsidian: Yes. I was...jealous of him. Not because I ever wanted Ross, but Ross was close to me, the only person close to me, and then he left me for Aaron because Aaron demanded it, saw me as a threat. He couldn't believe that I wouldn't reach out and try to take Ross from him.

Moonbeam: So did you have a part in hurting Aaron? You mentioned "the others".

Obsidian: I don't know! I don't remember what happened. It would have been fine, just me who made the mistake of taking them home, challenging them, knowing that even though they thought they'd have me, I'd somehow turn it around— I brought a threesome home from Manticore. They said they'd heard of me, craved me, Kain. Back then I loved to take the strongest men home and break them to my touch.

It started in my office at Manticore; I'd had a lot to drink that night. I demanded proof they could pleasure me, so one of them got down on his knees, so perfect. Devouring me, my cock, rolling my balls under talented, eager hands so I imagined pounding into him while the others watched, waited their turn.

Mask

Until I met you, that night was the best sex I'd ever had.

Moonbeam: :hushed: Shit! I've led a very sheltered life.

Obsidian: But I like you that way. I like your innocence, even as I want to tarnish it, pull you down in the mud and fallen leaves, invade you, have you, only me.

Moonbeam: Don't try to distract me. You know how easy I am. What went wrong that night? Tell me, Kain. Confide in me here.

Obsidian: It didn't feel wrong. It felt so good when one of them bit my neck. Christ, the rush, nailing some tight ass while he sucked on me.

CHAPTER 13

"LOUP GAROU?" Nick blinked. He was mixing paint the color of dyes someone might use on Easter eggs, not sure why *those* colors today except... he was happy after the night he'd spent with Kain, and those were happy colors, as light as soap bubbles, which is how Nick felt—or would feel if he hadn't suddenly needed to distract himself with something productive, aware that Detective Lisa Manners was here, even now questioning his would-be lover upstairs.

As if echoing the morning crushing the joy from their night, he suddenly focused on the runny crimson pigment and water and salt staining his hand and thought of Mark, of the sketches his friend had made, and swallowed thickly, living guilt. How could he feel this way, feel any happiness after Mark's gruesome death?

If this was a fairy tale, it was a dark one. Like Obsidian said, the castle was surrounded by sharp, bloody thorns. But I need to climb his walls. I need to be with him. In this fairy tale, the prince needs the pauper artist to come to his rescue....

"An Alpha werewolf. You don't believe they exist?" Finn smiled at Nick's blank expression. "I was seventeen and I met him one night in the woods near my home."

Nick put aside the paint and sat on the long table. He stared at Finn, who had amusement twinkling in his eyes, as if enjoying Nick's reaction.

"Werewolves are real?" Nick raised a brow.

"Ummmm. And other things. Dark, sexy monsters are all around us. And... darker *things.* Things you don't want to ever meet."

"I can't...." Nick gave a soft laugh and rubbed the back of his neck. "Finn, shit! That sounds like...."

"A fairy tale?" Finn cocked his head. "But isn't that what you've been painting this morning? Telemachus House as the castle of the mysterious and tormented prince and only you can heal him with your kiss?"

"Don't!" Hurt, Nick dropped his brush and his fists balled. "I didn't expect you to piss on my feelings! I thought you were my friend. Sort of," he was forced to qualify since Finn was an ambiguous companion.

"I'm not dismissing how you feel. I'm just asking you to open yourself to the possibility that there are things out there that are real, not fantasy. And anyway, about the master of our crumbling mansion—what does your gut tell you?" Finn's tone was serious, cool as running water. "After living under Kain's roof? All his secrets. All his fears. Don't you get he's a dangerous man?"

"Kain can be dangerous, yes," Nick whispered. "A little shady when it comes to getting something...." He flushed at Finn's ironic look. "Okay, *someone* he wants. But he tries. He tries to talk to me and he doesn't want me hurt."

"What does he want from you then?" Finn raised his brows, prodding.

"To enthrall me," Nick answered, very simply. "Or, to make me fall in love with him—but I don't think he sees it in those terms. Right now, he's using sex to entice me. And a roof over my head. And a job. Not inconsiderable ammunition."

Finn reached out and played with a strand of Nick's hair. "You can't really blame him for being drawn to you. You've got the personality of a sea urchin. And, just look at you, kitten."

Nick grimaced, since he wasn't exactly in love with his appearance. "Blond."

"If you ever did go to the clubs, you'd pick up more men than Kain did in his heyday. Because he was beautiful and intimidating, but you care about people."

"Chum in the water." Nick lifted a shoulder, indifferent. "But that's not me." In a certain mood, maybe, but he'd been so preoccupied with his passion for his art, and before that, with being Miguel's longtime boyfriend, wanting to believe they'd work it out.

"I don't know if it would be a good idea now, you clubbing. Kain's possessive side could come out. He's very protective of you. Willing to do anything to keep you, possibly."

"Do you think...? Mark?" Nick swallowed. "No, he told me he was sorry Mark was dead last night and I could hear the regret in his tone."

Finn just shook his head. "I hope not, Nick, but Kain.... He might not even remember hurting someone."

"His memory lapses. He mentioned them before, said you helped him with them."

"Yes." Finn held his gaze soberly.

Nick frowned. "And just now, when you talked about his appearance, you said he *was* beautiful."

"Mmmmmm."

Nick glared. "I will know him, Finn! But back to what you told me at the beginning of our conversation. Are you saying Kain is some kind of supernatural creature? A... *loup garou?*"

"He's something elemental, like a werewolf, yes. Why do you think this house otherwise? It's earthy, isolated. I told you I knew someone once...."

"So you're saying he's one of these shape changers?" Nick rubbed his forehead, trying to work it out.

"A werewolf? I don't know for sure," Finn said. "He's not exactly forthcoming. But I know Luke suffered from memory lapses and some of his kind were capable of terrible violence toward humans."

"Why did Kain hire you? Because you had experience with the supernatural?"

"When I first hit town, Kain and I *almost* had an interesting evening." Finn's lips curved and a wistful light came into his eyes. "Not his usual."

Nick looked away.

Smugly, Finn said, "So he's not the only possessive one."

"He's not mine. And I know he must have had… many lovers."

"Is that what your body tells you, that you're just one of many?"

"My body." Nick gave a rueful laugh. "*Primal.* I try to cool my body with my art. It's a safe outlet for expression."

Finn nodded. "It was that way for me and my Alpha, Luke. From the first night I met him, he was all I could think about. I dreamt about him, was sure sometimes he was even in the same room with me when I slept, watching me. Sometimes even now… I feel like he's around."

In a hushed voice, Nick asked, "Did he watch you when you slept?"

"Yes," Finn said, holding Nick's gaze.

"You called him an 'Alpha'?" Nick asked, shoving a paintbrush behind one ear as he both listened to Finn and tried to keep the color moving on his canvas until he could figure out what he wanted to explore.

"I was his human submissive," Finn confided. "I helped him control his… violent impulses. Some gifted humans live among us and having a mundane companion grounds them."

Nick's eyes widened. "Is that what Kain wants with me?"

"Yes, I think that instinctively he recognized you, what you could become for him, but he's newly made; he doesn't understand what he's asking, the danger he's putting you in."

"Danger." Nick wrapped his arms around himself. "But the sex?"

"It's like he's in your blood." Finn closed his eyes and his head fell back. "You want him too much; no matter what he's done, you feel like you could almost forgive him anything, but you have to stay strong, for him, for yourself." Finn's bright eyes opened again and he stared into Nick's. "Just how long do you think he's going to be able to hold off claiming you? If you were wise, you'd leave this house."

Nick gave his friend a cranky look, tired of him hinting that Nick should leave, but understanding that it probably came from a good place. "I guess I'm not wise."

"DETECTIVE." Nick nodded when Manners invaded the atrium, her sharp gaze taking in the art leaning against metal and glass walls.

"Mr. Anders." She was staring at the canvas Nick had done of Kain. Sensual lips wet with blood, tormented green eyes. "It turns you on that he's a killer?"

"Have you proof?" Nick swallowed, his heart thumping in his throat.

"Not yet, but I will. It's not like he's making it hard. Telling me he gets headaches, he can't remember…! Pathetic."

"I don't think he wants to hurt anyone."

"He seems pretty protective of you." She raised a brow. "He didn't deny he wasn't happy that Mark apparently made overtures to you."

Nick managed to keep his face serene. *Kain, what are you doing?* "Oh?"

"He told me to leave you alone, that you were innocent, untouched by this."

"He's…." Nick shrugged. "Just being nice."

"Uh-huh." Manners folded her arms, giving Nick a level look. "You ever visit his club, Manticore?"

"No, I'm a poor student and I was never into the club scene." Nick shrugged, feeling her glance slicing into him as if to spill his secrets—or more likely, any of Kain's he might be privy to.

Manners nodded. "For folks who like rougher play or just dinner and dancing, but the crowd is rumored to be somewhat... eclectic. Kain was a regular there until recently. Their floor show is stuff like submissives being flogged. You into that shit?"

Nick flushed. "That's hardly relevant. Kain told me he likes to watch, but that doesn't mean he hurt anyone."

"The little blond hustlers were regulars at his club. Didn't mind if someone roughed them up a little, by all accounts. Probably got off on it." Manners leaned close and whispered in Nick's ear, "They had bite marks on their necks and between their legs."

Nick shook his head, refusing to drop his gaze from Manners'. "I don't believe he's a bad person. He's merely isolated and lonely. And liking to watch sexual acts, that seems more like someone afraid to get close, don't you think?"

IN HIS bedroom, Nick lingered, restless.

So much for the wonderful night with Kain. His feelings of connection, of something deeper, had evaporated like a hazy fall mist in the harsh light of day.

He considered his laptop, waiting, and then glanced at his open suitcase. He could return to town, move back in with Marilyn, who would offer chocolate tea and sympathy.

Life would be simple again. Back in his rut.

And something told him, since Kain had been quiet all day, as if leaving him a choice, that this time he would let Nick go.

But was it what Nick wanted?

Moonbeam: When you were with your hired dates?

Obsidian: ...

Moonbeam: Did you...? Kain, were you intimate with them?

Obsidian: "Intimate," no. I fucked them and I bled them.

Moonbeam: Bled!

Obsidian: Some people are into cutting themselves and having someone suck the blood.

Moonbeam: ...

Obsidian: You asked.

Moonbeam: Do you ever think of doing that with me?

Obsidian: Yes. I try not to.

Moonbeam: What would you do to me?

Obsidian: Handcuff you in semi darkness so you couldn't look at me. Put my fingers inside you, stretching, and then my cock. I like the thought of you helpless, your blond hair shimmering in the light from the hallway while I fuck you.

Maybe you'd even have some paint on your pale arms or the side of your neck. Sometimes you don't notice it and I find that absent habit increasingly sexy.

Moonbeam: And would you bite me?

Obsidian: Christ, yes, I would bite you! I would spread open your legs and put my mouth to your inner thigh.

Mask

While you watched me, trembling, hard, I'd sink my teeth
in you and you'd come.

Nick made a soft sound, sitting away from his laptop and running his damp palms over his jeans. He noticed a bit of blue on the back of one hand and remembered how Kain said he liked that, how Nick wore his art on his body.

He was hard and perspiration darkened his hairline. His lips parted. On the edge.

But he also remembered Detective Manners' warning: *The victims had bite marks on their necks and between their legs.*

NICK couldn't bring himself to pack, and, hours later, a shadow leaned against his open bedroom door. Nick sensed Kain from where he was sitting on the window seat, knees pressed against his chest.

"Hey," Nick said.

"Hey." Kain moved deeper into the room, face tilted away from Nick's gaze, before he sat behind him, tentatively pulling him closer so Nick was resting against Kain's chest.

"You haven't left," Kain noted softly, a thread of pain, of almost-hope in his voice. "I waited all day. I was sure you'd leave."

"I don't know why," Nick said moodily. "Maybe it was what you said about how I forget to wash all the paint off my hands and body." He looked at the splotch of blue on the back of his hand. "I felt like you knew me, appreciated me."

"I watch you all the time."

Kain's hand covered Nick's, meshing their fingers awkwardly. The larger body looming behind him soothed Nick even as he felt the familiar rise of excitement.

117

Then Kain licked his neck.

Nick shivered and his head fell back in surrender.

CHAPTER 14

"MANNERS mentioned that club that you visit. The one you own?" Nick's eyelashes flickered as Kain gave him another long lick. He inhaled, shivering at the intensity, one hand clenching and unclenching over Kain's muscled thigh.

Kain was playing him slowly. Playing his body like one of Nick's works of art; preparing the canvas, choosing the colors, a masterpiece of drawn-out eroticism.

"I love what you do to me," Nick breathed, body on the edge.

"I know, kitten." Kain's fingernail bumped over Nick's erect left nipple. "I remember when Finn called you that, I wasn't sure if I approved but you are my kitten-boy, aren't you? You'll lick *me* one day when I ask. You're meant to be used, enjoyed... even passed around if I ask it."

Nick felt... ohhhhh. Panting, eyelids quivering as Kain whispered to him, luring him into a different world he'd never dreamed of.

Kain's hand moved softly down his body until it rested over Nick's erection where it strained against his clothing.

"But I'm not so sure I'll be able to share you after all. I'm a little... protective, as I mentioned to Detective Manners. I heard she brought up Manticore."

"Yes, and I want you to take me there, Kain," Nick asked calmly.

"Desperate to shake this mortal coil? You should know from what happened to your friend Miguel that it's not a place to go without protection." Nick only parted his lips as Kain leaned close and licked them, first the bottom one, slow, jungle-green eyes holding Nick's, as if testing him. "All right, I'll take you there, but I want you to stay close."

Nick took a deep breath, his heart pounding so hard he wondered if Kain could hear it. Was Finn right? Was Kain some kind of supernatural creature? And yet his own painting of Kain showed a side of him that Nick couldn't reconcile.

"That's it? Just... all right?" Nick swallowed, crushed in possessive arms, and quite satisfied that he was.

Kain licked under his ear almost affectionately and Nick made a thready sound, fingers digging into Kain's knee. "What if I find out that you're a—"

"Killer?" Kain whispered, eyes refusing to back down. "Maybe I am, Nick. Still think it's a good idea to stay under my roof?"

But when Nick hesitated, Kain stiffened, pulling away to climb to his feet, retreating from Nick.

Nick snagged his hand.

"I can't stay away from you," Nick confessed earnestly. "I know that you're doing all you can to protect me from whatever your secret is."

Kain gave a stiff nod, but his lips quirked. "I'm not sure how much longer I can leave you alone, safely tucked in your bed, Nick."

"So kiss me."

Kain looked surprised at the simple request. He had to know... to *feel* how aroused Nick was, and yet all Nick asked for was a kiss.

Maybe because a kiss could be a thing of real intimacy, unlike watching, unlike fantasizing on the keyboard?

Seeing he'd have to make the first move, Nick stood, going to him, studying the grooves of melted flesh on one side of Kain's face in contrast to the almost unearthly beauty of the other.

Mask

Kain had slowly let his guard down this evening so Nick had at last seen his face, but Nick knew better than to remark on the scars. His would-be boyfriend was impossibly touchy and needed careful handling.

"You know, suck face." Nick raised his brows, striving to keep the moment light. *Come on, just a little closer....*

"I don't kiss." Kain dropped his head, as if by reflex hiding the marks covering one side of his face. "Not since...."

"But you're such a sensual man." Nick kissed his chin, coaxing. "You must miss kissing. And I'd love to kiss you."

Kain growled and tugged Nick closer so that Nick's plump, welcoming lips met his in a kiss that a lover gives just before sex.

It wasn't enough. Nick moaned, fingers digging into Kain's shoulders restlessly. Kain hefted Nick high, still kissing, tongue caressing Nick's, *inside.*

Nick automatically wrapped his legs around Kain's hips, his groin rubbing against Kain's body. When he pulled back he was smiling, fevered, cheeks stinging from beard burn.

Kain.

And Nick whispered, "Let's kiss until we *hurt.*"

FINN leaned against the window in his suite, reaching out to press long fingers against the glass, seeing his own reflection, his own forlorn gaze.

If he closed his eyes, he could almost feel the heat between Kain and Nick lighting up the crumbling house.

Shit! Didn't that bring back memories?

Luke.

Was he still alive? It had been years, aching years apart because Luke insisted Finn grow up, insisted he was too young to take the final, irrevocable step as a human submissive to a werewolf Alpha.

But despite his reservations, Luke had marked him, though not as deeply as Finn suspected he'd bonded himself to Finn. But he wore a little mark just above his heart. A welt behind his neck. A bite on his thigh. So when Luke was close, Finn opened up, felt their connection sing through the tiny scars.

Sometimes in the past year, he'd sensed Luke, but he knew he had to be imagining it.

He thought back to that night, the night they'd first met....

A humid night, Finn walking the rutted track that led to his Aunt Marybeth's house. An owl ghosted across the road and headlights warmed Finn's back. He shielded his eyes and leaned his too tall eighteen-year-old body near the open window of the truck.

"Shouldn't be walking by these woods alone at night, boy," Mars Carmichael warned. "Strange goings on in these parts." Then his eyes widened as he saw who he was talking to. "Shit! Go ahead. Maybe something will eat ya!" He laughed and sped off, gravel and clumps of dried mud striking Finn's cheap sneakers, which he kept as pristine as possible.

"He doesn't like you," a voice purred from the trees.

Finn gasped, not having heard anyone trailing him. These woods... they had a bad reputation, but since Finn had one himself—and he had yet to earn it, darn it!—he was kind of fond of them.

And any place wild had always attracted Finn, made him feel at home. He loved the earth crumbling like devil's food mix in his hands, warm and connected....

"Guess he thinks I'll get eaten by the Big Bad Wolf," Finn mocked, but somewhat breathlessly, as a tall man wearing a black wife-beater and jeans was suddenly standing directly in front of him.

"Not a good night for you to take a stroll, cher," the man said, nodding to indicate the bright harvest moon. His eyes were so dark the

pupil and iris were merged, his hair loose bronze ringlets that fell to the center of his chest. A gold loop in one earlobe caught the light and a dragon tattoo snaked across one muscled bicep.

Finn licked his lips. Cher. The stranger must be Cajun, so calling Finn "darling" didn't mean anything. "I was preoccupied, sir," he said, using the manners that his Aunt Marybeth had drilled into him. She may be the town witch, but she went to church every Sunday and she made sure Finn came, even if he was rumored to be strange... a little off. But he was definitely handy to local farmers if their crops wouldn't yield—he had a way of knowing what might be missing in the soil or what kind of compost tea worked best.

"I'm Luke." The man cocked a brow. "I'll walk you home, earth fae."

Finn caught the sound of a low growl coming from somewhere amid the moss-hung trees leaning over the track.

"Don't pay attention, cher; they won't hurt you none." Luke took Finn's arm. At his simple touch, it felt for a second like a flare went off against the skin. Finn felt a quickening, as if he'd just tilled the soil for his aunt's vegetable patch.

"And why is that?" Finn asked. He could smell Bay Rum so close to Luke, and the scent made him almost dizzy.

"Because I'm the big daddy," Luke answered easily. He ruffled Finn's hair playfully, as if he were a child.

"Don't." The word was painful and Finn flushed at what he'd probably revealed with that naked exclamation. Don't treat me like a child. I am not. I want....

Luke paused, staring into Finn's eyes. "No one else ever see you have a thing for other men, earth fae?"

Finn shook his head, face red as one of the prize beets he'd grown last season for the county fair.

"Don't be looking at me with those big, yearning eyes, boy. Be careful what you invite."

Luke walked with him in silence, both of them stealing little glances at the other. But when Luke finally put an arm around Finn under the swollen moon, Finn knew he'd been claimed.

At the driveway where the lawn stretched out to Aunt Marybeth's, a Southern wedding cake of a house with white peeling paint and a long veranda, Luke stared into Finn's eyes.

"Please," Finn rasped.

"You're so young, cher," Luke reproved, stroking the planes of Finn's face.

"I know what I want."

A kiss. A sure kiss on his lips, Luke taking his mouth, cupping his jaw, exploring, so that Finn was so on fire he wanted to dry hump himself against the long muscular body, wind around him like a hungry, growing vine from his garden. He was on the verge of climax—

Luke broke away, eyes dark and haunted, face flushed and lips ruby from the intense kiss. He nodded to the patch of sunflowers. "You the gardener?"

"Yes," Finn said.

"Thought so. When I first caught your scent, I thought of the earth." Luke faded into the trees.

Finn hesitated before going in the house, sensing Luke was still watching.

"Thank you for my first kiss," he whispered.

"Don't thank me, little one," an amused voice answered him. "Best you stay away from me!"

Moonbeam: Tell me a bedtime story. I can't sleep and I'm too tired to paint. But you know how it is sometimes;

you can't stop thinking about things, images, even when your body needs to rest.

Obsidian: Out of practice.

Moonbeam: I heard you had a son. Didn't you ever tell him any stories?

Obsidian: ...

Moonbeam: I'm sorry. I didn't mean to pry, but when I dropped off work once in your office, I noticed a picture of a child on your desk and I figured... I've been wanting to ask you about him.

Obsidian: His name is Aiden.

Moonbeam: He's beautiful, Kain.

Obsidian: Yes.

Moonbeam: Why do I have the impression you haven't seen him since the fire?

Obsidian: No, I haven't seen him. He's only two, so he probably doesn't even remember me.

Moonbeam: That's not right. You should see him. I can feel that you care about him.

Obsidian: When I want your opini—! Nick, didn't you catch a glimpse of my face? I don't want him to see what I've become.

Moonbeam: He loved you, didn't he? He didn't love how you looked, he loved that you were his father.

Obsidian: He's just a baby. He doesn't know any better.

Moonbeam: You should see him.

Obsidian: No, I don't want him to be ashamed of me...or frightened.

Moonbeam: Kain, you wouldn't hurt him any more than you have me. And how you look doesn't matter.

Obsidian: It matters to me and most of the world.

Moonbeam: Okay, picture what I'm saying.

Obsidian: Huh?

Moonbeam: I know my prying stirred up some feelings but stop being so testy.

Obsidian: Start making sense.

Moonbeam: I just want you to imagine that I'm there with you now. It's pitch black in your room, but I cup the side of your face... artist's hand mapping your features... Here is smooth, perfect... There is pitted, rough.

Obsidian: Nick, don't...

Moonbeam: I don't care what the rest of the world thinks. What you think. You're beautiful to me.

Obsidian: Fucking crazy!

Moonbeam: :dryly: I believe that's been established. I'm living here with you, after all. Tell me something?

Obsidian: What?

Moonbeam: You're scarred but Finn implied that...you're not quite human.

Obsidian: Fire burns. It takes a long time to heal. Even someone like me.

Moonbeam: Why is Ross afraid of you?

Obsidian: You'd have to ask him that.

Moonbeam: He was angry when he came to the house but I sensed more.

Obsidian: I'd never—

Mask

Moonbeam: I know you'd never hurt him. Tell me more about how you were burned?

Obsidian: It doesn't matter.

Moonbeam: Maybe someone at the club will know.

Obsidian: Stay away from the club without me!

Moonbeam: Okay! Kain, I just want to understand you—

Obsidian: Obsidian has left the room.

CHAPTER 15

Obsidian: I'm back online since you asked for a bedtime story and I could see how restless you are. I resorted to searching through my dusty study, I'll have you know.

Moonbeam: I'm glad you're back. I hate that you go away when I get too close.

Obsidian: I've never been...close to anyone, not even before the fire. Ross was my only friend for a long time and he—

Moonbeam: I won't betray you, Kain. I won't leave you alone. My being here has to prove something.

Obsidian: Possibly that you are slightly insane. Okay, one bedtime story for an artist who can't turn off his great talent, but whose body needs to rest...

Once upon a time, Persephone was tending to her, uh, flowers.

Moonbeam: Great talent? I think I like that. As for Persephone, she reminds me a bit of Finn—you know he's got an uncanny green thumb with the remaining plants in the atrium? Anyway Persephone was the embodiment of the Earth's fertility, so an interest in botany tracks.

Obsidian: Smartass. Keep interrupting me and I'll spank you.

Moonbeam: Why does that make me want to interrupt?

Obsidian: Persephone attracted the attention of Hades, our villain.

Moonbeam: Interesting. But is he a villain? He really fits the mold of both hero and villain, like the classic misunderstood gothic hero.

Obsidian: Nick, this is my story, so let me tell it.

Moonbeam: Wrong, it's our story. And I think Hades was hot, though he acted wrongly by kidnapping Persephone and taking away her choice, but he was...lonely.

Obsidian: He took her away from the world she knew. He put her down in the dark where the only light came from fire.

Moonbeam: But don't you think he provided more? I'm sure he fed her well, as you do me, and I'm sure he was an incredible lover. I can see him in the firelight, tall, dark and hot... I don't think I'd mind being his "victim".

The story is a little old-fashioned, granted, since her mother bargains for Persephone's time and Persephone doesn't seem to have much to say about it—just a pawn tugged between her husband and her mother. But I think she ate the pomegranate seeds because she wanted to stay with him, she wanted to stop being a virgin and become a lover, and her mother always struck me as pretty fucking domineering.

Obsidian: What could Hades possibly offer that would equal living in the shadows?

Moonbeam: Sex. And the chance for Hades' lover to become his own man, to grow into his choices.

Obsidian: ...

Moonbeam: I mean, I'm sure he was shocked by Hades' taking away his choices, kidnapping him, but once he was living here, he wants...

Obsidian: What does he want?

Moonbeam: To have Hades inside him. Fire is the marriage of light and dark and what we make between us is fire.

Obsidian: Are you sure you want to go to the club later this evening?

Moonbeam: I'm sure. And thank you for giving me the choice, although I'm suspicious of you warning me off. I wonder if it's because you think I might learn more about you.

Obsidian: Interesting theory.

Moonbeam: On the other hand, you are entirely too calculating, so possibly you want me to understand something about you, something you can't express. Mixed messages. Good thing I'm patient with you, huh?

Obsidian: You might encounter someone I met, the night of the fire.

Moonbeam: You met him at the club?

Obsidian: I took him home. He was the one who...bit me.

Moonbeam: Oh. Well then, I want to meet him and follow your trail of bread crumbs, but one thing better be clear: Kain, he better not bite you tonight.

Mask

HEAD thumping painfully, Luke Munroe rubbed the dried blood from his lips.

Sunlight spotlighted one dank part of the tunnel, branching beyond the old wine cellar, directly over a table with fresh herbs reaching toward the outer world.

Finn. It looked like his doing. He was so good with plants, Luke's earth fae.

He tried to shift himself higher, his iron chains clinking dully. Iron, which no shape shifter could break, no matter how strong.

When the shadow fell, he braced himself for what was to come.

"ARE you sure you want to go there, kitten?" Finn asked, still a little breathless, as if from running an errand.

He ran a hand over Nick's charcoal silk jacket. He had helped Nick choose some clothes for his first night at Manticore with Kain so now Nick was wearing black pants and a matching silk tank top with the jacket, which Nick thought made his face and hair stand out like pale flame in contrast.

"Just remember what I told you about the dark, sexy monsters and… the other kind." Finn stroked Nick's hair, holding his gaze in the mirror. "The kind you don't want to ever meet. Be careful at Manticore. Stick close to Kain."

"The kind of monster maybe Mark met up with that night?" Nick swallowed, still feeling the burn of loss. What had happened to Mark was so sudden, so shocking… but he just couldn't believe Kain had had anything to do with it. He'd heard the regret, the thread of fear in Kain's voice when he told Nick he was sorry he'd lost his friend.

"I don't really care about the club," he explained. "I want to understand Kain. Get closer to the scattered pieces he's shared with me lately. He's a bit like a Cubist work, all planes and innuendo." He rubbed his chin ruefully, but then asked what he'd been burning to know for days, "Is he still, um, hiring young men?"

Finn sighed. "Sometimes after a few days, he does go to Manticore or other places, brings someone home. I don't think he wants you to know. He has strong drives, kitten. And I think he's still afraid of hurting you."

"I don't need to be protected from him! And I hate that he's with anyone else." Nick played with the bottles of aftershave that Kain had provided for his bathroom. He'd barely glanced at them since usually he showered, toweled off his hair, shaved, and then typically a fragment of art would live in his head and he'd forget all about everyday shit, except the basics, like underwear. Well. ..sometimes he even forgot about that, but only when his easel was set up in his bedroom.

Softly, he asked, "Does he take them down to his dungeon?"

"Yes," Finn said. "Kitten, you don't want to know about that side of him."

Nick disagreed. "What does he do with them?"

Finn gave an exasperated sound. "Usually lately he canes them, or watches them with someone else he's hired. He stopped using his dates sexually after you came to live here."

Nick breathed out a sigh and met Finn's gaze frankly. "You're wrong that I shouldn't know what he is up to," Nick said. "I want him. I want him so fucking much!" He was panting and defiant, tears pricking his eyes, and he was embarrassed, but Finn just pulled him into his arms.

"Nothing good can come of this," Finn said, shaking Nick, as if to get through to him. "One day you're going to be sorry you met him!"

"No way!" Nick vowed. "We artistic types are risk takers. I think I'd forgotten that, clinging to a safe rut of a job and a safe boyfriend. Now I won't settle."

Finn closed his eyes tightly. "I hope you don't regret going down this road."

Mask

THE car was the same jungle-green as Kain's eyes, low slung, expensive, but that's all Nick could make of it since he wasn't into cars. He climbed into the passenger side, heart beating fast with anticipation.

The sleek vehicle growled as it headed down the driveway before swinging onto the road.

Nick looked over at Kain, who was wearing a fedora and a black turtleneck. It made it harder to make out his features, except the light from his eyes, which seemed to glow in the semi-darkness.

Nick watched him, but his throat felt too tight for words, for their usual back and forth.

When he closed his eyes, he imagined the hustlers Kain hired, Kain taking them downstairs, handcuffing them, caning them, watching them perform and… biting them?

He shifted, his cock stiff even as resentment flamed in him. He wanted to be the one that Kain spent his lust on.

He wanted to take Kain's hand off the wheel and press it against his erection.

BEFORE they hit town, Kain pulled off onto the side of the road and down a deserted side street, shielded by trees.

Nick's heart was thumping, his gaze focusing on Kain's gloved hand, because there was something feral in his would-be lover's eyes that made them hard to meet.

"Get out of the car," Kain said, very evenly.

"Unbuckle your belt and hand it to me," Kain continued in a silky voice once they were both outside. But something was riding him, Nick could see. His nostrils flared as if catching Nick's scent and his irises were blown, hungry black rimmed by green.

He stood behind Nick and held out his palm, waiting for Nick to do what he commanded. Waiting to see if he'd be obedient and put himself under Kain's control.

Sensing he was being tested, Nick set his jaw and complied, hesitantly placing the curl of leather in Kain's hand, not sure if Kain meant to lash him with that belt, but if he wanted to, Nick would allow it.

Kain shook out the leather and the moment hung, full of possibility....

He gripped Nick's wrists together and wrapped the belt around them. "All right?" he asked. "I like you bound. Do you like it?"

Nick nodded, swallowing tightly. "Yes. Only for you."

Kain cupped the back of Nick's neck, thumb caressing the skin as he guided him so he was leaning over the side of the car. Then, he reached inside Nick's silk pants, helping himself as if Nick's body totally belonged to him, fingers brushing against his needy prick.

Nick's head fell back and he moaned at the invasion, the touch.

"Did you get hard when you thought I was going to use that belt on your ass?"

"Yes." Nick flushed. "I don't know why. I never thought I'd want that. Would it hurt a lot?"

Kain shook his head. "Only enough to test your obedience. You'd come like my good boy after I was done, face down on the ground, kissing my boot."

Nick was panting as Kain tugged down his pants.

"I like the Great Pumpkin on your boxers," Kain noted with amusement. "My innocent."

"Thank you, but I don't want to be innocent. I want to be yours."

Mask

A finger ghosted down Nick's crack, and his thighs quivered in reaction, clenching together. "I need you to hold very still," Kain ordered.

Nick had a sudden hunch. "This is something to do with the club, isn't it?"

"Yes," Kain affirmed.

Nick caught rustling sounds and then Kain's palm pressed him open, his touch firm and confident, making Nick aware of how many submissive men Kain must have handled. It was arousing, knowing he was being mastered by someone who understood his secret need.

As he waited, sweat beginning to coat his forehead, Nick's hands clenched, testing his bonds.

A too-broad something against his virgin opening. The fleshy head of Kain's cock.

"Breathe," Kain coached. "I'm going to open you a little."

"It's hard to do that!" Nick squeezed his eyes shut, his body wanting to undulate, to take more of Kain, despite the uncomfortable burn.

"Hold still!" Kain stroked Nick's tense back.

Broached, Nick tried to relax.

Kain leaned close and licked the back of his neck, whispering, "I'm going to come inside you. Don't move and don't come."

Nick made a thready sound.

"My slut boy, offering me your hole. And that's how I want you; I want you open to take it whenever I want. I want you to come only when I allow it, and sometimes I won't." Kain's prick nudged deeper, rubbing. "I'm going to come now and I'm going to enjoy it, but I don't want you to shoot, do you understand?"

Breathless, Nick replied, "Yes, Kain!"

"Good boy, good slut." Kain slapped his ass and in another second gave a choked-off sound.

Nick felt moisture filling him.

Kain pulled away and Nick could feel his gaze on his body, his hand cupping and squeezing his ass approvingly.

"My come is running down your legs. Do you like that?"

Aroused, shaky, and still burning from the first penetration he'd ever experienced, Nick whispered, "Yes. Yes, I like your come in me."

CHAPTER 16

KAIN continued to stroke Nick's body, gentling him down from being penetrated by a lover for the first time. More than a lover—a *master*, since that was the role Kain had assumed.

"Are you aching to come?" Kain asked, lips curving.

"Yes."

"I won't permit it yet."

Nick took a deep breath, biting his lip in disappointment. His body was singing, his nipples pointed stars, his cock hard, but he knew he was being tested.

He held Kain's gaze and then instinctively fell to his knees, bound hands in front of him.

Kain's eyes darkened further at this sudden unasked-for submission. Roughly he said, "Christ!"

Nick let his gaze drop, waiting....

"Open your legs. I want you to expose yourself to me. I want to see that erection I won't let you touch."

"Yes, Kain." Nick wobbled a little, careful with the pebbles on his bare knees.

Seeing his awkwardness, Kain's lips quirked and he drawled, "You never hear about pebbles when you read hot stories on the Net about submission. I'll make sure the next time you kneel for me, it's on a more comfortable floor."

"Thank you, Kain."

Kain's leather boot appeared. Nick held his breath, aware of how vulnerable he was in this position, kneeling, his legs spread and open, his balls and cock prominently displayed.

Kain nudged Nick's erection with a very carefully measured out touch. The suede was both rough and soft as it stroked Nick. His lips parted and he looked up at Kain, silently pleading.

"Not yet, kitten. Now kiss it. Kiss my boot and thank me for marking you."

Nick pressed his lips against Kain's boot, but he didn't say exactly his scripted words. Instead he went with his heart. "I love you," he whispered, "Kain."

Kain's breath hitched, and then he was leaning against his car, his gloved hand tangled in Nick's hair, and it was entirely natural that Nick put his eager mouth on Kain's penis, licking away the traces of come, pleasuring Kain, while Kain widened his legs and enjoyed his attentions.

NICK ran a finger around the rim of his tea martini, taking in the Moroccan decor and ambience of Manticore.

He and Kain were seated in rattan planter's chairs with a low painted table shared between them. Lanterns made of hide and colored in jewel tones of peridot, garnet, crimson, and topaz hung at varying lengths throughout the semicircular club. The space had a sense of intimacy and yet also a quality of voyeurism since it was easy to spy on the activities at other tables where some sat… and some knelt, as Nick had for Kain.

Seeing other men and women choosing to do that brought that moment back, and Nick felt his chest tighten as he remembered what he'd offered Kain, both with his vulnerable body and with his words.

Had he actually said them? He hadn't even known himself until they rose from inside him and spilled from his lips like a gift.

But he didn't regret it. Kain had to know why he had stayed, why he believed in him, why he wanted to surrender completely.

He nodded to his dominant lover, who was slouched deep in his chair, so the light couldn't quite reach his face. "It's, uh, quiet here tonight. What did you order? I can smell spices but...."

Kain shook his head, looking moody and closed off. "You wouldn't like the taste."

Nick shifted restlessly and the moisture still damp between his thighs made him flush. Kain hadn't permitted him to dry himself, just ordered him to put his pants back on. His lower body also throbbed where Kain had taken him so he could feel an afterimage of the experience, almost feel Kain still inside, hard, commanding, pleasuring himself while he deliberately restrained Nick.

"*Kain!*" A slender man with flowing black hair with a dramatic white streak stood next to their table, holding Kain's gaze. "Who is this exquisite boy? I could smell him from across the room. Delicious!"

Kain's gloved hand tightened on the arm of his chair. "He is mine," he warned, very softly.

Nick stared into Mediterranean blue eyes which were looking at him with the appreciation that an art patron might have for a painting. He went with a hunch. "Do you work some of the floor shows here?"

The man's lips quirked. He had creases by his eyes, giving away that he was slightly older than Kain. "I'm Siren. You've heard of me?" He reached out and sifted Nick's hair through his fingers, making Nick gasp at his daring. "Moonbeam finally visits our world of fire and darkness."

"How do you know that name?!" Freaked, Nick glanced over at Kain but couldn't make out his expression, only that his hand was still clenched over his chair arm, as if Kain were restraining himself.

"I met your Miguel one night," Siren admitted casually. "He shared some of your correspondence with Kain. It rather disheartened him, and I could see why—you and Kain obviously had something hot going!"

"Oh." Nick flushed at hearing his former boyfriend's name mentioned. Then his eyes narrowed. "Something strange happened to him the night he came here. He doesn't remember, but it's possible someone set him up."

Siren's brows rose. "Oh, dear me. Well, Kain probably told you this club is a little... unusual. It's best to come here with a protector and I did try to warn your friend to take it easy."

"Uh-huh. How did you meet Kain?"

Siren gave Kain a peaceful look and Kain's mouth tightened. "I visited his home."

"The night of the fire?"

"Yes." Siren pulled out a blown-glass perfume bottle from a bronze beaded bag. It was pink, shaped with undulating curves, reminiscent of a genie bottle. "For the pulse points." He nodded to Nick. "I use it on the submissives in my act."

"He doesn't know...." Kain leaned forward and the scars on his face caught the light. He looked like he wanted to say more, but closed his mouth after a glance at Nick.

"Yet you brought him here." Siren frowned, studying Kain's face. "Kain, if you would only allow me.... The scarring."

"Don't ever touch me again!" Kain growled, green eyes dangerous.

Siren grimaced. "If you wish to go on punishing yourself...." He placed the perfume bottle on the table and cocked a brow at Nick. "On the house, beauty. Now you'll have to excuse me; there is a ceremony about to start below stairs."

Nick leaned forward and lifted the wand from the bottle, curious. "Orange blossom," he said after catching the scent. "Fresh, zesty. Not what I would expect in a place like this."

"You probably assumed he'd offer you something smoky and spicy but Siren mixes custom scents for certain patrons. I'm not surprised he chose flowering fruit for you, Persephone," Kain said. His gloved hand extended and hesitated, and then he ran a gentle fingertip over the back of Nick's hand as if in apology for his abruptness.

Nick felt the familiar tightness under his breastbone.

Kain.

Softly, Kain asked, "Do you want to try it?"

"I am curious but I'm also wary. Is this what happened to Miguel? He was offered scent in a bottle and somehow wound up in a public orgy? I don't want to make a fool of myself."

"I'll keep you safe." Kain turned Nick's hand so the inside of his wrist was exposed. He waited to read permission in Nick's eyes and when he did, he used the wand to anoint his skin with a single drop.

Nick stared at his wrist, seeing a drop of color, like crimson pigment that expanded into thinner clouds, diffusing to lime on his skin.

"It enhances," Kain explained. "Touch. Emotions. Siren mixes it for certain submissives."

"How'd he know I was one?" Nick asked wryly. "Never mind. I'm probably putting out a neon vibe right now that I'd like to kneel at your feet and rub my face against your hand."

Kain's eyes widened and he swallowed thickly. "Is that what you want?"

"You're so easy," Nick said, teasing. He took a deep breath, trying not to reach for Kain, touch his hair… lick his skin. He was obviously feeling the effects of the special oil. "He works for you?"

"He runs the place for me."

"And yet you can't seem to stand him?"

"My… relationship with Siren is complicated."

"Um-hmmm." Nick wanted to push for more but sensed he would get nowhere with Kain. "Everyone is downstairs for this ceremony?"

"Yes, but—" Kain hesitated.

"I want to see." Nick held Kain's eyes in challenge. "You brought me here."

"All right." Kain stood. "But I don't think you're ready. And Nick… about Miguel."

"Yes?"

Kain took Nick's hand and stroked the lifeline in the center of his palm, paying special attention to the fork that divided it. "Whatever happened to him here, it had to be something he secretly desired if the oil was involved."

Nick swallowed. "I know. He… was unable to reach completion sexually for a long time."

"So for him, it was a good thing." Kain pressed cool lips to Nick's hand. "And for me, kitten, since you came to live under my roof."

Nick climbed to his feet, nervous for some reason. This place…. What wasn't Kain sharing with him? Kain's uneasiness made Nick uneasy.

Shyly, he brushed one of his lover's hands with his own. "Thank you for saying that," he said. "And don't be so grim. I'm sure you're worrying over nothing. How different can this place be?"

BLOOD struck Nick's face, the motion strange, stretched out, so that the droplets seemed to take an age to reach him. He gasped and a hand covered his shoulder, steadying him on the stairs that led down to a circular stage. The space was cavernous, yet intimate, like a caught breath, like a heart beating….

Feeling the effects of the special oil, Nick stared at two men lost to themselves in the audience.

"That man," Nick rasped, a little dizzy as he stared from heavy-lidded eyes. "Cutting himself with a razor."

Nick watched as the man's companion sucked the beaded drops from the stranger's bare chest, the gesture strangely tender.

"He's feeding his submissive," Kain said. He tugged Nick forward.

Nick opened his mouth to question Kain.

A body slammed into him—

He staggered, breath knocked from his chest, reeling.

Blurry movement, so fast he only had the impression of Kain's hand shoving someone away.

A young man hit the curved wall with the dull thump of flesh.

Nick stared into the wide cocoa eyes of a boy, panting, nude.

His panicked gaze seemed to catch Nick's, pulling him in.

"Are you okay?" Nick instinctively reached out to the trembling stranger and their fingertips grazed. At their touch, he experienced something like an electrical charge, *raw feeling*, gripping him in the throat, making his eyes sting with tears as emotion walloped him.

Then Kain was there, pulling him back from the powerful exchange. Cooling, protective touch, shutting out the noise.

The stranger looked from Nick to Kain and Nick saw awareness dawn in his eyes. "You belong to one of *them*," he rasped, almost accusing.

Two men wearing black leather vests and pants pushed through the crowd and took charge of the young man, guiding him back to a cage in the center of the stage as Nick and Kain watched.

Nick whispered, still feeling what the stranger had been experiencing. "…*Scared!*"

Kain held him firmly. "It's the drug."

"No! I felt him!" Nick struggled, looking up at Kain, pleading, tears running down his cheeks from the moment of unbearable connection. "Please, help him! I know you can! Please, for me, Kain."

Kain's face was stony. "I know you can't understand this, Nick, but he asked for this."

As Nick watched, trembling in Kain's arms, the young stranger was guided onto a table, two men pressing him down, holding his arms while a third lifted something from a smoldering brazier.

Nick screamed.

White pain! Something burning a mark into his skin!

Nick grabbed his skull.

The world tilted. Riding Kain's shoulder, jolting up the stairs.

WARM, concerned blue eyes. "Here, have a little more."

Nick coughed, throat raw, as he came back to himself. "What is that?"

"It's just whiskey. You were in a state of shock," Siren reassured. "Kain thought it would help you."

Nick spied a rigid Kain standing close by, face white, fists balled as he stared at Nick in Siren's care.

The memory of what he'd seen, the emotions of the young man, once again swept through Nick. A red ball expanding in his chest—

He was on his feet, his hand cracking against Kain's cheek.

The scarred side of Kain's face turned red from the imprint.

"*Branded.* They branded that boy!" Panting, tears cold on his cheeks.

Mask

"Yes," Kain said, looking removed. He walked away, leaving Nick trembling, arms wrapped tightly around himself.

CHAPTER 17

"TAKE a look now," Siren prodded, not unkindly.

Nick swallowed, hesitant, not wanting any more shocking surprises at Manticore, but Siren had insisted they return to the amphitheater and talk to the young man whose encounter with Nick had been so distressing.

Now Nick looked into the cage, seeing the boy with cocoa eyes was reclining, looking relaxed as a white-haired, bearded man licked the brand on his chest.

The boy moaned and pressed the older man closer, as if enjoying his touch, and a wall of desire, like looking through the rising sparks of a bonfire, hit Nick.

He steadied himself against one curving wall, taking a deep breath and struggling for composure. He was obviously still feeling the effects of Siren's oil. "He wanted what happened?" He looked blankly at Siren, who appeared satisfied with the outcome of the evening's performance.

"He signed a contract." Siren pulled a sheaf of papers from under his gray and blue shot Thai silk jacket. "They've been together a long time but the final bond is hard on any human submissive. It has to be, since living with one of us isn't easy."

"Contract." Nick's fingertips grazed the paper as he scanned it. "Human submissive?" Nick remembered Finn had used that term. He rubbed his forehead, trying to understand. "But he was *scared*, Siren. I could feel it, almost like it was happening to me!"

"Of course Carlos was scared, kitten—may I call you that? I know Finn does." At Nick's nod of acquiescence, Siren gave a smile calculated to charm and continued. "He was about to become a human slave to a shape-shifter, belong to him in ways that will test him constantly. And branding *hurts.* But Leo couldn't let him go since he's deeply in love with his boy."

"So this ceremony…. It's like a make or break between humans and shape-shifters?"

Siren nodded. "Leo was struggling because every full moon, his possessiveness for Carlos was making it hard for him to interact with the other wolves in his pack. They had no choice but to take the next step in their mating."

Nick saw Carlos was smiling now as the older man, Leo, pulled away. He could make out that the brand on Carlos's chest represented the head of a wolf, the skin pink but, unbelievably, almost healed! Had Leo done that somehow for his young lover, taken away his discomfort so quickly?

Nick's hand fell, papers fluttering. "There is so much I don't know. I feel like the new kid at school. I don't know where recess is held, I'm wearing the wrong clothes, I'll never blend in and maybe—" He closed his eyes tightly, not wanting to say it.

"What?" Siren asked, very gently.

"Maybe it won't work between Kain and me because I can't become a part of his world." The thought spilled out raw, acid burning, and it didn't make Nick feel any better to share his fears. Siren couldn't answer him on that score, only Kain. He sighed. "So why didn't Kain stop it when I asked?"

Siren's face was very serious. "Kitten, you must be feeling like you've stepped totally into the unknown. I know it must be… terrifying."

"If I understand what's going on, I can filter and deal with it. It's being in limbo, interpreting shadows that makes me crazy," Nick admitted before continuing in an aching whisper. "I need to know who Kain is. It's all I've wanted all along."

"Okay, information I can give you." Siren reached out and stroked Nick's shoulder. "To put it simply, Club Manticore is a venue for a mix of creatures that don't always get along. If Kain had interfered in the final bonding of Carlos and Leo, it could have been war, and even an outsider like our employer knew that."

"Kain's an outsider too?" Nick blinked, taken aback at this new insight.

Siren nodded. "So maybe it doesn't matter to him how much you blend into our world, but only that you accept *him*, hmmm?"

Nick dropped his head, considering, afraid to hope again and stretch out on a brittle branch that might suddenly crack under his weight.

Siren continued, as if sensing Nick was looking to see Kain in the events that had unfolded that night. "Leo is an important man to the shifters. He needs to be in control of himself and having a much younger, very hot, and somewhat slutty man as his chosen companion has been hard on him. I think he would have tried to kill anyone who got between him and Carlos."

Below where Siren and Nick were standing, Leo had lifted Carlos into his arms. The young man curled his arms around Leo, head buried against the older man's neck. They left the cage, followed by the other men, who were obviously bodyguards of some kind.

"Leo is a *loup garou?*" Nick guessed.

Siren nodded, blue eyes respectful as he nodded to Leo. "Yes, the most powerful pack leader in this city. Carlos is an artist like you, but he works with found art. He lives the sweet life since Leo is in real estate and has done very well for himself and he likes to pamper his boy."

"A werewolf in real estate?" Nick shook his head. "Fuck." He ran his hands over his arms, suddenly chilled. "And Carlos really agreed to the branding?"

"Yes, but it took some time before Kain would agree to host it here. He wanted to be sure it was what Carlos truly wanted." Siren ran a finger over his full lips. "Have you ever seen horses mate? It's raw, even violent sometimes, but they do it and the outcome is beautiful foals. It's like that sometimes between demons and humans, but here at the club, we try to offer the human submissive some protection."

"Oh." Nick's lips quirked, though he still felt like broken glass inside. "And is the human always the submissive one?"

"Nope," Siren said.

He couldn't take it all in. But had he been wrong? Had he gotten everything so very wrong?

Kain!

He'd left the club, scarred cheek blooming red from Nick's slap.

Branded ugly.

Nick's breath caught as he saw the events of the evening in another light.

"Why won't he let you heal him?" he asked Siren now. "You said…. It seemed you might know how to do that."

Siren folded his arms, one brow lowering as he seemed to consider Nick's question. "You'll have to ask him that." He studied Nick, examining him with clear appreciation. "None of us can touch you, you do know that?"

Nick blinked. "Uh, no."

"Do you have any idea what would happen to you, coming to a place like this, if you weren't so obviously wearing Kain's scent?"

Nick ran a hand through his hair, flushing with embarrassment as he remembered just *how* Kain had marked him. Broaching, penetrating… leaving his scent. "I figured it was some kind of claim."

"It was keeping you safe." Mischief gleamed in Siren's eyes. He leaned close and suggested, "But that doesn't stop *you* from taking one of us. What do you say? I love cool blonds. I'd love to wear your scratches, even let you bite me."

Nick's lips parted in shock. "Are you offering…?"

149

Siren nuzzled Nick's neck and sighed somewhat wistfully. "You smell of him."

Nick swatted the other man away. "It sounds like it's *him* you want!"

Siren made a sad face. "If you have me, it's like having you both, since you are bonding."

Nick shook his head in disgust. "Kokopelli."

Siren grinned, obviously catching Nick's drift. "The chaotic god of the South West. You know he has a big cock. I think I like your comparison; it's very flattering."

"Huh. You just like creating chaos," Nick grumped, giving in ruefully to Siren's draw. Even though he had doubts about him, he was almost irresistible. "I guess that's what you'd expect of a *loup garou.*"

"*Loup garou?* I'm not." Siren's eyes changed, greens, ambers backlighting the blue. He kissed the back of Nick's wrist with old world gallantry. "I am a warrior fey."

NICK found the green car waiting outside the club, the keys in the ignition.

Kain had left him a safe way to get home.

He paused, touching the night dew on the hood. *Aching.* How could he go home to Kain now, after he'd torn at the thing between them? He could drive to Marilyn's, stay with her. Probably that was what Kain expected.

Jaw tight, Nick climbed behind the wheel and made his choice.

Mask

Moonbeam: I'm sorry I hit you. That's not me, or the me I've always been. I don't have any excuse other than... Love. It sometimes is like having my skin peeled away. Obsidian? I hurt. Please talk to me.

Obsidian: Why did you even come back here? I thought you were done with me. It would be better for us both if it were just...done.

Moonbeam: Wait! This sounds like you expected my reaction, even hoped for it. And you were sure I'd leave after your setup. See you for the monster you are, ditch you. And then you don't get hurt, right?

Obsidian: If you left.

Moonbeam: What?

Obsidian: It might hurt.

Moonbeam: For me as well, can't you understand that? I know you played this out like a game in your head, Kain. You wanted to shove me away because I was getting too close and I think it hurts you to let me in.

Obsidian: ...

Moonbeam: Let me close to you.

Obsidian: I wasn't the one to walk away.

Moonbeam: I'm coming to you. I thought of going to Marilyn's, tea with chocolate, safe, even considered being with Siren, and I know after what happened tonight that I shouldn't be able to fix this, whatever this is.

I won't let you push me away. Not if we fight. Not if I fuck up.

NICK went deliberately to his studio first, grounding himself by touching canvas, paint, taking a deep breath. His throat tightened as he thought of the initiation at Manticore. He'd promised Kain he'd stand by him, taken his hand and vowed not to turn away.

Okay, well, it hadn't worked out. He'd screwed up. What now?

"I have a prince to rescue," Nick muttered.

His hand grazed some scarlet pigment and touching that, touching color he had mixed himself, used, brought him back to ground zero.

He didn't understand Kain's world. He wasn't sure he liked it. Fine.

But right from the beginning, Kain had touched him, woken him.

Nick slowly removed his clothes, feeling he was taking a step with everything he folded, set aside. Expectations, fear of exposing himself to hurt; it was time to let go and make his own initiation.

Nude, he ran a line of scarlet pigment over one slender hip, the line warm, a tattoo he created himself.

KAIN was sitting at his desk in his dilapidated study in a pool of shadow, his laptop still open at the last line of their broken communication, his hands on the keys like a pianist stalled in composition.

Seeing him like that, Nick ached, throat, heart.

He discarded his robe and went to Kain, knelt at his feet and put his head on his lap.

Kain didn't speak, but his face tilted so the light couldn't reach the scars on his face.

I did that. I made him afraid, ashamed again.

"Shattered," he whispered. "And you didn't exactly stick around to explain shit to me!"

Kain's hand clenched in his hair, tugging gently so Nick looked up. Seeing Kain's expression, Nick hopped onto his lap, legs going around him, ankles hooking, his erection brushing against the one hidden under Kain's clothing, his arms looping around Kain's shoulders.

Kain's hand stroked a line down his side, finding the mark of scarlet in the dark where Nick had instinctively brushed himself with color. Would Kain read the meaning behind painting his skin?

Initiation. I gave myself to you, and I want to show how you touched me, changed me.

Finally, Nick's patience was rewarded. Kain's lips brushed his throat.

"I love you," Nick repeated, not hiding.

Kain gave a stifled groan, giving in, his teeth entering Nick at last.

CHAPTER 18

NICK gasped, an initiate passing another threshold, hands digging into Kain's skull, pulling him closer, his balls tight, his nipples erect, his breath, his body, expanding, contracting, a focused heart beating, living the moment for Kain.

Joined.

He heard Kain make a soft sound, a feeding sound, as if he loved Nick's taste, as if everything before had been prelude for this and even Kain hadn't known until he'd taken Nick this way.

But the feeding moved more than Kain. Nick felt heavy, weighted down, even as his desire rose to fever pitch. He didn't want to break Kain's hold; he wanted to invite him deeper, to take it all—

A human submissive has to be strong, were Siren's words.

Nick frowned, wondering why the other man had somehow intruded in this moment, but he couldn't hang onto the thought because his head, even his vision, was fuzzy. When he opened his eyes, he thought he could see furry light surrounding the ivy dripping from the ceiling. Instinctively, he knew that was the vine's projected growth, the energy radiating from it.

And… he could make out scratching sounds between the walls, as if some small animal had climbed in through the gaps in the ceiling.

Unable to process, he was at least chained to Kain by sex. He rubbed his cock against him. "What's happening…?" he murmured dully.

Kain was kissing him, as if he were a dessert that he'd tasted and now wanted to revel in. Nick's chin, his lips, one finger following the hollow of his earlobe, the line of his throat, and then Kain was again feeding on the blood pounding in Nick's throat.

Nick was lit up, so close, his pulse thundering, hungry for this new closeness, needy, slutty, everything Obsidian had promised he'd want to be for the right man.

Hoarsely, he had to ask, "Is this how you treat your whores? Drink from them, touch them?"

Kain lifted drowsy lids, his face flushed, Nick's blood on his lips. "You want to be my whore, Nick?" One long finger stuttered over the still sensitive place Kain had broached, shot his seed inside, marking Nick.

"I never imagined this kind of…." Nick bit his lip, not wanting to say the word that came to mind aloud, mating. He was trembling spasmodically now, chilled, his heartbeat sounding louder in his ears, the dim light of the room wearing a strange nimbus, like a moon through misty clouds. "I never let anyone inside me before you."

Kain's hand tugged Nick's hair and he rubbed his lips against Nick's throat, losing himself. "I know you were untouched. I wanted to shove it deeper, Nick!"

Nick blinked, licking his lips, even as his cock jumped at Kain's crude truth. "You're not the most, um… politically correct boyfriend," he mumbled, smiling faintly so his insecure lover could see he was okay with that.

"Don't be nice, don't be good," Kain encouraged against Nick's throat. "I need to soil my innocent. I want you to be the man you were when we first met online. I would tell you stories of what I liked to do to the young men I hired…. You couldn't get enough."

Nick pulled him closer, feeling like a merman who had ensnared his lover, wanting to tangle him in seaweed until he drowned.

The cold touch of Kain's fangs and... *drowning.*

Lost in this new mating, Nick felt again a chilly finger poking his spine in warning, but he was feasting as much as Kain was feasting, experiencing the intimacy he had been denied even when Kain had briefly entered his body.

Kain was making purring sounds while he kneaded generous handfuls of Nick's ass.

"I think I want you to come," Kain mused. "But come the way I want, for my entertainment."

More than ready now that Kain, his master, his lover, would allow it, Nick's lips parted. "Yes, Kain."

"Spread yourself over my knee." Kain helped Nick, who was trembling now, still feeling spacey, but so aroused he gasped as his cock rasped against Kain's clothing. "Get that ass nice and high for me." Kain rubbed it appreciatively when Nick was positioned to his satisfaction. "If I branded you, it would be on your inner thigh and I'd make you display it by spreading your legs as you knelt for me."

Nick was panting now, his hairline dampened with sweat. He mouthed the back of Kain's scarred hand, letting him know silently how moved he was at Kain's words and actions, playing his fantasies perfectly.

"You like the idea of showing the world how slutty you are for me, don't you?" Kain's voice was smug. "But right now I have an urge to prove to you how slutty you are when we're all alone."

Nick stiffened when he felt something cool brush his ass.

"No, don't look, kitten. I want you to relax and trust me. Focus on my voice, on pleasing me."

Nick nodded since he wasn't sure he could speak through his constricted throat. His heart was beating fast again, this time with anticipation. Kain was going to let him come!

Mask

Kain made an approving sound at Nick's submission and something came down on Nick's rear end in a hard swat. He moaned at the shock, the inevitable slight humiliation in being spanked, but his cock loved it, loved everything about it as he rubbed himself against Kain.

"Up a little higher, kitten," Kain said. "I want to give you a good spanking. I'm using rolled-up newspaper since you haven't earned the right to be spanked with a proper tool, like a paddle. Maybe after you've performed for me a few times, humped my leg, or sucked my cock perfectly, I'll use one on you. Would you like that?"

Nick's cheeks were bright red, both his ass and his face. He wanted to hide from what he wanted, but there was no hiding from Kain. Kain was Obsidian, who knew him better than anyone. And Nick had spread himself for Obsidian online long before he'd done it here in reality.

"Yes, I want that. You know I do," he husked, clutching Kain's muscular leg and holding onto him. He tipped his ass a little higher and was rewarded by some harder swats, one finally catching the edge of his balls so he cried out, caught between sharp pain and ecstasy.

"Ask your master," Kain prodded, rubbing smooth, warmed skin. "Ask for your relief."

"Kain, please."

"I'm not convinced."

Bastard! Yet Nick was smiling. Kain was feeling playful, a big cat, toying with Nick.

He chose to answer Kain's question, knowing it would ignite him. "I want to be your whore. Teach me...."

"*Nick!*" Kain's fingers dug possessively into Nick's raised bottom.

"Teach me to be your whore," Nick finished.

Kain's hand slid into his crack and he pinched Nick's opening, still swollen from accommodating Kain. The slight pain, the reminder of what he'd offered, how he'd been willing to lie at Kain's feet and suck on his leather boot if ordered—

"Kain...." Desperation threaded through Nick's voice. He needed Kain to say yes, needed his approval.

"Come, Kitten, come for me like a good whore!" Another swat of his vulnerable ass and... Nick was conscious of his balls tightening, the backs of his feet arching, toes curling, a fire roaring up and out through his fingertips, through his cock as he came, spattering like a naughty boy all over Kain's pants.

He wilted, sweaty, tears standing on his cheeks.

"Nick, your scent. I can't...!" Kain rasped. He lifted Nick high, Nick's hair swaying, his body limp.

... Sharpened teeth caging the pointed nipple over Nick's heart.

Nick's fingers clenching in Kain's hair, and unbelievably, his penis stiffening again, sensitized. It hurt to be hard again so soon, but Kain's teeth inside him, drinking him, drinking deep—

"Ohhhh! Kain, I can't—T-too much!"

"Nick!"

He faded, sinking beside the chair, body feeling cold and rigid, unable to do more than look up at Kain, pulled down by an undertow, cold now, not feeling it when his head hit the floor.

Kain's hand on his neck, his chest, yelling his name. Haunted green eyes, suddenly misty with tears.

Don't worry, Nick wanted to say.

"KAIN, you have to leave! You lost control and look what you did?"

Finn's accusing voice.

Nick frowned, head moving on his pillow. The sounds, scents, all wrong for the cool breath of Telemachus House.

His eyes opened and he saw his Kain, head in his hands, sitting in a chair by the twin bed where Nick lay. He licked his dry lips, so fucking thirsty.

"Kain?" he rasped, wanting his lover's reassurance. He hated seeing him like that, looking so lost; it made Nick feel more vulnerable somehow, like something must be really wrong.

Kain looked up, staring at him almost blankly.

His hair was wild peaks and he was wearing the same clothing he'd worn when Nick gave himself over to him. No hat or high collar to disguise the ridges bisecting one side of his face, as if Kain didn't care for once if others saw him and stared at his ruined features.

Nick reached out. Of course he reached out, unable to bear Kain looking.... The effort made perspiration dot his forehead and his hand dropped, trembling like a broken string on an instrument.

The chair fell behind Kain. He loomed over Nick's bed, tentatively touched the back of his hand.

"I'm sorry," he whispered. "Finn's right; I went too far. I should have stayed away, should have been more careful with you. Christ, Nick, I was afraid you wouldn't wake up!"

He closed his eyes tightly, fist balling, before he swallowed and stepped away from the bed.

Nick's lips parted to speak but Kain strode from the room, the door swinging back and forth behind him his only answer.

Nick turned to Finn, who sighed, reaching for some orange juice. "You're in the local hospital, kitten. You, uh, lost a lot of blood."

Nick took in the drip going into his inner arm as he tasted the juice. His tongue felt swollen and his head was thumping like a dull, sodden drum. "Why did Kain have to leave?" he demanded, a little cranky. "I'd like to understand what's going on exactly. What happened between us."

"Kain's afraid of hurting you. Of who he is."

Nick's eyes closed and he curled his knees up to his chest.

159

After a moment, he felt Finn's hand, warm over his own cold, open palm.

Moonbeam: You can't stay away from me forever, you stubborn man. I'm going to be fine.

Obsidian: I did this to you. Because of what I am now.

Moonbeam: I was there too. It wasn't your fault alone! We screwed up together.

Obsidian: I wanted to keep drinking you.

FINALLY, Nick had given up on waiting for Kain, fallen asleep, still weak as… yes, a kitten.

The slight draft of air on his skin woke him, reminding him of his home with Kain. His eyelashes fluttered and he glimpsed a familiar shadow.

"What's that?" He strove to keep his voice light since he sensed Kain was like a wild animal now, wanting to hide from him.

"Finn suggested I should bring you…." Three tattered roses fell at Kain's side. His hand was dripping blood.

Nick made a soft, scolding sound and reached for Kain, tugging him closer. "Idiot. What did you do?"

Kain sank to his knees beside the bed, the flowers, missing petals, wilting already, mashed against Nick's sheet-covered legs.

"Those roses look like they were in a car accident," Nick observed wryly.

"The fucking gift shop was closed so I broke in."

"Cut your hand."

"It'll heal."

Already it was closing, Nick noticed with wonder. He lifted it and put it to his lips, licking the residue. Kain's pupils yawned hungry black as he watched Nick taste him.

"Thanks for leaving the evidence in my room. They'll think *I* broke into the gift shop," Nick teased, knowing Kain needed to lighten up. He looked as if he were in shock as if he could use an IV as well.

"We can't be together."

Tears stung Nick's eyes, but he fought them off, telling himself it was just the fucking blood loss.

Again he remembered Siren's words: *a human submissive must be strong.*

This. This was what he meant. When he and Kain had mated, they'd done so in innocence, and Nick hadn't known he had to be strong.

Kain's head pillowed against his thigh and Nick stroked his hair.

Strong. I will be strong for him.

He whispered, "It will be all right."

 CHAPTER 19

"FINN," Nick breathed, touching the front door to Kain's dilapidated house. It was late, but he couldn't sleep, hadn't slept well since that night Kain had visited him in the hospital with his broken roses. The ache for Kain wouldn't go away. His touch. The way he gave Nick what he had never dreamed he'd crave. His... bite.

He looked up at the camera poised in his direction, knowing Finn had to be watching, knowing he'd been relieved when Kain had stayed away from Nick, but now Nick had recovered and it was time to try to scale those walls to his lonely prince again.

"Please, I need to see him." Nick leaned his flushed face against ungiving wood. "It's not over between us. It's not that easy."

BROWN, umber, thundercloud gray, nightmare black, ashes of roses....

"No, no, *no*, none of these work!" Nick shoved paint, canvas aside, panting. He wanted to rip the damp works and unsatisfying compositions in half! He wanted to tear at them the way that his need for Kain was slowly tearing *him*. An itch just under his skin he couldn't answer.

Marilyn made a rough sound and reached out to rub his shoulder, blinking as she took in the debris of his frustration in her spare room. "What a mess, honey! I'm sure you're just having a bad, uh, week."

"I can't. Create. Do you know how that feels?" Nick glared at his best friend. "*Do you?*"

Marilyn raised her brows. "I think you need to leave it, stop taking out your feelings on it and deal with the real problem—*calmly.*"

"Okay, I'm freaking out," Nick admitted, shoving back his hair, the movement tugging lightly on the bandage on his neck, almost redundant now that it had been a week since Kain had bitten him, nearly drained him. But that was then and this was now, and Nick needed Kain. And the bite hadn't been so bad. Hell, it had been amazing, which had been the problem!

"It's like not breathing when I can't work. All the colors are...." Nick turned away from what he'd been mixing, the tones as sober as a businessman's suit. Not spontaneous eruptions of color. Not Nick.

Not *Kain.*

Marilyn growled, as if picking up Nick's frustration. "It's all *his* fault, this man you're seeing. First he just about stalks you online, from what little you've admitted, and I'm not impressed that you wind up in the hospital because you fell over and cut yourself while under his roof. He hasn't even bothered to see how you're doing!"

Nick shook his head, giving a rusty laugh. "Marilyn, it's more than that." He put an arm around her, glad he had her, his former boss, his unlikely pal. Even though she was so much older than he was and a straight woman with no artistic abilities, they clicked. "Kain... he's disappeared! Finn says the night he came to see me at the hospital he put his assistant Cassandra in charge of his company and just... vanished."

Marilyn sat on the chair next to Nick and took his hand. "I'm sure he's all right. Didn't you say he could take care of himself? And the way he manipulated you into living and working with him. What did I tell you? The man's a classic bad boy."

Nick's lips quirked. "Like from one of your novels?"

"Don't give me that! Jane Austen knew what she was talking about. Mr. Darcy had a lot to learn before he was whipped into shape, didn't he?"

"Right," Nick agreed. "Well, *my* bad boy is a regular tortured hero and I'm worried about him. Under the tough act, he's… fragile."

"Yeah? Fragile is usually the secret side of the Alpha male, luring you like the proverbial moth to the flame." Marilyn sipped some of her rose-chocolate tea, fascinated by Nick's love life as always. Nick had the feeling that she'd found his relationship with Miguel rather dull, but she had loved to hear about Obsidian-Kain, his online admirer.

Nick made a face.

"Sorry, it must be different to live it than read about it."

"Yeah, uncomfortable, mostly, and right now my gothic hero is being a pain in the ass," Nick said, feeling a little defeated. He might have been the one who wound up in the hospital, but physical wounds were sometimes the easiest to heal.

Kain's eyes the night he'd brought the roses….

"He needs rescuing."

"Well," Marilyn said. "You better stop painting and get on that, hmmm?"

"MY PLACE," Ross said, showing Dr. Armand Leyland into his brightly painted apartment—maybe too bright. Kain had once teased him that it looked like he'd taken giant crayons to the walls. Purple, blue, red….

"A rainbow," Armand said now, as if sensing Ross's unease. "Appropriate."

"Yep." Ross shrugged out of his fall coat and took Armand's. He couldn't believe this gorgeous and brilliant man had any interest in him. Had actually asked him out when Ross had called him to tell him his handlebars had been modified for his new mountain bike. Ross took pride in his work and he'd tried to hand-build something special for Armand, to take the demands of the rugged sport.

"Funny, my…." Ross swallowed. "My first boyfriend commented on the same thing, that my walls reminded him of a rainbow."

Armand spotted a picture of Ross and Aaron, still smiling on the dresser Ross used to store files in his tiny living room. "You still think of him?"

"Sometimes. He was a wonderful man though he had a real temper. I'm ready to move on," Ross admitted, not wanting to talk about the past. Spending time with the hot doctor was just what he needed after a week of receiving black roses. Shit! He'd vowed not to think about that anymore, but he wished Kain would knock it off.

Now what? He blinked, staring at his small galley kitchen, almost an afterthought to Ross since he rarely cooked. Oh, right, he'd offered to make Armand dinner so they could go over the specs of the new custom design he'd created. His heart picked up. He wasn't a great cook, but maybe pasta would go over okay, he thought, trying to stifle the usual cloud of self-doubt before it could choke his enjoyment of the evening like weeds in a garden.

He wished, and not for the first time, that Kain hadn't changed after the fire, that he hadn't let Aaron die. Right now he could use a best friend to get some advice on handling the dazzling Armand. Ross swallowed thickly, remembering it had been Kain who had helped him prepare for his very first date with Aaron.

Fuck. How could he think about Kain? He hoped that bastard rotted in hell after what he'd done. He certainly wasn't the fun-loving man Ross had grown up with and looked up to when they'd been in school and first figured out they were both different. Kain spent all his time locked away in that ruin of a house now, almost as ruined as his life.

"I thought you weren't seeing anyone?" Armand teased, suddenly handing Ross a black rose wrapped in cellophane. "I found it just outside your door."

Ross froze, heart thudding in his ears, not wanting to take it, touch it. He'd have to call Finn, confide in him that he'd received another; it had been Finn who reluctantly put up the possibility that Kain might have sent them since Kain was not himself lately. If that was true, maybe Finn could talk to Kain, get him to knock it off again.

"Hey, Ross, you've gone white! What is it?" Armand put an arm around him, protective, breaking all the first-date ice. For a moment, Ross allowed himself to absorb Armand's strength, liking how comfortable it instantly felt. He'd missed having someone.

But he couldn't share this. "It's nothing."

Armand studied him, cocking his head. "You can talk to me."

Ross turned his back, realizing that as much as he wanted to leave behind what had happened, he wasn't free to date Armand.

"I...." He looked over his shoulder. "Tonight was maybe a mistake."

"Ross? You're frightened, I can tell."

Ross gave a rough laugh, rubbing his jaw with shaky fingers. "Frightened. Yeah." What if Kain *hadn't* sent the roses? It was something that Ross had wondered sometimes, when he was lying alone in his bed with only the sound of his heart beating so he switched on a light.

But if it wasn't Kain, then who was bent on scaring him? Ross just couldn't think of anyone.

DETECTIVE MANNERS folded her arms as she spotted Nick walking toward the club Manticore. "That close call you had not enough to warn you off?"

"It was nothing like what happened to those other boys, Detective," Nick managed evenly, annoyed. Why did everyone believe the worst of Kain, even Kain himself?

"Not at all!" Manners mocked. "He didn't by any chance give you any roses, did he?"

Nick remembered Kain's bloody hand offering tattered red roses at the hospital. "Uh."

"Because Forensics found traces of a charred black rose with each of the victims."

"Oh. No black roses. He's not the murderer, Detective."

"Uh-huh. Funny how the week he goes out of town or some shit, we have no murders," Manners noted.

"DOES Kain know you're here, kitten?" Siren demanded, hands on his hips as he came over to Nick's table in Manticore. It was the same table Nick had shared with Kain and he ached, feeling Kain's absence.

"He's... not around." Nick raked a hand through his hair.

Siren slid on the chair next to Nick's. "You look strung out. I'm sorry. He's not...." He chewed his lip, obviously not knowing how much to give away about Kain.

"Dead?" Nick shook his head. "But he's not exactly normal either, thanks to you."

"Making Kain into a dark fey is not something I regret." Siren shrugged. "He was the most beautiful man I'd ever seen and now he'll be beautiful for a very long time."

"He didn't tell me.... There are things I need to know about what he is," Nick pressed, getting to the reason why he'd come to the club.

Siren sat back, musing over his drink. "Warrior fey were created to be the enforcers in the fey armies. We are stronger, have sharper senses, and we often live close to the earth—as Kain has chosen with his dilapidated house. Some of us make it a mission to take care of the otherworldly creatures that can pose a danger to fey, shifters or humans."

"But you take blood?"

Siren nodded. "It's the *Turgold*, the bond made by blood. An adult dark fey craves it, takes it from lovers until he or she meets their mate. When they do, the need takes on more power. We want to become a part of our chosen one."

"Which maybe explains the trip wire Kain and I set off. Tell me more about what happened the night you made Kain a... dark fey?"

Siren sat back, raising a brow. "How much did he tell you?"

"What do you think?"

"Not a lot."

"I *need* to see him."

Siren lifted a languid hand. "Don't worry, kitten; he can't stay away from you for long, whatever he thinks. You are bonded, a fey to his chosen human."

Jaw flexing, Nick sighed. "I'm glad you think so. So far he's proving you wrong."

Siren's blue eyes narrowed on Nick's face, as if taking in his upset for the first time. "You went too far with him, didn't you?" He nodded to the bandage and Nick flushed. "Kitten, it would be better if you and Kain learned from us. I—we can teach you both how to bond safely."

"I'll keep it in mind but right now I just need to find him. I've tried his work and his house is shut up tight, so…."

"Uh-huh. Well, if Kain is playing a game of hide-and-seek, where does your heart, your body tell you he's hiding?"

"I…."

"Come on; you're bonded. What is the first place that comes to mind for a fae?"

Nick didn't have to think. "He would not leave familiar ground."

"No, he would not," Siren agreed.

Mask

LUKE moaned at the pain at his wrists and ankles from the iron shackles. Iron, so he couldn't change, couldn't get free, couldn't help—

"Finn," he whispered, sensing his mate was close, by a certain warm earthy note in the dank tunnel that he'd know anywhere; it was what had brought him here, doomed him.

"Luke, you were so rough last night. You never used to be like that," Finn said, forlorn.

Sickness gripped Luke's throat. *Oh, Finn. Oh, no.* Knowing what had happened, rage made him writhe in his bonds, so his wrists bled and his eyes bled, but still he could not change.

THE door of Kain's mansion was still barred to him. The windows dead of light.

Why had he come out here? Nick sighed, rubbing his chin.

Just because Siren suggested that Kain might stick close to home....

Nick folded his arms, not sure what to do next, shivering in the foggy night air. Probably he should go home. Try to work on his next assignment.

Instead, pulled by instinct, he circled the house, into the wild garden he'd been warned more than once by Finn wasn't safe.

THE moon was a misty spotlight as Nick walked under the moss-hung trees, stepping on crunchy clumps of tall grass. He passed an ornamental lake, water murky, ice rimmed, the heroic marble of a man stained brown, like mottled flesh.

Something grabbed his ankle.

"Uhhhhh!" Clawing, kicking out, he cried, "Shit!"

Dirt, leaves, he slid, fighting, pulled into the earth. His hands rasped against rotting wooden boards, a pale, dirty face, pale as a drowned body. Pulling him deeper, covering him.

He stared into feral green eyes.

Kain, nude, green and brown spattered, a wild creature, coming out of the earth and pulling him down onto the shards of an old veranda?

...Tearing cloth, mud-streaked hands gripping his hips, raising him, grunting as his sex butted against Nick's, pushing, awkward, fighting to get close....

"*Wait!* Kain, wait, what's happened to you?"

His clothes torn aside, white-knuckled hands spread him. Kain's teeth flashed, and Nick cried out.

Kain's wrist, dripping blood on his erection while Nick watched, dazed, remembering that Obsidian had warned him this was a dark fairy tale.

And then Kain reached, positioned, *took.*

Kain fucked him, hard, savage, almost dry.

Filthy, flattened against cold ground and shards of wood, head bumping against the side of his prison from the force of Kain's thrusts, Nick let him.

 CHAPTER 20

KAIN'S skin was blue, like an ancient warrior Celt, washed by the pigment of the earth, his tangled dark hair dry, rough, crowned like a wild prince with leaves and twigs, and his eyes—

It was his eyes that made Nick surrender.

Innocent, lost, groping for contact, Nick had a feeling that Kain had lain in the earth, curled in the fetal position, hiding, but Nick wandering so close had somehow roused him, ignited their bond. Blind, he'd reached out of the dark for Nick.

Not desire, not love, because that was too complex for a reduced beast. *Need.*

Nick cupped Kain's cheeks, trying to kiss him as Kain's penis skidded warmly against his leg, leaving a wet trail of want. Kain lifted his leg, hungry again, even though he'd just had Nick, hammered him like an animal, his hands restless as he gripped the shreds of Nick's pants, which he'd clawed off in his haste to mate.

"*Uhhhhhh!*" Nick gasped, not quite ready to take Kain again, but he didn't resist. Dragged down here in the dirt, it felt oddly right. Kain wanted him this much and Nick was his, even if this wasn't all he'd wanted.

Kain to the side of him, impaling him, penis buried deep inside, too-full, slick now with semen and blood. Nick clawing, clods of dirt under his hands, pressed into the earth, as Kain grunted.

The next moment, he pulled out and rolled Nick over onto all fours, as if he needed to possess Nick from all angles. Nick gasped when his legs were kicked wider, Kain ramming, fucking, opening him.

When Kain's teeth entered the back of his neck, Nick stiffened, his cock immediately reacting to the sharp invasion. Unbearably hard, spurting now, Kain's hand wrapped around the front of his throat like a possessive collar.

Mashed to the ground. Pounded. Used.

BLOOD warm from another bite on his shoulder blade trickled. Kain lapped at it, licking the side of Nick's throat as well until the blood stopped seeping and healed.

Nick jerked him close, giving a choked laugh. He wasn't sure if he was close to tears or…. His body was singing complaints, singing satisfaction.

"Kain…."

Still flushed from the collusion of their bodies, Kain sat up, looking into Nick's eyes, and Nick saw *him* and not the monster ascendant. Kain reached out and stroked the hair off Nick's forehead and then gave him an aching kiss.

His penis firmed against Nick's leg.

A little raw but hardening in response, Nick let out a puff of breath when Kain pushed inside again. He didn't penetrate deep, just rubbing the tip in and out. This time was face to face, a dance with Kain holding Nick's gaze, thumbing away the tear running down his cheek.

"I don't know how I feel," Nick whispered, another tear brimming. "Destroyed. Remade."

Kain didn't speak, leaning his forehead against Nick's, stroking with his body. Not so rough now.

Mask

NICK woke in Kain's bed, tangled against him like a bit of seaweed washed up on a beach after a storm, both of them still filthy, sticky.

He sat up and winced, shoving the hair out of his eyes. "Shit," he said, feeling the bruises, the bites white throbs on his shoulder and neck, his opening raw, coated with Kain's dried spend.

The spark of a match.

Nick's eyes flared as he swallowed thickly, not sure who he was coiled against, the man or the beast? He watched as Kain lit three candles by the bed. Was he ready to face him now? Shit, he felt like hiding, like going to his studio in the house and processing what had happened on canvas after canvas in spattered color, jewel drops of feeling, before facing Kain in sober sepia light.

Soft, pitiless, Kain asked, "Did you want it?" His head dropped. "Oh, fuck, did I…?"

He had only a second to consider and knowing Kain, he went with the truth.

"Yes, I wanted it."

"How could you? I all but…." Shame heated Kain's unmarred cheek. His face was turned away, hiding the scars, hiding the beast.

"No. I went searching for you." Nick leaned his head against Kain, squeezing his eyes shut, hands clenched against Kain's tense upper arms. *Listen to me.* "Subconsciously I knew what I might be inviting. I always knew with you, that you could be… wild."

Kain jerked away. "Yeah, a real encounter with Tarzan. A rough, messy, awkward fuck in the dirt. Very nice."

"Primeval, yes," Nick contradicted. "And I don't believe things are always ideal between… mates." He cupped Kain's cool cheek, stroking, gentling, seeing the acid of self-loathing acting on his lover and wanting to give him ease, as he had in the tangled garden of the night. "It's nice to be missed."

Kain gave a reluctant smile. "I can't believe you. I grab you by the ankle and pull you into the pit of the old cellar and… have you, and you see it as a Valentine."

"A grubby Valentine, maybe. Believe in me, Kain. I told you I want to be with you, how I… feel about you. I don't know exactly what that means, but I won't be made afraid."

Kain's gaze fell. He muttered to his thigh, "Was it that bad?"

"Dummy! I came twice." Nick lifted a shoulder. "Good, bad…. Is that even relevant for us anymore? If I were to text Siren right now, what would he say about the chain of events that led to what happened between us?"

Kain opened his mouth, paused.

"Come on, give. *I* certainly did earlier."

"He'd say…." Kain's gaze was fixed on his hands now. "It was your fault."

Nick's eyes widened. Then he chewed his lip, considering. "Because the human submissive has to be strong? The one to put the brakes on."

The tips of his ears pink in a way that made Nick's throat grip tight, Kain nodded. "Nick, there are times when I do lose control of myself. I want to taste you, roll in you. Sometimes even hurt you."

Nick sat up, crossing his legs, wincing a little, but determined to talk, to push this, until he settled this with Kain. "So is there some… training program for all this? Siren hinted there was. Like couples therapy for supernatural beings and their humans?"

Kain admitted with obvious chagrin, "You saw something like it at Manticore the other night, but you didn't like it."

"I didn't get it," Nick corrected. "Not at first. But Siren took the time to stick around and explain it to me, not run off, sure I'd be revolted."

Kain bent his head, the angle hiding the scars so that Nick reached out and lifted his chin, deliberately bringing them into the light. Siren had called him the most beautiful man he'd ever seen, and Nick could see what he meant from the untouched part of Kain's face, but he also found that the seams and pits of Kain's harsh experience with the fire were growing on him. If Kain chose to wear them, it would make no difference to Nick.

"You'd be safer away from me."

"I told you I don't want to be safe," Nick growled.

OUTSIDE Ross's apartment, Dr. Armand Leyland reached into his pocket and pulled out a single black petal from the rose he'd shown Ross.

Ross had been shaking.

Armand ran the silky petal over his lips, reliving the moment. The smoky fear smell that Ross exuded. It hadn't occurred to him that anyone, any*thing* could threaten him but Kain when Armand had set him up to seem the villain.

Now he was obviously beginning to suspect there might be more to it, and it terrified him. Kain had been a safe villain because Ross must have known deep down that Kain would never truly hurt him.

For a while, Armand hadn't been sure how he'd approach Ross. It wasn't possible until he gained more power, more control. Experimented.

Finn had helped.

He fingered the petal, smiling now. Smiling as the glamour faded and his true face looked up at Ross's window, still lit late into the night.

KAIN swept Nick off his bed, gravely holding his eyes as Nick looped his arms around his neck. He carried him into his bathroom and placed Nick carefully on a towel-covered stool while he ran hot water in a huge soaker tub. It was neon-orange, seventies renovation and the inevitable vines curled from the ceiling, but the water was *hot*.

Dazed, still thinking about their conversation and the very physical prelude to it, Nick stared at the yellow and orange checkerboard mosaics on the wall as Kain licked him, like a wolf with a cub. First the scratches on Nick's pale arms, Kain inspecting them carefully and making soft sounds when he found finger-shaped bruises, the legacy of Kain's hands, his need.

Seeing he was getting worked up again, and not in a good way, Nick commented, "That mosaic is fucking ugly."

Kain looked up, surprised. "Uh, yes."

"Darling, I think we need to redecorate."

Kain shook his head at Nick's antics. "Does nothing keep you down?"

"Yes, being apart from you," Nick admitted, very seriously.

"All right. Now lean over the tub," Kain directed.

"Why?"

"Why do you think?" Kain raised his brows. He'd licked all the bruises and scratches away but one place was less accessible....

Nick blushed, but let Kain position him so he hung over the brimming tub, bottom raised. It reminded him of when Kain had swatted him with rolled-up paper, so of course he got hard.

Kain spread him and tongued his ass.

Nick trembled, ambushed by the sudden emotion gripping his throat at this intimacy, somehow feeling more exposed with Kain's hands opening him, with his tongue buried inside, with the knowledge that just as Obsidian had seen almost every part of him exposed in cyberspace, now Kain saw him physically.

It stung at first, but with every lick, eased.

Soon Nick sighed at the sensations.

And he felt Kain smile against his thigh.

It will be all right, he'd promised Kain days ago. Now, reunited the way they needed to be, maybe it would be.

IN THE water, sleepy against Kain, and slightly horny from his tender care, Nick noted in surprise as the bright lemony light caught Kain's face clearly, "Your scarring…. It's softened!"

Kain gave a rigid nod.

"Was it Siren? Did you let him help you?"

"No, it was you. That night I almost drained you…. Blood of my mate."

"Oh," Nick said. He reached for some soap, wanting to spend some time running it over Kain's lean body. It was amazing to be here with him, sharing the normalcy of a shared tub.

"You should go back to your room," Kain warned, jaw flexing. "Or it could happen again. I'm new to being a fae and lately… not myself, according to Finn."

Frowning, Nick hesitated with the soap short of touch. "Is the room mine again?" He'd been banished to Marilyn's, after all. And he was still pissed over that.

Kain raked his glistening wet hair back from his forehead, looking frustrated. A familiar look when he and Nick locked heads. "Nick, I don't want you to leave my house, do you understand? If I had my way, I'd chain you to a wall in my dungeon and visit you to fuck you and feed you." Kain took the soap and used it to stroke Nick's skin, as if he couldn't keep his hands off him. "I'd never let another man even look at what is mine."

Nick covered Kain's hand. "But you won't do that because most of the time, you are not your monster. And besides, I thought you thought the idea of sharing me was sexy."

Kain shrugged. "Under certain conditions, maybe. As long as we both know it's for my pleasure and you're completely mine."

"You could have really hurt me, but you didn't. Things are looking up."

"If you'd fought me…." Kain closed his eyes tightly.

"That's a moot point since I didn't want to fight. I wanted," Nick meshed his fingers with Kain's, "to be fucked."

"Nick…."

"So I belong to a supernatural being." Nick cupped Kain's scarred cheek, something he was making a habit of to get his point across. "We'll just have to find a way to deal with that part of you. I go to school to become a better artist, so all we need is to be better educated, right?"

"Why don't I trust you when you sound so fucking reasonable?" But now Kain's arms were firm around Nick.

Nick gave Kain an innocent look, but it didn't look like Kain was buying it. "We're agreed that we have to talk to someone who might know about this stuff. Like… Siren?"

Kain growled.

Smiling, Nick ignored him, taking command of the soap. It was time to take advantage of the size of the tub.

 # CHAPTER 21

"FINN."

The familiar hoarse whisper from beyond the kitchen door, summoning him. Hearing it, Finn blinked, blade raised to chop fresh herbs. He was making a raspberry and lavender cake. He liked to fill the center with oozing fruit and sugar and like the finest European pastry; it relied on simple flavor and not too much processed sugar to—

"Finn!"

No, he didn't want to open that door. He didn't want to go in the tunnel and see him.

Chained, bleeding wrists. Iron. Iron so Luke couldn't break free.

Though part of him screamed not to turn the knob, he did, just like always.

"HERE'S your medicine, Kain," Finn whispered, as if wary of Nick overhearing him. "It... will help with the cravings. Maybe help keep Nick safe from you; I know you've been worried," Finn outlined.

Nick was packing up his art supplies for class, and he turned to glare at Finn. This was going too far with interference between him and

Kain; he didn't want Kain encouraged to keep secrets, especially from him. He opened his mouth to tell him off but Kain did it for him.

"What do you know about my 'cravings'?" Kain growled, glaring at the mug that Finn was thrusting in his direction. "I don't want to drink that shit."

"I've helped you before." Finn frowned, wide eyes on Kain's face. "Are you forgetting again?"

Kain looked away, swishing the liquid in the mug.

"Kain, you can't kid yourself about this! Not if you really care about Nick. Or do you want him to wind up in the hospital again?" Deliberately, as he left Nick's impromptu studio, Finn switched on the lights in the room, which Nick had left turned off so Kain could visit comfortably with him.

"Fuck!" Kain cursed, raising a hand to shield his eyes.

Nick folded his arms, determined he was going to be a part of this. He wasn't sure what Finn was up to. "Is sensitivity to light something all fae suffer from?"

"How the fuck would I know?" Kain scowled.

Nick raised a brow. "Peachy! That's just great; have this big, life-changing experience and hide here in a big, falling-down house and don't try to become functional, don't try to understand yourself."

"I run a company." But Kain dropped his gaze, flushing a little.

"Better than you do your life, apparently," Nick said. His voice softened. "You need to know yourself; go into the shadows and shine a light."

Kain reached out and sifted a hand through Nick's hair. "Brat. Where did you get such smarts?"

Nick shrugged. "An artist needs to tell the truth in his work." He stepped away from Kain, wincing from the movement and trying to hide it. He was still a little raw from the night before. He colored now, remembering crushed leaves, churned-up earth… and Kain. *In him, on him.*

"Just how late is this night class?" Kain didn't look happy so Nick suppressed a smile. He was certainly acting more and more like a boyfriend, which suited Nick. He saw the fae stuff as a quirk; they just had to learn how to deal with it and then they could enjoy spending time together.

"Late. I'll crash at Marilyn's," Nick suggested. "I haven't spent much time with her lately and I miss her."

Under his breath, Kain admitted, looking a little embarrassed, "I don't want to let you go."

"But you will. Your possessiveness is sexy when we play, but I like spending time with my friends." Nick shoved another sketchbook into his knapsack and then hit the light switch, so that softer candlelight dominated again. He smiled at Kain's look of relief. "I'm not the reclusive type. I'm just in love with one."

"Thanks," Kain said, giving Nick a shy look, as if he liked hearing certain words from him. "Although I do feel managed sometimes. Anyone ever tell you that you're bossy?"

"That's because you are managed." Nick didn't deny it. "And don't mention it." Then Nick nodded at Finn's mug, which he had been obediently sipping from as they talked. "What's in that?"

"Fuck knows." Kain took another swallow. "Supposed to help with the blackouts. And he's right; I can't risk them now you're staying under my roof." In a husky voice, he said, "Can't risk *you.*"

"Uh-huh." Nick swallowed, hearing the words Kain didn't say. But he frowned, wanting to ask Kain more about the stuff. Unfortunately a glance at his watch warned him he'd have to table it tonight.

"Nick. You did enjoy what we did, yes?" More color stung Kain's cheeks. "I know you came but…." He took a deep breath. "Fuck!"

Seeing Kain still needed reassurance, Nick retraced his steps, cupping Kain's scarred cheek as he held his gaze. "I liked it."

Kain closed his eyes, nuzzling Nick's hand.

"And if I hadn't, well, sex isn't an exact science. It would be nothing to be embarrassed about if I didn't come perfectly every single time." Nick bit his lip in amusement at Kain's appalled look. "As long as I do most of the time, right?"

"I'm not embarrassed! And you will come perfectly every single time!"

"Okay." A smile tugged at Nick's mouth as he slung his bag over his shoulder. At the door, he glanced back at Kain as an odd grief tightened his throat. Maybe it was better they spend some time apart. Last night had been so fucking intense and then they'd had to talk, to rebond, to heal....

"Happy Halloween, boss!"

Kain grunted.

Siren sauntered over to Detective Manners, who was standing near the bar in Manticore. "You wished to speak with me?"

Manners nodded, giving Siren a narrowed glance. "Looked you up. You don't seem to have any last name."

"No."

"Some kind of rock star thing?"

"No."

"Uh-huh. About your whereabouts the nights of the murders...."

"We've been over this, Detective." Siren now had an edge to his voice. "I have witnesses that place me here at the club. Unless I could be two places at the same time?"

"Men you were with, huh?"

Siren nodded.

"Who you could have paid to cover for you."

Mask

"I could have, but I did not need to." Siren pushed back his long black hair, blue eyes flashing at Manners. He didn't miss her scent changing, reacting to his looks. Everyone wanted him, human or demon, but few took him seriously it seemed. Or at least the people he wanted....

"Tell me about your boss, Kain Mitchell."

Siren's fist clenched. "What of him?"

"You know him well, do you?"

Siren swallowed thickly, heat moving through his body.

...Sinking his teeth into Kain's throat. Kneeling behind him as he fucked one of the others, body coated with sweat, beautiful, defiant.

Then they'd all been on him. Fangs sinking into his thigh, his neck, his chest, his three "lovers" tasting him, taking him.

Mateo had tried to mount Kain but he'd weakly kicked him away, even as he was fading....

And inexplicably, Siren intervened. Leaning over Kain, seeing the haze in his eyes. "I want inside."

But Kain only flipped them over, his erection pressing against Siren, his hand fisted possessively in his hair.

Startled, Siren stared into his green eyes.

"No," Kain said, "I will have you."

"He is extremely... strong willed," Siren said, touching the scar on his own neck, given him by Kain that night they'd exchanged blood by accident—transforming Kain into a dark fey.

"I think he's my guy."

"I did some digging of my own, Detective Manners. I discovered you are ambitious and are working toward becoming chief of police. It would certainly help if you were to find this mysterious killer."

"Politics has nothing to do with it!" Manners spat. "Or do you like someone going around torturing, burning, and killing blond hustlers? Especially when they are your regulars?"

"Politics *always* has something to do with it. Whether it's the Roman Senate or what is happening here in our fair city." Siren spoke from experience. "And no, if I find out who is doing this... he will be destroyed."

"Destroyed?" She slapped a hand on the bar. "This is my business."

"Not entirely." He gave her a stony glance.

"Whatever, but you better stay out of it! And the next time Mitchell experiences one of his convenient blackouts, I'll be there."

Siren blinked. "His *what*?"

Manners turned to leave but paused. "Weird shit goes down in this club. You want to know what's also weird?"

"What?" Siren raised a brow.

"One of my vic's bodies is missing. Just... gone from the morgue. I guess you don't know anything about that?"

"No, I don't, detective, but it's very revealing, don't you think? Thank you for the information. I'll look into it."

Obsidian: Nick, you almost didn't come.

Moonbeam: Well, hello to you, Obsidian. Yes, I'm enjoying this lecture very much, thank you.

Obsidian: ...

Moonbeam: All right, yes, but I did so it wasn't a big deal. I admit our encounters haven't been quite what I wanted. Yet. Something is missing.

Obsidian: It wasn't a big deal! Clearly you have much to learn from me. I wasn't myself. I do care about pleasuring you—very much.

Moonbeam: No kidding you weren't yourself. Burying yourself alive in the back forty will do that. Remember what I said about knowing yourself? You need to work on that.

Obsidian: I...

Moonbeam: Are you trying to apologize?

Obsidian: No!

Moonbeam: Okay.

Obsidian: It won't happen again.

Moonbeam: You mean you won't...?

Obsidian: If you hadn't been so raw, I would have done more.

Moonbeam: It did hurt a little, Kain, but what was missing was the intimacy. I want that with you sometimes, even though what you do fulfills every fantasy I've ever had.

Obsidian: ...

Moonbeam: I wanted you, don't doubt that, but I want to be more to you.

Obsidian: I took you like an animal.

Moonbeam: ...

Obsidian: You want to be away from me now. I felt that when you left.

Moonbeam: You misunderstood; I just need some time to process. I...never let anyone inside before. It wasn't how I envisioned it. And you aren't the easiest boyfriend.

Obsidian: I would take it back if I could.

Moonbeam: I don't know if I want you to. I just need to understand. Me. You.

Obsidian: What's to understand? I'm the monster who just about grabbed you—

Moonbeam: It wasn't like that! Kain, it was a mistake for you to retreat that much. I want you to promise me you won't anymore. Not from me.

Obsidian: When I was inside you, I didn't care about anything but you under my hands, taking my cock.

Moonbeam: Fuck, stop saying that...

Obsidian: Why not?

Moonbeam: Because I'm getting hard and I have to stand up and give a presentation soon. I'd prefer to do it sans woody.

Obsidian: Oh.

Moonbeam: Yes, oh. Before I completely chicken out, because you're not here, looking at me—

Obsidian: Yes?

Moonbeam: You know I'm horribly in love with you. Not singing-in-the-rain love, but a burning in my gut, consuming me from the inside.

Obsidian: ...

Moonbeam: Shit. I shouldn't have said that, right? You're going to ignore that I said that.

Obsidian: Nick, let me drive you to Marilyn's after your class.

Moonbeam: I don't think that's a good idea. We really need a little breather.

Obsidian: There's a killer loose. I'll wait for you. You don't even have to look at me, talk to me, since you don't want—

Moonbeam: Do you even listen to me? What part of I'm in love with you do you not get?

Obsidian: Has left the room.

Moonbeam: Because if we're in a thing, like a relationship-thing, then we need to communicate. Hello? Damn it!

KAIN had to pull onto the side of the road, sweat prickling his hairline. He squeezed his eyes shut, hands rubbing his temples. He had to get to Nick, make sure he was safe, but his head was pounding, the first sign.

No, oh, no.

Not tonight.

Red pain....

NEAR the university, where he was hoping to intercept Nick Anders, Dr. Armand Leyland followed a scent, an invisible ribbon of warmth in the foggy night air until he came to the body of a student, schoolbag splashed with blood, insides tangled like seaweed, staring blue eyes, blond hair, in the pale, dead face.

He had to fight down the part of himself that wanted to roll in the blood, touch the still-warm corpse.

Of course, he knew who had killed the boy.

NICK paced outside the school. Kain was twenty minutes late. Why was he waiting for him? Oh, yeah, because they needed to hash some things out.

"Nick?" A hand gripped his arm.

He jumped and then gave a weak laugh. "Oh, it's you! Fuck, you *scared* me!"

RED eyes, bleeding. Hands clenched into the bark of a tree, holding on.

Watching from the shadows.

Nick wasn't alone. Someone... with him.

Mark?

Mark had kissed Nick. Mark screaming the night he died. Mark was dead. This had to be just another of his hallucinations.

Everything jumbled in his head. Pain. Protectiveness. Rage.

 CHAPTER 22

"MARK, how is this possible? I thought you were dead!" Nick hugged his friend, tears pricking his eyes. "Shit, oh, shit! They even had me identify the wrong body and it was fucking awful, thinking you were dead!"

"Poor Nick," Mark whispered in his ear, pulling Nick close. "Were you upset? You were always so wrapped up in your art... and lately, *him.*"

Mockery. Jealousy.

Nick blinked, stiffening, then flushed self-consciously at the slap at both his dedication to his work and his relationship with Kain.

"Mark, you okay?" He pulled away from his friend. "Where have you been? You missed Kelsey's lecture tonight. Fuck, you've missed a bunch of classes."

"Let's just say my priorities have changed." Mark smiled. "No thanks to your boyfriend."

"Kain thought you were dead too. He regretted it."

Nick searched his friend's beautiful light eyes, seeing the same old Mark, except he was pale under the streetlamp. So what were his instincts trying to tell him?

"You've been sick or something? Where have you been all this time, Mark?"

"In a manner of speaking. You could ask Finn." Mark raised his brows.

"Finn! But he thinks you're dead too! He went with me to the morgue and he was really upset." Nick ran a hand over his jaw as he thought it out, shuffling the pieces into a new, unexpected pattern. "I wondered if maybe you were with him the night you disappeared and he wouldn't admit it for some reason of his own. Possibly because he was afraid suspicion would fall on him and not just Kain."

"So you don't entirely trust him?" Mark raised a brow. "Smart! Yes, I was with Finn. He actually gave me a tour of the grounds on Kain's estate. They are quite extensive... and dangerous. Did you know there is an old wine cellar with a tunnel leading to it from the house?"

"Kain mentioned it. I think Finn keeps some herbs and stuff there." Nick frowned, uneasy. "I still don't get why he didn't say he was with you that night, and that you were okay."

"Maybe he felt guilty. Or maybe he just forgot." Mark shrugged.

Nick crossed his arms, pissed. "That's really unlikely! What could make him forget something so serious? And it's such a weird coincidence, don't you think? Someone who looks so much like you, even wearing my jack—" Nick broke off and his eyes widened as one possible answer hit him.

A few weeks ago, he would never have dreamed of the idea, but since then he'd rubbed shoulders with shape-shifters and been claimed by a dark fey.

He swallowed thickly, taking a step back from Mark, back toward the brighter, safer lights of the university. "And about Kain," he clarified, trying to buy a little time until he showed. "We have an unusual relationship. He's not what you'd call normal. Something... happened to him."

"Really?" Mark didn't blink, stalking slowly after Nick. He reached out so fast Nick didn't see the movement, playing with a strand of Nick's hair.

Nick jerked away from the touch of chilly fingers. "Hey, don't!"

Mark shrugged, not looking very remorseful. "Sorry. It's just that… we had a moment."

"We did," Nick agreed, trying to keep up a calm facade, although his heart was pounding and the back of his neck and his armpits were abruptly clammy with sweat. "But I think that window is closed."

"Closed, huh. So did you let him have you at last, Nick? Are *his* bruises on your skin? A man like him, you're right; he can't be gentle."

"Uh." Nick couldn't believe how things could skew so quickly. From shock and joy at seeing Mark… to asking questions… to suspecting the truth. "What happened between me and Kain is not something I want to talk about with you, Mark. Ever."

Primal. Kain coming out of the earth and bringing Nick down, claiming him. And after, licking him, caring for him.

He had a feeling that Mark would understand the first, but not the second, experience. And anyway, hadn't he wanted to get away from Telemachus House so he could put in some thinking time and figure out what was going on? He'd hoped to have some time to talk with Marilyn, who always was a great guide. She might even have read enough supernatural romances to give him some kind of idea of how to deal with Kain, who didn't seem interested in understanding what he was now.

He took a deep breath, hating that he felt afraid of his friend. "Do you want to borrow my notes for class? I'm waiting for Kain now. He'll be here any moment," he offered casually, hoping Mark would back off.

Mark reached out for Nick's offered art portfolio bag, and opened it, pulling out sheets of Nick's careful sketching and notes and then letting them flutter to the damp pavement. "Naw."

"Mark, what the fuck!" Nick knew then that this wasn't his friend anymore. Mark had been a passionate artist, and he had always respected Nick's work. "Oh, shit! What happened to you?" Chills whispered down his spine.

"Nick Anders?"

Nick glanced at the muscular blond stranger with compelling blue eyes who stepped out of the trees near campus. He almost sagged with relief since the last thing he wanted was to be alone with Mark!

"Yes?" he rasped.

"I'm Dr. Armand Leyland. I'm a friend of Ross and I've been looking for you." Leyland stared at Mark and his expression tightened into a snarl. *"Get away from him; he's disgusting!"*

Too fast, way too fast for Nick to have any chance to evade him, Mark snatched Nick's arm.

"Mark!" Nick gasped in pain at the tight grip. "Fuck, that hurts!"

"He's mine," Mark growled. "Back off!"

"Let him go, creature!"

"Creature?" Nick gave Mark a blank look. "I thought you were a—"

Mark smirked. "Entertain me with your theory."

Nick swallowed. "It was you at the morgue. You were wearing my jacket and it would just be too unbelievable a coincidence that you would go missing and someone who looks exactly like you winds up—"

"Dead," Mark growled.

"Yes." Nick raised his chin. "So I think you must somehow be like Kain, a fae."

Mark shook his head slowly, still with that unsettling little smile. "Not quite."

"Can't you smell him?!" Leyland grimaced. "Nick, close your eyes and then *look* at him."

Something in Armand Leyland's eyes. The certainty.

Nick took a deep breath and then squeezed his eyes shut, feeling like a little boy who wanted to hide under his covers; he wasn't sure he wanted to know what Mark had become. But hadn't he told Kain that they had to shine a light on the shadows in their lives?

Mask

The smell hit him first. Not the clean scent of damp earth and man, as when Kain erupted from the ground, but something like rotting cat food.

Nick's eyes flared open.

Mark stared back at him through milky eyes, fluid seeping down one pitted cheek showing burns, torn flesh... and a beetle crawling through a hole in the skin.

"*Shit!*" Nick fell back and Mark allowed it, eerie smile on his lips.

Nick covered his mouth, afraid he'd vomit. Mark was nothing like Kain or Siren, who both possessed an almost unearthly grace.

Armand Leyland stepped between Nick and Mark, giving off a welcoming vibe to Nick in that moment of Alpha and protective. "*Revenant,*" he cursed.

"You know what I am?" Mark grinned, blood coating his lips from rotting gums. "Then you must know poor Nick is no match for me."

Armand shoved Nick toward the woods. "*Run!*"

NICK crashed through the brush, branches striking his arms, stinging his cheeks.

Getawaygetaway.

How was it possible that he was so close to the place where he'd sat through a lecture, just minutes earlier? It was like his life, mundane, normal, boring even, had been a thin membrane over what lay underneath.

He'd been touched, changed, as soon as Obsidian hooked up with Moonbeam in a chat room.

Shadows swayed in a sudden gust, foggy air making a nimbus around the balls of light from a nearby running track that cut through the parkland.

Breathing ragged now, looking over his shoulder but seeing no sign of Mark—or the thing Mark had become—, Nick remembered coming here recently on a warm September afternoon and sketching, oblivious to what was to come.

It felt like another life. It was another life.

He'd also lost track of Armand Leyland, his mysterious rescuer. And there was no sign of Kain, who had promised to meet him. Shit, where was he?

A branch snapped against his face, a sharp wakeup call.

Pay attention or you'll wind up dead... or worse, like Mark. You have to take care of yourself now. Kain will kick your ass if anything happens to you.

Gut twisting greasily. Throat tight.

Oh, Mark.

Panting, he came at last to a familiar small clearing where he'd often done some sketching in warmer weather. He knew the spot was located near the campus bus stop. As he trembled, listening intently to every small sound, wary of stepping in the light, he glimpsed the colorful costumes of trick-or-treaters passing on the sidewalk through gaps in the brush. Children escorted by parents. Fuck!

A twig snapped like a shattered bone behind him.

Caught in the net of this new nightmare, he swallowed, sweat running down his cheek. Shit! He didn't want to look behind him.

He just knew it would be bad.

Slowly he moved his head by inches, struggling to suppress the sound of his breathing, to not give himself away to what hunted him.

Mark's ruby dripping smile.

Mask

"Happy Halloween, Nick! Did you think I'd forget our favorite sketching place? It's certainly the perfect night to meet a real monster, don't you think?"

"Mark. God, I'm so sorry about what happened to you, but you can't want to hurt me," Nick breathed. "I really cared about you."

Mark's milky eye widened. "Oh, I do care about you. That's why I'm going to do to *you* what your lover did to me."

Nick made a soft, disbelieving sound. "Kain wouldn't do that. He wouldn't hurt anyone I loved." Kain, primal, taking. Kain, gentle, diffident in the wake of his dominance. *Please, no. Don't let it be him responsible for Mark being like this!*

Nick grappled to make sense of things. If he dashed out onto the street would the creature Mark attack those kids?

The sick twist in his belly said *yes.*

Trapped. He was truly trapped. If he went forward, he endangered innocent people. If he stayed here, Mark would—

A hand snaked out of the wood. Dirty, fingernails crusted with blood. Yanking Mark under the trees—

Shaking, Nick caught the sound of a choked-off cry of agony.

The finality of the snap of bone.

Chilled, Nick waited, heart pounding in his ears.

What now?

Kain stepped into the dim light, defused by swirls of low-lying mist, nude, twigs and leaves caught in his ragged hair, hand up to protect his sensitive eyes from the nearby streetlamp.

He hesitated, staring at Nick dumbly, hunger burning silent in his green glowing eyes.

Nick let out a deep sigh, arms wrapped around himself, still trembling. He closed his eyes tightly.

"Oh, thank God!" he whispered before opening his eyes again and confronting his lover. "I guess I really did need a ride home, uh, not that you're exactly dressed to offer one."

Holding Kain's innocent and feral gaze, knowing better, knowing he had to think about things, and maybe this was the time to break it off. Remembering how Kain had taken him, Finn's warnings, what Mark had accused Kain of doing....

Remembering all that, Nick went to Kain, feeling it was as inevitable as the rise of the moon. He cupped Kain's scarred cheek and then embraced him, resting his head against his cool shoulder.

"Thank you for saving me. Shit, I was so scared!" Nick took Kain's bruised and bloodied hand and kissed it.

Kain only stared back with glassy eyes, looking totally out of it. "Nick," he rasped. "My Nick." Shaky, torn fingers combed through Nick's hair.

"Come on; we better find you some clothing!" Nick took Kain's cold hand firmly, protectively.

CHAPTER 23

MY NICK.

Nick could still feel the words like a warm pressure expanding in his chest as he walked through the woods near campus, his hand firm on Kain's, guiding him. Kain loved him. He was scared to say it because of the darkness, the questions, surrounding his life, but Nick was sure of it.

Kain lifted his head, and a minute later, Nick caught the sound of a jogger running toward them on the path.

He tugged Kain behind a tree to hide his nudity. When the footsteps faded, he breathed a sigh of relief against Kain's neck.

Kain was shivering spasmodically, his eyes so dilated in the dim light that only a thin rim of bittersweet green remained. "N-Nick."

"I'm here." Nick plucked twigs, leaves, from Kain's hair. "Shhhhh, I'm here."

"Red, hurting," Kain mumbled. "Did I h-hurt you?"

"No, you saved me. Don't you remember?"

Kain shook his head slowly. "Never remember. I... didn't hurt?"

"No, never." Nick took one of Kain's hands and stroked it gently, wishing he could touch all of Kain, his torn body, his tormented mind.

Unable to give Kain what he needed with words, Nick wrapped his arms around him, ignoring the blood, the chilled skin. And, after a moment, Kain rested his head against Nick's shoulder.

"It's all right," Nick whispered. "You did what you had to. Now let me take care of the rest."

NICK peeled off his jacket, passing it to Kain.

Kain stared at him, making no move to take Nick's offering.

Nick made a soft sound of exasperation, mainly at himself. Kain was reduced to his most primal. Dangerous... but also innocent, vulnerable.

"We won't be able to get to Marilyn's if you don't wear it," he told Kain. "And we need to get out of here so I can take care of you."

Kain slowly slipped on the jacket, which was just long enough to cover the essentials—barely.

"HE'S IN costume," Nick told the wary driver who was obviously reluctant to give Kain a ride.

"As what, fucking Tarzan?" the man asked, shaking his head.

Sighing, Nick pulled out his wallet and offered triple the fare.

"COME on; you're shaking!" Nick kept his tone soft, which seemed to reach Kain. He hated seeing him like this, but at the same time, it felt right to take care of him. "Step into the shower so I can rinse you off and get you clean," he urged. "Please, Kain, just let me help you. I want that, more than anything."

Kain looked back at him blankly, green eyes dazed, still seeming out of it, except every now and then his eyes would snap into focus on Nick's face.

Nick rubbed Kain's arms. Did the fey suffer from exposure? He didn't know, but Kain did not seem himself.

"I just want to help you," Nick whispered. "You saved me, saved us both." He pressed a gentle kiss against Kain's lips, wanting to imprint comfort, safety, gratitude that they were together.

HOT water struck Kain's back, rousing him, stinging his eyes. He took a deep breath, wishing he could remember what had happened. Just... red mist images.

And Nick.

Familiar depression caught him, making him want to sink down, sickened by what he was; he fell to the shower floor and put his head on his knees.

"Hey, I go to get a fresh bar of soap and you crash. Literally." Nick was suddenly there, inside the tiny wet space with him. He gently tugged a strand of Kain's hair.

Kain looked at him, one dull, sullen ache.

"Shhhhhh." Nick was all around him, refusing to leave him alone, his body a slight, strong imprint that Kain could feel, could hang onto.

"Did I hurt someone?"

"You stopped Mark from hurting me," Nick said. "And Mark... he wasn't Mark anymore. I think we'll need Siren's help on what exactly he was."

He helped Kain stand up and picked up the only bar of soap he'd been able to find, scented with lilacs, reminding Kain they were at Marilyn's apartment. No wonder the shower booth was so small, not that he said anything to Nick, who was earnestly cleaning him off. But Kain didn't want to be seen by anyone else, wanted to go back to his mansion and bury himself in his rooms.

He squeezed his eyes shut, feeling the soap stroking his back, Nick paying careful attention to the scratches Mark had inflicted.

As if anything could make him clean after everything he was afraid he'd done, everything he'd experienced since he'd become a part of a dark, secret world.

Nick soaping the scarred side of his face jolted him from reverie. He covered Nick's fingers, staying him.

"The scars are a part of you, and I'm not going to pretend they aren't there," Nick stated, almost primly. "Siren implied you choose to wear them."

"Why would I do that?" Kain raised his eyebrows.

"To punish yourself, probably." Nick shook his head. "I'm not going to let you go on doing that, because it's just dumb."

"How can you stop me?" Pushy. Nick was so pushy, and prodded him to believe in himself.

Nick wound his arms around Kain and rested his head against his chest. After a pause, Kain's hand came up automatically, caressing Nick's back.

"Behold my strategy," Nick murmured.

"THIS bed is too fucking small," Kain groused. He was spooning Nick, scrubbed clean by him, head buried between Nick's neck and shoulder. At first Nick's warmth and scent had been soothing, but now Kain could feel need rise. He couldn't be close to Nick without wanting to possess him, hammer home with cock and touch that Nick was his. "We should go home."

"We will when we've both had some rest. Last night...." Nick breathed. "Shit, do you know what made Mark like that?"

Kain lifted a shoulder. "No." Then he cleared his throat, feeling Nick's tension translated by his tense muscles. "I know he was your friend. Sorry."

Nick looked over his shoulder, sad smile on his face. "Thanks."

"For what?"

"For thinking of my feelings."

"I'm not very... accustomed to doing that."

Nick closed his eyes, seemingly serene. "You're missing the point."

"Which is?" Nick distracting him, as usual. Capturing his interest. Pushing away nightmare.

"The point is you're trying."

Kain grunted.

KAIN'S eyes snapped open, jerking away from Nick and unbearable temptation.

"What is it?" Nick grumbled sleepily. "You were sleeping."

Kain sat up, back to Nick.

Nick also sat up, wrapping his arms around him from behind. "I'm not afraid of you," he reminded Kain.

"I almost drained you dry. And the night you came looking for me, your first time, I was out of control." Kain's head bowed.

"You're a new, uh, warrior fey, right? So I figure you are on a learning curve."

"More like I've driven off a cliff," Kain said wryly.

Nick ignored Kain's pessimism, chewing his lip.

Always wanting to help him, Kain thought with a rush of something alien. Tenderness? He'd never felt it for all the tricks he'd known as both human and fey.

"You need blood, right? If you hurt anyone, you wouldn't need that."

Kain shook his head, wishing it was that simple. "I don't need that much, except that I have a special craving for yours. I wish I could remember, Nick."

"Okay, start with what you do remember."

"*Pain.* Flashes. I saw… someone young, screaming." Kain swallowed thickly. "And then he was dead. I saw Mark dead. And you, I saw you and I wanted to drag you away from him and put you in chains so you'd never—"

Nick lifted his wrists. "Hmmmm, I seem to be chain free."

"Very funny."

"Just because you *think* something, that doesn't mean you act on it," Nick said quietly.

"I made you run."

Nick shrugged, uncomfortable. "It's… a lot to take in. I just needed some space. It was more like regrouping than running."

"I should go."

"*No.*" Nick kissed Kain's cheek and then his lips. "I belong to you. Don't I?"

Kain's hands combed through Nick's hair. "I want to please you, make you beg, make you come."

"Well, that sounds horrible!" Nick said dryly. "How will I ever endure it?"

"Brat." Kain's lips quirked in a reluctant smile.

Mask

ARMAND stood under Ross's window, looking up at the light still burning. He knew Ross was home, and wondered what he was doing. Reading specs for new bicycle designs?

He wanted to knock on the door, enjoy Ross's innocence and his fear. Knowing he was the source of that fear just made it more delicious.

But he decided he'd had a busy enough evening. Mark had proved to be a disappointment. He should have easily captured Nick, but he'd gorged himself on a student before Nick had even shown, dulling his senses.

Kain had snapped Mark's neck when he'd finally managed to corner Nick but wanting to clean up the mess once and for all, Armand had cut the head off the revenant so it could not rise again.

Mark had served his purpose.

Armand would just have to make another revenant.

KAIN fastened Nick's hands to the bed rails of his headboard. He paused to kiss the back of his neck and Nick shivered. He was on his knees, facing away from Kain. He hadn't even blinked when Kain had torn up and used Nick's old painting T-shirt to tie around his wrists.

He was breathless, flushed, anticipating.

So trusting.

"Do you remember one of our early conversations, about rimming?" Kain asked.

Nick stifled a soft sound, biting his lip. "Yes, I told you I'd never tried it."

Moonbeam: I'm not sure how comfortable I am telling a stranger my sexual fantasies. I only just met you!

Obsidian: Tell me, Moonbeam.

Moonbeam: Well, there is one. I'm...I'm tied to my headboard and a man, a stranger I can't see comes into the room and—

Obsidian: Yes?

Moonbeam: This is embarrassing.

Obsidian: Share. You know you want to tell me.

Moonbeam: He puts his tongue inside me, licking me, invading me. Not asking me for permission, just—

Obsidian: You want a man to do that to you?

Moonbeam: :blushing: Oh, shit, Miguel's home! I— Never mind! He's my boyfriend and—

Obsidian: Moonbeam, I'd love to eat your ass.

Moonbeam: Moonbeam has left the room.

KAIN spread Nick's ass cheeks open and licked a line down his body, pausing to suckle his hanging balls.

Nick gasped, arching his back. The fact that his hands were tied made him even hotter. He tugged at his bonds, moaning as Kain's tongue found him, pressed inside him. "Kain!"

"I want to do this to you back at the mansion. I have a spreader bar I'd fit you into so you couldn't close your legs, leaving you totally open, slutty…. Would you like that?" Two of Kain's fingers gently penetrated him. Kain seemed totally focused on pleasuring Nick, stimulating him.

"*Yes!*" Nick bit his lip hard to stop himself from begging. He loved it when Kain treated him like one of his hustlers. He'd fantasized about it for weeks, even knowing he shouldn't think about such things.

"I want my tongue in you, marking you."

Nick whimpered, as Kain's fingers toyed with him, sending sparks to his nipples, his balls, his needy prick.

"Does my whore want that?" Kain's voice was rough.

Panting, Nick felt a thrill that zapped him at Kain's language. "Yes," he whispered.

"*Say it,* Nick." Kain licked under his opening, making Nick cry out as he toyed with his trembling body. So close!

"Your… your whore wants you inside. Your tongue, Kain, please!"

Fingers spreading him and then Kain. Deep, making a husky sound of approval at Nick's taste, Nick's willingness as he pushed his ass back, inviting Kain to have him, take all of him.

Possessed, Nick's body arched as Kain's hand found him, gave him a cursory stroke, almost insultingly easy….

And then Kain's tongue was gone and he felt the scrape of teeth on one ass cheek. He shuddered, heart galloping. "Yes," he acquiesced.

Kain bit his hip, teeth sinking into flesh and Nick—

"*Fuck, yes! Your whore. Yours, Kain!*" He shot, his cock gripped in Kain's hand, his climax under Kain's control… just how he wanted it.

CHAPTER 24

"SO FINALLY you come to me for advice?" Siren toyed with his long hair, coiled in a ponytail, and leaned back in his chair, considering Kain. "After treating me without respect for how long?"

Nick held tight to Kain's tense arm, watching his impassive face. He ached to push, but he knew Kain needed to do this himself. Knew Kain had only asked for help because of Nick's prodding.

"*You* made me."

"And you were delicious."

Kain made a growling sound.

"However much you want to deny it, I gave you pleasure and protected you from the others."

Nick could see how well that went down. He cleared his throat. "Kain, uh, I mean, *I* need your help, Siren. He needs to know more about his own nature and how to… keep me safe."

Siren inclined his head. "That is wise and important. A strong human submissive should be valued. Be seated, kitten."

Kain pulled out a chair for Nick. "I'm not sure I like you calling him that," he remarked, raising an eyebrow at Nick.

Nick suppressed the need to roll his eyes. He didn't mind Siren finding him hot. Kain reached out with a casual brand of possessiveness, caressing the back of his neck.

Mask

If it acts like a boyfriend....

He took heart that maybe this second visit to Manticore would be easier with Kain's support.

"I regret you will probably never allow me the pleasure of experiencing Nick."

Kain folded his arms.

"Hello!" Nick huffed. "Can talk for myself and everything!"

Neither Kain nor Siren looked away from their macho eye lock so Nick decided to break it up. He pushed up his sleeve and rested his arm on the table, clearly displaying dark bruising on his inner wrist.

Kain frowned. "Why didn't you show me that?"

"We, uh...." Nick flushed, remembering being tied to his bed at Marilyn's, Kain's tongue in his ass and then his teeth.... His hand found the fresh bite on his hip and rubbed against it through his clothing, savoring the secret erotic memory. "We were a little busy."

Kain ran a thumb over Nick's purpled flesh. "I didn't do this?"

"No, it was Mark," Nick reassured his lover and then looked at Siren. "My friend Mark. He was a sweet person, very talented." Nick took a deep breath. "He was dead... and then he wasn't."

"One of us?" Siren raised a brow at Kain.

Kain shook his head, grimacing. "His face.... Rotted flesh."

Siren's eyes narrowed. "Who would dare?"

"What was Mark?" Nick leaned forward. "What happened to make him like that?"

Siren's eyes were stormy Mediterranean. "A revenant, created by a fey to serve him or her." Again he looked to Kain. "Did you cut off its head?"

Tightly, Kain answered, "I broke its neck in the woods near Nick's university."

"Then it might still walk. Samuel," Siren signaled a boy with pale skin, spaniel-brown eyes, and shaggy blond hair.

"Siren?" There was a thread of insolence in the voice, which surprised Nick. From what he'd seen, most of the clients at Manticore fawned over Siren.

"That's 'Master' Siren to you, bratling. Take a team and explore the woods near the downtown university campus grounds. You are looking for," Siren's lips tightened, "a revenant, made by one of us, so be cautious."

The boy's eyes widened.

"If you find it, do not approach it unless it tries to feed on someone. I want to know whom it belongs to."

Samuel swallowed, but nodded obediently.

Siren reached out and snatched his wrist before he could leave. "Take at least five of the bouncers with you, and… be careful."

A mixture of emotion moved over Samuel's face: surprise, irritation, the crackle of furtive and reluctant attraction. He yanked his wrist free and stalked away.

Nick raised his brows at Samuel's singular behavior.

"He works for me here at the bar," Siren said. "Doing odd jobs."

"Did you make him?"

"I'd like to." Siren smiled but his eyes were serious. "No, someone not as nice as I am made him, kept him, until I helped liberate him. I'm afraid the lad is most ungrateful, but I have hopes one day…."

Sensing Siren didn't want to discuss Samuel further, Nick asked, "What will happen to Mark if they find him?"

"He is *not* Mark." Siren shook his head. "Don't make that mistake, Nick. A revenant has another name in the language of the dark fey: *g'lethe marbara*. It means, the 'finger of evil'. He is better put down, believe me."

"So I could have made Mark?" Kain interrupted, brows lowered.

"No!" Nick glared at Kain.

"Yes," Siren said, very calmly. "A revenant is made when one of us takes too much blood by accident or design and does not give back our own. It's... an abomination, a thing that is dead and sustained only by fae magics."

"But Kain took a lot of blood from me," Nick prodded. "And I didn't—"

"He didn't take enough to kill you, and besides, you're a bonded pair, so it doesn't work that way." Seeing Nick's eyes widen, Siren nodded. "Oh, yes. I was at the hospital, monitoring you during your stay. Kain asked it of me."

Nick looked at Kain. He replied in a hushed voice, "Oh."

Kain's gaze dropped. "So I'm still not in the clear."

Siren shook his head. "No, you're not."

DETECTIVE MANNERS strode into Manticore, flashing her badge at one of Siren's bouncers. Her gaze roamed the Mediterranean decor until it homed in on Kain.

Nick tensed, putting a protective hand over Kain's wrist.

"It'll be all right," Kain said, seeming to immediately pick up on Nick's concern.

"But she thinks you're a killer!"

Kain's face was closed off as he climbed to his feet. "Remember how you found me, roaming the woods, completely out of it? She may be right, Nick."

Jan Irving

"HE SUFFERS from blackouts?" Siren probed as he and Nick watched Kain talking to Manners at the bar.

Nick nodded, biting his lip. "Is that common for the dark fey?"

"No," Siren said, shaking his head. "We have exceptional memories. And now that Kain's mated himself to you, it should be steadying him, helping him find balance. I don't understand why he's experiencing them."

"I don't believe he hurt anyone."

"Nick." Siren sighed. "He is capable of it. It is what we are: hunters, predators. The Fey of Light created us to hunt down dark creatures, after all, to be their muscle in the supernatural world."

"He has never hurt me. I mean, not really," Nick qualified. He flushed under Siren's interested gaze. He leaned forward and whispered, "Something is... happening between us."

"You are a bonded pair, a fey warrior and his submissive." Siren nodded.

"He's afraid with me, of going too far."

"And yet he seems to have pleased you; you are touching the mark he left on your skin."

Nick's eyes widened. He had been rubbing it again, his fingers seemingly unable to stay away.

"You feel a burning; it stimulates you."

"Uh." Nick shrugged it off, embarrassed.

Siren leaned forward and offered with more earnestness than he'd thus far shown, "Nick, you need to let him bite you often. He is a member of my line of the blood so he will eventually be very powerful when he centers himself. You need to help calm him, and the dividends of that will pleasure you both."

"Is that what you want with Samuel?" Nick pushed back, needing time to process Siren's suggestion.

Siren's face hardened. "Samuel is a fey of light. His kind doesn't dirty themselves with common warriors. We're dogs to them."

Kain returned, immediately putting a hand on Nick's shoulder as if needing contact.

Nick reached up and covered his hand automatically.

Siren smiled, quirking a brow. "Shall we try a little experiment as your first lesson in bonding, gentlemen?"

Obsidian: This is stupid.

Moonbeam: Come on. Siren pointed out this place is wired for cyber, uh, conversation and now it's locked up for the night and we're totally alone. Didn't you tell me once that we were engaged in an online flirtation?

Obsidian: You were safer then. I just couldn't stay away.

Moonbeam: I don't want to be safe, not anymore. Sleeping Beauty is awake now and he wants to experience the world. In fact, he'll get pissy if you keep trying to push him away... Please, let's try this? I don't begin to understand this fey-human thing between us, but I can feel how powerful it is.

Obsidian: It's growing stronger.

Moonbeam: I need you inside me. I want you to bite me.

Obsidian: Christ, Nick! Don't tell me that!

Doing what Siren had recommended, Nick closed his eyes and let his feelings guide him. His inner compass spun, his rational mind, his shyness... his desire.

He pushed off his jacket and before he could think about it, also tugged off the T-shirt underneath. From across the room where Kain was using another laptop for their experiment, he heard a soft growling sound. It made him smile.

Kain reacting. So predictable.

He ran a hand over his own chest, trying to experience his skin, his body, the way Kain might, the silky feel, the pebble of one of his nipples. He pinched it.

Obsidian: I can't be responsible if you keep provoking me.

Moonbeam: I only took my T-shirt off.

Obsidian: You're licking your lips and touching yourself. Performing for me. I am not made of iron. Don't tease me!

Moonbeam: You once told me to let go. To let myself accept that I like being under you.

Obsidian: I created a monster.

Moonbeam: I keep touching the bite mark on my hip. The first time you bit me, it didn't feel as sensitive, but now I want to touch it and remember how you made me come, how you controlled me.

Obsidian: Show it to me.

Nick stood, staring at Kain across the room as he removed his jeans and let them fall, then tugged at the waistband of his boxers, displaying the pinkened mark on the blade of his hip.

"Come here," Kain ordered softly. "Come closer so I can touch it."

Heart thumping, cock hard, Nick went to Kain.

Mask

He stood looking down into green eyes, bright with hunger for him, aware as always of the differences between him and Kain and how they turned him on.

"Siren said we should go with our feelings," Nick suggested.

"Then take off the boxers and... I think I want you on your knees," Kain purred, finally getting into their play.

Color flushed Nick's chest, his nipples tightening so that when Kain brushed one with a callused fingertip, he moaned.

His penis, the mark on his hip, throbbing in tandem like a primitive drumbeat.

He shrugged off the boxers and knelt, putting his cheek against Kain's knee, holding on to it, feeling need pulse between them, like an unanswered question.

"I want.... Nick, suck me. I want my perfect little cocksucker—" Kain broke off when Nick undid his belt and hurriedly pulled him free, his own penis distended from his body, flexing, as he opened his mouth and took Kain, running one hand in approval up the shaft, exploring the length, the texture.

I want to suck you. I am your perfect little cocksucker. His feeling translated into the way he touched Kain, the way he squirmed, burning, empty, unfulfilled.

Kain's hands tangled in his hair, holding him there, making him take it all as he thrust up, fucking Nick's eager, innocent mouth.

"*Sit.*" The order, not unlike what you'd tell a dog, only made Nick hotter. Freed by Kain's hands, he sat back on his heels.

Hot semen spurted over his chest as he stared into Kain's eyes, panting. Kain holding his penis, thighs bracketing Nick.

Still holding Kain's gaze, Nick reached down, touched Kain's spill, brought it to his own lips to lick the taste of Kain off his own body.

Silkily, Kain asked, "Want to get off?"

"Yes!" Nick gave an excited laugh. He loved their games.

Kain shifted one of his booted feet between Nick's thighs and raised an eyebrow.

Eyes saucered, Nick read his suggestion. Could he actually do it?

Kain's spend drying on his body, Nick wrapped his legs, his arms, around Kain's leather-covered leg.

"Hump it." Kain pressed against Nick, exerting pressure on his balls, his needy cock.

Staring into Kain's eyes, it didn't seem wrong. They'd talked about this and many other acts of submission. He wanted to be this way with Kain.

Moving, thrusting, head back, holding Kain's eyes, seeing that he was just as caught, anticipating, just as aroused by the forbidden between them.

"You little slut," Kain whispered, combing a hand through Nick's hair. "I want you to do this in public sometime. I want everyone to see you hump my leg and know you belong completely to me."

Kain's comforting touch in contrast to his words, so wrong. Thighs clinging, grunting now, lost in a sensual dreamworld, needing to come, *please—*

Kain's index finger circled his parted lips and then entered his mouth.

Nick bit it, needing something inside him.

Penetration.

He spurted over Kain's leg, crying out, not hiding his pleasure, white hot, flying.

Kain's.

Suddenly Kain lifted him onto his lap where Nick wilted, satisfied, glowing.

"Say it again."

"Say what?" Nick asked groggily, but he knew.

Mask

"You know. Nick…."

He leaned close to Kain and whispered in his ear, "I love you."

CHAPTER 25

"DID I pass the test?" Nick asked when he spotted Siren lingering outside the club, smoking. He wondered if the black-haired fey was aware of what Kain and Nick had shared in Manticore. He was surprised that the thought didn't embarrass him because of everything they'd done….

But Nick had been a full partner.

And anyway, he was in love with Kain, even if Kain wasn't exactly ready to be loved.

"A first step," Siren said. "Nick, I was relieved to see him here, but don't tell him that since there's no telling how he'll react. If you want to know more about what you and Kain are experiencing, I can set you up with a bonded pair to foster you."

"Relationship counseling for feys? I'm sure Kain would love that!" Nick agreed ruefully, folding his arms. It was fucking chilly now that it was November.

"And I'm sure that if you want to do it, you'll find a way to bring him on board." Siren raised a brow. "From the moment he met you online, he was obsessed. I'd see him use the laptops in the club sometimes, totally lost in your conversations. His expression at times could be very… revealing." Amusement warmed Siren's eyes. "As well as his scent."

"Um, I don't even know if I want to know!" Nick raised a palm.

"I could feel his desire for you," Siren answered simply.

Nick flushed, remembering how incendiary those chats had been. He'd loved it! He hadn't recognized at the time that it was foreplay. That Kain was wooing him. "I'm not sure if or when he'll agree to exploring more with your help. He doesn't like to bring others into our circle; he's a very private man." Nick rubbed tired eyes. "A pain in the ass sometimes but I love him."

Siren's eyes were serious, even a little wistful. "He is fortunate."

The green sports car growled at the curb and from the driver's window, Kain glared at the loitering Siren, talking to Nick.

"Nick, the revenant; we discovered someone did cut off its head."

Nick swallowed thickly. "Mark." He let out a breath of grief.

"Unfortunately, we were not able to remove the remains, so the police will have questions."

Nick nodded. "Thanks for the heads up. I tried to get Kain clear."

BACK at the house, Kain put his hands in his pockets, watching Nick as he paused at the head of the stairs leading to Kain's rooms, running his hand over the banister.

"Do you feel a little... self-conscious?" He looked over his shoulder at Kain. He'd exposed so much of himself, given so much. Did Kain ever feel the same way?

Kain cleared his throat, rubbing the back of his neck. "Share a brandy with me?"

In Kain's study, a fire crackled. Kain fed Nick a sip of brandy from a shared glass. Nick was sprawled over his lap. Kain caressed his hair, pausing to lean close and sniff.

"I need a shower. I must reek of—" Nick flushed, remembering he was still sticky with Kain's come.

Smugly, Kain said, "I like how you smell."

"You would." Nick covered Kain's hand and took another healthy swallow. "Tell me about the blackouts. How often do they happen?"

"My face…. Finn made up a mixture for the pain in the first days I came to live here and I lost days, nights."

"Ummm." Nick stroked the back of Kain's hand. "What happened the night of the fire at your loft?"

Kain's head sagged back against the wing chair.

"Kain, why does Ross hate you?"

"He wasn't supposed to be there!" Kain growled, staring into the fire. "He brought Aaron over unexpectedly. I'd been a shit, a total shit to both of them because he was my best friend and I couldn't—"

"You were afraid you were losing him."

"Not *afraid.* I just didn't like Aaron. He was extremely territorial and I knew that." Kain paused, took a deep swallow of his brandy. "That I'd lose Ross." He lifted one shoulder in a shrug. "I did anyway."

Nick reached out and stroked Kain's arm. "I think he still cares about you."

Kain's green eyes widened in surprise. "Why do you say that?"

"Because he's so pissed at you. You don't feel that way about someone unless you love them."

Kain took a deep breath. "One of the men I was with made a pass at Ross. I intervened and it would have been fucking fine if only Aaron had left it alone but he insisted on sticking around long enough to tell me off. I was dizzy from losing blood, from… from drinking from Siren. I passed out."

"The feys you brought home, they fed on Aaron?"

Kain gave a jerky nod. "I think so. There was a fire. I must have....
I don't remember how it got started. Ross was trying to get to Aaron, but
I managed to pull him out. He told me he hated me, that it was my—"
Kain swallowed. "He loved Aaron and I killed him. Somehow I killed
him. I went back to the loft but it was an inferno. I couldn't find Aaron's
body."

"That's how you were burned, wasn't it?" Nick smoothed a hand
over the grooves and drawn, shiny skin of Kain's scarred face. "Trying
to give Aaron back to Ross."

"It doesn't matter."

"It does to me, and one day it will again to Ross." Sensing that
Kain was feeling raw on the subject, Nick changed the topic. "I should
shower. Get some sleep so I can get to class."

Kain nodded, bleak hazel eyes fixed on Nick's face. "Nick, I'm not
good with.... I've been alone so long."

Nick waited, feeling that something important, something he'd
wished for, was about to happen.

"I want you to stay."

Nick meshed a hand through Kain's, looking at their tangled
fingers.

"Okay," he agreed quietly.

CHAPTER 26

WARM water dripping from his fingers as he raised his hand. He watched droplets fill, sparkle, grow, dangle... fall.

The moment stretched, like the water falling, and he wanted it to go on forever.

Lips against his neck, nibbling lightly, gently.

Kain.

Soaping his hair.

Nick let his head fall back. This. This was what he'd been craving for so long. A new ease between them. It had finally come when Kain had asked him to stay with him, seeming to know at last that Nick accepted him, was not afraid of trying to build a relationship with a dark fey.

He still wanted the words, but right now Kain's touch made him live them.

A soapy hand slid down his chest, polishing one nipple with a bar of sandalwood.

"Like that?" Kain teased.

"Yes," Nick breathed. "Kain, I know you worry sometimes about dragging me into your world, but I have no regrets. When I met you, I was in a safe rut. I wasn't satisfied or I'd never have been so drawn to you."

Kain's cock slid naturally into the divide of Nick's ass, thrusting against slippery skin. His hand found Nick, curled around him, worked him.

Nick made a husky sound of pleasure, feeling as if his backbone was melting from Kain's loving ministrations. And something clicked back into place, the void created by his breakup with Miguel, like grass growing over a scar in the earth. Now Nick was ready for another boyfriend. He hadn't been looking for it, but it had always seemed to him that life scattered rose petals when you *weren't* looking for them.

Their hands slid over his body, meeting, tangling together, symbolic now that Kain had asked him to stay. Kain's teeth in the tender groove between Nick's neck and shoulder—

As easy as a wave hitting the beach, Nick came on caught breath, dimly aware of Kain spilling against him with a growl of completion, before he slumped forward.

"Don't fall asleep," Kain scolded, still pressing his cock against Nick's skin as if he couldn't get enough of that. Well, neither could Nick. "You said you wanted to get cleaned up."

Nick turned around, lazily watching Kain soaping his legs, kneeling so he could do a thorough job. He was becoming a very attentive boyfriend, touching Nick often, which suited Nick.

"I lied." He quirked a brow.

"Oh, did you?" Kain came to his feet and nuzzled the bleeding spots on Nick's neck, sucking so the mark was briefly a live connection, sparking between them, channeling raw feeling.

"This feels so natural," Nick said. "I love belonging to you."

"Well, it's not." Kain stiffened slightly, obviously still not comfortable with his darker side.

Nick grabbed his hand, stubborn. "Different is not wrong!"

Chiding, Kain said, "Nick, don't be naive."

Nick kissed Kain's chin, accustomed now to the eyelid that sagged on the ruined side of his face. He hoped Kain would allow himself to be healed one day, but not because his appearance turned Nick off—just because he knew it would mean Kain had stopped punishing himself and was allowing himself happiness. "I'll keep repeating myself as long as needed."

Gripping Nick's hair. Kain said, "Stubborn brat."

"I don't believe you made Mark what he was."

"Based on what?" Kain raised a cool brow. "What's your evidence?"

"Based on the fact neither of us even knew what he *was*."

Kain's expression flattened into a mask. "Siren pointed out it could happen by accident as well as design. You don't want to believe, but it could have been me."

"How do you know that?"

"Because when he kissed you, I wanted to kill him."

"Kain, you don't remember much about that night you became a fey, do you?"

Kain shook his head.

Nick chewed his lip. "Somehow this is all connected. What if one of the men you took home is our killer somehow?"

"WHERE did you find that thing?" Kain raised a brow when Nick entered his bedroom wearing a brown and yellow kimono with large bronze-orange chrysanthemums.

"Finn lent it to me when I first came to stay here."

"Hmmmm." Kain ran a hand over Nick's skin.

"It has a habit of falling off my shoulder." Nick climbed onto his bed, onto Kain, secretly delighted to find him still here. He hadn't run away. That had to be a good sign.

Nick wanted to sleep with Kain all night. It was still new.

"So I see." A palm slid over pale rounded flesh and Kain pressed a kiss to Nick's collar bone.

Smugly, Nick said, "You think it's sexy."

"Apparently you can read my mind, little one."

Nick pouted.

"You know very well how you look." Kain reached for a mug by the bed, taking a sip.

Nick intercepted it, staring into the ruby depths. "Kain, what is in that shit Finn makes for you?"

"Pig's blood. And some herbs for the pain."

Hushed, Nick asked, "Are you sure that's all it is? The other night when I found you, you were totally out of it."

"Finn didn't turn away from me when I—" Kain put the mug down. "I had a blackout. It had nothing to do with him."

"Turn away from you like Ross did, you mean?" Nick cupped the ravaged side of Kain's face. "Kain, I'm convinced that Ross still cares about you although he's obviously misguided about what a good man you are."

Kain made a rude noise which Nick chose to ignore.

"But it concerns me, this almost innocent faith you hold for your friends. Even when they hurt you."

"How the fuck do you know Ross still—?" Kain sat up, as if to leave.

Nick wrapped his arms around Kain's tense neck. "Because how could he stop?"

Kain's head fell.

"And Siren said that the fey don't suffer from blackouts."

"I don't want to talk about him."

"You stubborn ass."

"Speaking of ass," Kain drawled, eyes glinting.

Nick combed the hair back from the scars. Kissed them.

"You're beautiful."

"You're delusional."

But Kain was smiling.

One piece at a time, Nick was going to help Kain get back his life.

Which meant he had to find a murderer.

LUKE closed his eyes and tugged again, ignoring his wrist, slippery with blood. He was weak since the creature who kept him locked under the earth didn't feed him.

A mere human wouldn't have survived weeks of captivity, but Luke being a shape-shifter had, though he would have to feast, have to hunt. Soon.

He caught the sounds of footsteps and paused, waiting to see if Finn would enter the tunnels.

Finn. The pain and rage rose.

Patience.

He was an Alpha *loup garou.* He would endure, he would wait for his moment, and then he would kill.

His left wrist popped free of the iron shackle.

Mask

ARMAND suppressed a smile when a hot apple cider with a Starbucks label was thrust in his direction. Perfect. He didn't even have to try, Ross was so easy.

But then, he knew all his habits, all his weaknesses.

It had been so enjoyable putting him at odds with Kain. Almost as enjoyable as tormenting Kain, making him question his own mind and soul.

How the powerful had fallen.

"Ross." He pretended wide-eyed surprise.

"Pretty cold out here," Ross said, shrugging, obviously a little shy with the new man in his life.

Savoring the irony of that, Armand took the hot drink, pretending to sip it to give himself some time to consider what buttons he would push. "Fancy running into you here at your favorite coffeehouse."

"Uh-huh. But haven't you been watching my apartment night after night? Or did I just dream that?"

"Uh, yeah." Shit! He had sworn Ross couldn't see him. Had Finn spoken out of turn? He'd bloody him for opening his fucking mouth if he had.

"So you've appointed yourself my protector or something?" Ross shifted a bag with groceries and bicycle parts poking from the top.

Armand shrugged. "You were so frightened of that black rose you received. Old boyfriend who won't leave you alone?"

Ross blinked. "No, worse. I thought it was my former best friend, but Finn said maybe I was wrong."

Finn, you've been a very bad boy. Daddy will have to punish you.

Armand pictured Finn, white-eyed, helpless and sweating on his bed. A rolled-up towel shoved in his mouth to keep him quiet so Kain didn't hear his cries for help. Pinching his nostrils and cutting off his air.

Going to behave now?

Finn nodding, frantic, face washed with tears. Removing the gag so he could listen to the hopeless choked-off sobs.

Finn putting an arm over his face. Shame washing his cheeks.

Broken again.

"Good boy, my good boy." Licking the tears as Finn shuddered....

"Hey, where'd you go?" Ross interrupted Armand's reminiscence, cocking his head. "Looks like somewhere good from that smile."

Armand raised an arch eyebrow. "You have no idea how good. But you will, someday soon," Armand promised, loving that Ross had no idea of the double meaning of his words.

"Well, anyway, Finn and Kain's new boy toy, Nick, don't think he's involved. And I'm beginning to wonder...." Ross's voice drifted off and he shivered, as if feeling the chill fall weather prod him from outside, or sensing the approach of a predator. "Anyway, I don't know if I want to be alone tonight. If you like, you might as well come up to my place, uh, have some soup with me. It's so... cold this fall, and they found another couple of bodies near the university grounds."

"That's very close to where you live."

"Yeah."

"You're sure this Kain couldn't be responsible?" Armand seeded.

"I hope not," Ross whispered. Then, cheeks pink, he waited to see if Armand would take him up on his offer of supper.

"What kind of soup?" Armand pretended interest, but he was focused on Ross's fear. He could taste it on his tongue.

"Campbell's." Ross shrugged. "I'm not much of a cook."

"Don't worry. I'll come over and keep you company," Armand said. He had some time to kill before he dealt with Finn... and Nick.

Mask

FINGERS clawing the bedsheets, Nick woke abruptly.

The hell…?

Huffing, he swallowed, feeling a little sick as he listened to his pounding heart and tried to shake off the dream.

A man with long hair and burning eyes, chained to a wall in a dank tunnel, a discarded straight blade, curls of skin like wood shavings.

Nick rubbed his arms, telling himself sternly it had been nothing real, even if it was a surround-sound nightmare.

Cold, the room was cold.

He frowned, sitting up, sweat drying between his shoulder blades.

Scary dream. Just a scary dream. But why was it so fucking cold in his bedroom?

He wasn't alone, so he didn't need to be afraid. Kain was with him. Kain had chosen to sleep with him because Nick had asked.

He looked at his lover, touched his skin, found it as chilly as the room.

"*Kain!*" Suddenly a little freaked out, Nick shook him, but Kain remained impervious, body limp.

Shit! Another blackout? Or had Finn drugged Kain?

Nick snatched his kimono and wrapped it tightly around his body before climbing off the bed and heading for the thermostat. The numbers glowed in the comfortable zone and yet the room was freezing.

An arctic puff of air at floor level made his toes curl. Coming from outside his room?

It was the last thing he wanted to do, but he had to know what was happening. He turned the doorknob then leaned cautiously into the hallway, looking around.

"Fuck!" Icy November air. "What the…?"

It had to be a window, or—

He strode down the hallway, silk snapping against his skin, echoing his irritation. What the fuck was up with Finn? First giving Kain something to knock him out and now the house was freezing?

At the top of the stairs, he paused, transfixed, heart thudding.

In the entranceway, fog rolled into the house like invited spirits.

The front door stood open.

# CHAPTER 27

A SHADOW extended slowly over the flagstones in the entranceway. The silhouette of a figure, robe rippling in the late-autumn breeze, and a hand, fingers like the long branches of a tree, pointing up the stairs.

Toward Nick.

Colder now than he had been from just the late-fall draft, Nick took a step back.

And the floorboard creaked under his bare feet.

Shit! Be quiet. So quiet.

He knew whatever was out there, absolutely, was what had met up with Mark that fateful night.

And it was coming for him. It only made sense. The unlocked door, Kain drugged out of his mind, helpless.

So what? The next morning he'd wake up and think he'd... hurt Nick? Killed him?

Oh, fuck, that would not be just Nick's end, but Kain's as well. No way could Kain live with that!

And maybe... someone knew that?

In a silvered mirror with a peeling frame the color of forest lichen, Nick caught the reflection of his own terrified eyes. A swaying jasmine vine, shriveled from autumn nights, undulating from the ceiling behind him, wrapped sinuously around the broken crystal cascade of a dome chandelier.

Weirdly, his surroundings called to mind the wreck of the *Titanic*. A ship of ruin, like this house.

Definitely going to talk to Kain about modern renovations if I make it through the night.

He caught the slight sound of a footfall.

Inside. Inside the house now.

He covered his mouth, heart banging in his ears.

Quiet. God, be quiet!

He fell back against the hallway wall, out of direct sight to anyone—anything—climbing the stairs. Closing his eyes and trying to think what to do. He couldn't stay here and he couldn't leave Kain alone in his bed, helpless, drugged. And Kain was in no shape to save him.

So it looked like it was up to *Nick* to save Kain. Up to Nick to figure out how to outsmart the thing stalking them.

He retraced his steps carefully but quickly back to the bedroom, his pale toes curling into chilly hardwood, trying to keep from making a sound while his pulse raced, as if urging him onto a run.

When he got to his room, he breathed thanks that Kain had left the lock intact, even though it had once been a bone of contention between them. Now that lock might buy Nick some time.

He closed the door behind him, easing it, and then pushing the bolt home.

He couldn't help make a slight noise and as if he was somehow connected to his stalker, he felt its interest turn in the direction of his bedroom.

It knows where I am. It knows I'm awake.

Lips parted, sweat coating his forehead, Nick backed away from the door, but before he did, he caught another faint sound—the same creaky floorboard he'd stepped on in the hallway groaned.

Mask

KAIN was slumped on Nick's bed, scarred face crushed against his pillow, looking like a beaten little boy, wiped out.

Seeing him like that, knowing the cost to him if Nick didn't make it....

That won't happen. I'm not going to let anything happen to him, to us. "Kain, can you hear me?" He breathed in a whisper, shaking his lover. Kain didn't stir.

Nick swallowed, bracing himself, and then his palm swung.

He struck the unblemished side of Kain's face, his palm leaving a red imprint. Belatedly, it occurred to him that he'd made a sound his pursuer might clearly pick up on, but they needed to get out of here, both of them, now!

"Can't leave you, *can't!*" Nick lifted a limp arm around his shoulder and hefted Kain upright on the bed. "Kain, please!"

Eyelids flickering, Kain moaned softly.

And the doorknob to Nick's bedroom twisted once, decisively, the tumblers making a loud, distinct sound.

"Oh, God, oh fuck!" Whatever it was on the other side of that door, Nick knew he did *not* want to see it. He squeezed his eyes shut, panting, "Kain, please. I can't leave you here and if I stay—" *Something's going to hurt me and if I'm hurt you'll—*

He didn't like to think about it, but a cold lump lodged in his chest.

As if sensing Nick's need, Kain licked his lips and lurched forward; his ankles twisted and he nearly hit the floor.

"P-P—"

"What?" Nick looked over his shoulder toward the door, eyes wide. The doorknob rattled again... then kept rattling.

231

Jan Irving

Shit! Kain, come on, we have to get out of here!

"P-pa—" Kain leaned against the paneled wall, sweat glazing his face, the grooves of his scars standing out in relief. Harsh, like what had made him what he was now, and again Nick thought it all had to be connected somehow. It didn't make sense otherwise. It was almost like someone was haunting Kain's life. Shadowing him, wanting to smash the things he cared about.

His friendship with Ross. The safety of his home. The sanctity of his own mind, so that he doubted himself. And now, the man who loved him, who had faith in him. Nick.

"Someone hates you. Hates you enough to want to *hurt* you before he—"

Kain snatched Nick's arm urgently despite his wobbly legs. "Passage," he said, very clearly this time.

Nick stared at him, blank... but then his eyes widened. "A... secret passage? I know that there's a tunnel under the house where Finn keeps the wines." Nick ran his hands frantically over oak and walnut marquetry.

Telemachus House had originally been built by a banker in Victorian times, Nick knew from Kain, and despite its jarring seventies renovation, it retained a lot of its original architectural quirks—including a way to find safety for him and Kain?

A despairing whisper from behind the door: "*Niiiick. Nicky. Nick, let me—*" Scratching. Fingernails. Claws?

Nick shuddered at the voice. It sounded almost affectionate.

Kain kept his focus on the wall, leaning against it, running his hands over it, even though his eyes were only half-open, his expression slack and groggy.

Trying for Nick.

A panel suddenly yawned open at floor level. Small, something that would be hard for Kain to navigate with his wide shoulders....

232

"Kain!" Nick tugged his hand. "Come on; we have to get in and go through it!"

Kain's green eyes snapped on him. Tight on his face and before he spoke, Nick knew what he would say. "You f-first, Nick. I need you s-safe," Kain mumbled, pushing Nick roughly toward the passage.

The scratching at the door had intensified. Clawing. Like an animal lost in the need to *get inside the room.*

"Nick," the thready voice called. "Niiiiicky, I came f-for you."

"No!" Nick flattened himself against the wall, panting. "We don't have time for this! *With me*, Kain! That's how it has to be."

Kain wavered on his feet, his face paling as if he was on the verge of passing out.

And Nick pushed him so he fell against the passage, shoving him by his bare ass, not caring about the groan of wood as Kain struggled through the gap. Behind them, the doorknob rattled once and then stopped.

Bang! Bang!

Wood splintered.

Nick could make out Kain's pale feet. And then a big hand, reaching for him—

They fell in and the panel slid back into place, leaving him and Kain panting in the darkness.

Kain crushed him in his arms for a second. Nick squeezed his eyes shut, face buried against Kain's neck. "Oh, shit. Oh, God," he whispered, trembling.

"Touch. Nick, t-touch—"

Nick frowned, trying to understand, but then Kain shifted forward in the cramped space and he understood. Kain wanted him to keep a hand on him as they navigated in total darkness.

Nick snagged Kain's foot, following him on hands and knees, gritting his teeth as his left knee pressed down on what felt like broken glass.

Anything was better than what they'd left behind.

"*Niiiicky!*" The voice came from his abandoned bedroom.

SOMETHING caught his robe. A stray nail he couldn't see, probably. He tugged, sweating, heart still pounding, still terrified of that thing behind them. He couldn't free his robe, so he let it fall, abandoning it, body instantly pebbling with goose bumps.

Dark and close. Odd breaths of air and sound traveled the passage, as it stretched past the rooms of Kain's house.

Once Nick thought he heard the sound of breaking glass. Coming from his room?

At last Kain paused, chest heaving, dragging Nick so he sat on his lap. Possessive arms wrapped around him. Naked, shivering, Nick wrapped his arms around his warrior fey.

"K-keep you safe," Kain muttered against his hair. "N-no matter what."

Aching with love, dirty, sore, chilled, Nick clung.

"I know," he whispered. "Same goes."

LIGHT through the cracks in the paneling warmed Nick's cheek in bars and he blinked, seeing in the semi-darkness the gleam of Kain's feral green eyes, feeling the caress down his back to cup his bare ass.

Mask

"Fell asleep," he croaked. "I guess… we're safe now?"

He sat up, running a hand through his hair. His body was aching, scratched, but he was alive and he was with Kain.

Kain seemed to be feeling the same relief because he didn't answer Nick, but lifted him higher and covered his lips in a deep kiss.

Nick wound his arms around Kain, tight, tighter, thrusting against him helplessly, needing release at Kain's hand, at Kain's pleasure.

Kain, his familiar scent, his protection, his need of Nick.

Drowning….

Abruptly there was only one thing he wanted. He didn't care about their filthy surroundings, any more than he had when Kain dragged him beneath the earth and plowed into him, took him for the first time.

The terror of the night before fanned his hunger. Wanton. *Take me, fuck me.*

Kain made a rough sound and suddenly Nick was on his back, knees up around Kain's hips. Kissing, teeth clicking, Kain's finger up him, clenching around it, dry, so it hurt a little, but the *fullness.*

He needed to be fucked.

Panting, he squirmed, but Kain pressed a firm hand over his belly, holding him in place. His cock reacted to that silent domination, twitching between his spread legs.

Holding Nick's gaze, Kain rubbed his arm once against a long nail. Blood spattered, hitting Nick's face and chest, and then Kain held the long scratch over his cock, anointing himself. Cutting into his own flesh to protect Nick, to ease Kain's entry into his body.

Eyes stinging at what this gesture said, Nick whispered, stroking Kain's arm, "I love you."

Kain spread Nick's legs wide, so each of his feet were splayed on opposite sides of the passage, his ankles high. Nick's lips parted, seeing the hungry way Kain looked at him, as if loving how slutty Nick must look, open and accessible.

235

Fingers wet with blood entered him. Two, so Nick hissed, his body arching at the burn. But it felt good, after the terror of the night.

Kain prodded him firmly, adding a third finger to fuck Nick while he gasped and his head rocked from side to side. "Please, Kain," he pleaded.

"My slut needs me?" Kain's eyes shone gem-green, struck by sunshine through a crack. Beautiful eyes. Eyes Nick wanted to see look at him just like that.

"Yes," Nick whispered. "Your slut needs it."

Kain palmed his heavy cock, swollen and sticking out from his body. Nick's dimple contracted as he watched him fit it to his slighter body.

"Kain!" He gripped Kain's hips in welcome, urging him to take. Mounted at last, Kain's eyes holding his as he guided himself, pushed inside. Too thick, broaching gently, back and forth until Nick was slippery with Kain's want and the blood Kain had spilled to try to spare Nick discomfort.

But then Kain couldn't wait any longer.

Nick cried out at the first firm thrust, body open wide.

Kain rocked, hand fisted in Nick's hair. "You slut, you whore."

"*Yes!*" His legs knitted around Kain. "Your slut," he whimpered. "If you'd ever hired me like the others, I'd have come back, let you use me for free."

Kain's eyes flared. He bent close to Nick and muttered, "After we figure out what the fuck is going on and take care of it, I'm going to use a marker on your ass one night—that's a special paddle with words cut into the leather."

"What will it say?" Nick rasped.

Kain covered him, body, prick, and lips. "*Mine,*" he muttered before sinking his teeth into Nick's neck.

Mask

Nick's eyes were heavy as his penis jutted out, untouched but so close... head falling back, surrender, *ecstasy*.

CHAPTER 28

"THIS is a mistake; Kain didn't kill that boy near campus, Detective!" Nick trailed after Detective Manners. "And he didn't cut the head off that… body you found."

"No mistake, your boyfriend's involved somehow. We identified the headless corpse as your friend Mark. I suppose you know nothing about how his body just left the morgue and went out for candy on Halloween?" Manners pressed. She'd been hammering at Nick, but he knew Kain wasn't guilty—not the way she assumed. Mark hadn't been a victim this time, but a predator, and Nick the prey.

"Kain was with me." Hair still wet from the shower, ruffled from Kain's touch, the juncture between his neck and shoulder freshly bitten, throbbing. His body also throbbing. *Claimed.* Claimed again by Kain.

"And you'd say anything to protect him, wouldn't you? A taxi driver identified him as a passenger leaving the area that night and the apartment of your friend Marilyn Walters is certainly convenient to the university and the nearby green space where the bodies were discovered."

Kain appeared then, scarred face turned away from the early winter setting sun.

"Nick, stay the fuck out of this!" he rasped, brows lowered.

"Cuff him," Manners ordered.

"*No!*" Nick reached for Kain, pressing his head against his chest as Kain's hands were cuffed behind his back. He squeezed his eyes shut on the prick of tears. "It's just for more questioning, right?"

"Take care of yourself," Kain ordered, sending a stern message with his eyes, reminding Nick of how they'd both been hunted the night before. "For me, Nick."

"It's *you* I'm worried about!"

"Promise me."

"Come back and make sure I do." Nick craned up on his toes and kissed Kain, one heated press of lips, and then they were pulling him away.

No, Kain.... Nick clenched his fists, protectiveness, tenderness, *anger* flooding him. Someone was setting Kain up. Who was it? Nick was determined to find out and put this behind them.

"How can you...?" Manners grimaced.

Wondering if she meant the scars, or her suspicions about Kain, Nick pitched his voice so Kain could catch his words. "He's the most beautiful man I've ever seen, Detective. And he hasn't hurt anyone."

AT THE university later, Nick typed in his latest password: *great minds have purposes, little minds have absurdities.* It struck him as an apt phrase right now. He knew Kain was innocent, but it seemed the more he pushed, the more people wouldn't listen. And Kain himself wasn't much help, still confused and owning guilt Nick didn't think belonged to him.

Signing on and watching the chat room open, it struck him as full circle, how Kain and he were communicating this way again. He decided he didn't mind if they continued to use this medium.

Moonbeam: Are you okay?

239

Obsidian: It's not me I'm worried about. Nick, I was terrified something would happen to you last night and it would have been my fault.

Moonbeam: Not yours. Finn drugged you. I'm in the art library at the university and I'll stay at Marilyn's tonight if you won't be home. I promise I'll take care. It's not like I want to be attacked. All right?

Obsidian: I suppose I'll have to trust you to show some sense. Just refrain from playing boy detective. Despite Manners cuffing me I'm officially only here for questioning. My attorney is wrangling with the cops now and I hope to be free to take you home soon.

Moonbeam: There was no sign of Finn back at the house.

Obsidian: I can't believe he's a part of this. He has a good heart, Nick. I know you can see that too.

Moonbeam: It seemed like Finn wants what is best for both of us. I can't reconcile what he's almost certainly doing either.

About last night, when that...whatever it was went after us, that secret passage was certainly useful. You've made use of it before, haven't you?

Obsidian: I told you I liked to watch. It was part of an old servant's staircase.

Moonbeam: You used it sometimes to watch those hustlers you hired?

Obsidian: Yes.

Moonbeam: Tell me more...

Obsidian: I liked to watch them touch themselves, slide a dildo in and fuck themselves on it. Satisfied? I could order them to do what I wanted, but they couldn't see me.

Moonbeam: Did you also use it to watch me?

Obsidian: Yes.

Moonbeam: And did you like what you saw?

Obsidian: I wanted to break through the walls and take you. Nick, are you all right? Manners interrupted before I could examine you. This morning I just had to get in you.

Moonbeam: I'm...a little tender. Lube would be nice. And a more comfortable place to fuck. In fact, the place needs to be renovated.

Obsidian: All right.

Moonbeam: I was just joking. I know you only renovate a home together if you're... If it's a serious thing.

Obsidian: I said all right.

Moonbeam: You said more than that.

Obsidian: I want to do you again. I want to come home, find you in your studio, shove you over the table and come inside your tight little asshole.

Moonbeam: :Squirming:

Obsidian: You want that. My dick up you, in you.

Moonbeam: I've been thinking of that special paddle you told me about. The one that says "mine".

Obsidian: I'd love to pinken your ass with it. I'd do it with a mirror above our bed so you could see it as you held perfectly still for me on all fours.

Moonbeam: Keep it up and I'll have to put a book over my lap.

Obsidian: ...

Moonbeam: Kain?

Obsidian: I know I should stay away from you. After last night... I tried, but you are so fucking stubborn, the way you wouldn't let me go!

Moonbeam: :rolls eyes: Oh, yeah, just me. Kain, about the boys you hired, was it ever like last night? You fell asleep, lost time, and when you woke up—?

Obsidian: They were gone, yes! I assumed they'd left since our business was...consummated.

Moonbeam: What if what nearly happened last night to me, also went down with them? What if that thing came and—

Obsidian: I don't want you to be alone! Not for a second, Nick, promise me.

Moonbeam: I won't be. Gotta go. Gotta meet someone.

Obsidian: Who?

Moonbeam: Don't be jealous.

Obsidian: I am not jealous! But someone did stalk you last night.

Moonbeam: Of course not. We'll call it "slightly possessive". And don't growl, Kain.

Obsidian: :growls: Who is it you're meeting?

Moonbeam: Someone who can help us...

Obsidian: NOT that fucker Siren!

Moonbeam: Moonbeam has left the room.

Obsidian: Nick! I'll spank your pleasantly round and interfering ass red if you—! FUCK!

Obsidian: Obsidian has left the room.

Mask

NICK leaned his art portfolio against the brick wall outside the fine arts building. The wind was cold, like chilly fingers trying to get under his coat, so he raised his collar, shivering, trying not to flash back to the night before and the chilly breath that had run through the house when a stalker hunted him and Kain.

Speaking of which, Kain would not like him waiting out here, after dark, but they had to be free of this mystery.

He was yanked against a hard body, a hand covering his mouth.

He bit down savagely.

"*Ow!* Fuck!" Siren released him. "You didn't have to bite so hard!"

Nick quirked a brow. "Nice, coming from a warrior fey. Aren't you supposed to be tough?"

"But not impervious to pain!" Siren was sucking the edge of his hand. "I did some investigating of Dr. Armand Leyland, as you asked. He's doesn't have a home address and he's not a registered physician. Not in this state, not in any of the neighboring ones."

"So *he* could have something to do with what's been happening to Kain!" Nick reached out and gripped Siren's arm, hoping that finally he'd hit on a real clue.

A little smile played over Siren's lips. "Maybe, but didn't you say he rescued you from the revenant? I think it more likely he was the one who cut off Mark's head."

"What if… he was somehow connected to what made Mark the way he was?"

"It's possible if he's another warrior fey or a revenant who can mask his appearance, like your friend Mark did. In fact, it's very strange that a newly made revenant like Mark would have that knowledge. It points to him being someone's pawn." Siren shrugged. "I have my people out looking for him."

"Thanks. I want to speak with him again. He mentioned Ross, so I've been wondering what his game is." Nick chewed his lip. "I also want to know where the fuck Finn is and why he drugged Kain!"

"One mystery at a time, kitten." Siren pulled out a Blackberry and tapped it for a few seconds. "I'll see what I can do, but in return…." His voice drawled off suggestively.

"I'm not fucking you." Nick rolled his eyes.

Siren blinked in surprise. "Why would you assume I—?"

"Just a feeling."

Siren shrugged, reaching out to push a long swatch of Nick's hair behind his ear. "I'll settle for another bite."

"What?" Nick laughed. "But you said you didn't like it!"

"Bite my neck. Trust me; I'll like it."

Nick gave Siren a doubtful look.

"Fine. Tell Kain I hope he manages to handle this on his own."

"Okay!" Nick swallowed. "But close your eyes first."

Siren leaned against the building and obediently shut his eyes.

Nick studied him uncertainly before looking around and seeing they were alone. He shifted closer to Siren, heart pounding. If Kain found out he'd done this!

He decided to get it over with quickly, instinctively going for the same place Kain bit him, pushing back Siren's silk shirt, his lips brushing against the strong neck.

Siren shuddered, hand snaking out to bury itself in Nick's hair as Nick bit down gently.

"Break the skin!"

"I…." Nick bit harder, hearing Siren give a sensual gasp.

And then his own vision blurred.

Mask

He saw himself and Siren in a bedroom. Siren's wrists were tied to the four-poster bed and he was also gagged with a black silk handkerchief. His muscular ass was high and waiting like an offering as Nick climbed on the bed behind him.

As if waiting for his orders, Nick glanced at a shadowy figure sitting on a wing chair. Fingers waved languidly, giving Nick permission.

Cock hard and ready, Nick licked his lips and pulled the black mesh of his thong off his sex. Without preamble, he shoved into Siren, who made a muffled sound of need.

And then he was humping him, hands running over silky skin undulating with muscle, reveling in his control over the beautiful black-haired fey—

Nick fell away from Siren. "What the fuck was that?"

Siren flushed. "Uh. Just one possible future."

"You like being submissive?"

"Quiet! Do you want the entire city to hear you, boy?" Siren's normally serene eyes sparked annoyance. "And no, it's not that simple."

"*That's* why you wanted Kain the night of the fire?"

Siren played with the cuffs of his long leather duster. "He won't have anything to do with me."

"No, he won't," Nick agreed. "Why do you keep what you want a secret?"

"Only an Alpha fey can rule the city," Siren said simply. "Archaic. Just because I sometimes, under special circumstances, like it up the ass doesn't make me weak."

Nick smiled in perfect understanding. "No, it doesn't."

CHAPTER 29

FINN curled up in what had been a bathroom in the fire-gutted building. Wind tore through boarded-up windows, touching the fresh lumps of bruises. He lay in the fetal position, shivering, despite his long legs aching with the need to stretch.

The door creaked open and a shadow fell.

Luke. Is that you, Lu—?

NICK looked up from his ceramics class, elbow deep in red clay, to glimpse Samuel lingering at the open doorway to the studio. He immediately recognized him as the intense young man who worked for Siren.

Heart picking up, he scrubbed the worst of the mess off his hands and headed for the hallway.

Maybe he would finally have some good news for Kain and they could put this stuff behind them.

SAMUEL folded his arms, eying Nick.

"What?" Then Nick considered the vibe between Samuel and Siren. "Nothing really happened between me and your boss," he clarified.

"Please, what do I care what he does? He's the biggest slut in this city," Samuel said in disgust, but Nick caught the live wire of pain buried in Samuel's dismissal. He didn't want to, but he obviously *did* care about Siren.

"Good thing. Can you imagine if you hooked up? He'd be Samuel's Siren."

A smile barely touched Samuel's lips, his spaniel-brown eyes warming slightly. "If I ever make a move, he *will* be."

"Whoa," Nick said, eyes widening. Samuel might play the role of Siren's servant, but he had a feeling it would be a different story if they ever got as far as the bedroom—or any accommodating surface.

Samuel was a strange combination: pale hair, dark eyes, and a secret fire burning. Siren had no idea what he was toying with.

"We can't find Dr. Armand Leyland anywhere. It's like he's a ghost…. Just traces," Samuel said. "But we did find someone else. Someone who was living on Kain's land up until recently."

Nick frowned. "You mean Finn? I'd like to talk to him, find out what the fuck is going on! He drugged Kain."

Samuel shook his head. "No. Not Finn."

"INTERESTING." Nick's finger grazed the carving of an antelope in Luke Munroe's apartment.

"It's a Chi—"

"Chiwara, I know. A carving of the antelope used for rituals in Mali."

"Very good, cher." Luke eyed Nick, pushing back his bronze hair so a dragon tattoo flashed on one bicep, dark eyes narrowed on Nick's face. "I'm impressed."

"You sound like one of my professors." Nick gave a wry smile. "I'd really like to understand how you ended up a captive on Kain's land. I'd swear he had no idea! Was it Finn again?" Nick's eyes narrowed.

"Well...." Luke cleared his throat, as it was still raspy from his captivity. "It's slightly embarrassing." He stretched his tall frame, which was too thin.

Samuel had told Nick that if they hadn't found the shape-shifter wandering the woods near campus the night they'd been nosing around for Kain, Luke might have died; he'd been starved and delirious, searching frantically for Finn.

"I know you're a shifter. Maybe start there since Samuel told me that much. May I sit down?" Nick propped his leather portfolio by the door.

Luke nodded wearily. "I'm not sure I could stop you if I wanted to at the moment, cher." His mouth firmed. "But shifters heal quickly and I am especially motivated."

Nick sat down on a couch with a fire-red throw made of mohair. It looked like something else Munroe may have picked up in his travels. Obviously this had been his home base for a while. "Let's start with your interest in Kain."

Luke shrugged. "I'm not, not especially. He was just Finn's employer. For a while I wondered if they were something more...." His dark eyes flashed.

Nick held up a palm. "Finn told me himself that they'd never gotten that far. They are just friends."

Luke made a growling sound that seemed to penetrate Nick's flesh and make his bones vibrate. *Primal.*

"So you're his Alpha, the man Finn is in love with."

Unexpectedly, Luke's eyes filled. He turned away sharply and Nick realized that in his debilitated condition, he was probably revealing more to a stranger than a proud man would be comfortable with.

He went to the small galley kitchen and poured a glass of water, returning to hand it to Luke silently.

Luke drank it, eyes holding Nick's. "Finn still feels that way?"

"Yes," Nick answered gently. "I think not a day goes by that he doesn't think of you."

Luke closed his eyes tightly. "I meant to let him go; he was too young for the kind of commitment I needed."

"Becoming your human submissive."

Luke nodded.

"But you, you weren't too young to bond with him?"

"You're very wise, cher," Luke noted. "I needed to know he was safe. I let him go and it was like… removing a part of myself. I followed him to this city and tried not to kill any man he slept with."

"He's not too young for you now."

"No. I was going to get in touch with him again when he began acting strangely. I tried to talk to him one night and that's when *he* tricked me."

"Finn?"

Luke shook his head. "The monster that holds him enthralled. I think it can change its shape, but it's almost certainly a revenant."

Nick's face twisted. "Like Mark. If it looks like Mark, it would have to be able to hide its appearance."

Luke nodded. "I taught Finn how to disguise himself, take on the appearance of another. It's just a simple glamour. I think maybe the thing forced him to share this knowledge."

"This revenant has been killing for months and using Finn to make Kain think he was responsible."

Luke nodded. "I want to feel its neck under my teeth, but first I must find Finn, make him safe." Luke's fists balled. "I'm so fucking weak, but Finn... he's my earth fae."

"I think the revenant also stalked Kain's friend Ross, turned him against Kain. Whoever is behind this wants some kind of revenge against Kain. Wanted to take everything from him."

Luke's eyebrows rose. "Finn got caught up somehow."

Nick leaned forward, elbows pressing over a *National Geographic* on Luke's coffee table. It seemed to center around wolf packs, which struck him as fitting for a shifter's apartment. "Just to be clear on one thing: he's not going to hurt Finn."

"I'm sorry?" Luke blinked.

"Kain. He'd rather die than hurt a hair on Finn's head. He hasn't admitted it to me, but I think he's found the idea of Finn betraying him damn near unbearable. He doesn't let people close easily."

"Nick, you're obviously emotionally involved, so how can I trust you? I can't let Kain hurt Finn. I didn't let Finn bond to me, but I was unable resist bonding myself to *him*. If he falls...."

"Luke." Nick climbed to his feet, touched Luke's arm. The skin was chilly to the touch. He looked into Luke's shadowed eyes, trying to reach him.

"He wakes me up, you know?"

"Where you live, I know," Nick agreed. "Kain's not a sentimental man, but his actions...."

"Okay." Luke's shoulders slumped. "What we need to do now is figure out where Finn might be. Um. Want some tea? I've been drinking some homeopathy shit to bring up my body temperature somewhere normal."

Nick shook his head. "Help yourself. You know, I keep going back to the night of the fire in Kain's apartment. So much went down that night. Kain changed and was marked. His best friend wrote him off and…." Nick mused. "Someone died."

KAIN leaned against the low-slung body of his green sports car. All he wanted was to find Nick, drag him home, protect him, but when he raised his gloved hand, it was trembling. He clenched it into a fist.

Manners had hammered him over and over again, no doubt for the prestige of solving the serial murder case, but Kain couldn't remember. He hoped to God he hadn't hurt anyone but—

Was Nick right? Was Finn somehow tied up in this? His fingers found his scarred cheek, rubbing…. Finn had been there for him through some very dark times.

"Do you think it's wise to seek out Nick while you feel this way?" A mild voice interrupted his thoughts.

"What the fuck do you want?" Kain growled, not happy to see Siren lurking near the police station.

Siren shrugged. "Maybe I feel responsible. I did make you, after all."

"Make me what?" Kain's lips twisted. "A monster?"

"Surely that's for you to decide?" Siren lifted his brows. "I've just been with your Nick."

Kain's eyes narrowed and settled on a bright mark on Siren's neck.

Siren smiled.

Kain took a deep breath, tamping down his instinctive rage. "He didn't let you touch him."

"So sure?"

"Yes." Kain squelched the doubt. "Nick wouldn't be disloyal. It's not in him."

Jan Irving

"You're fortunate," Siren agreed.

"I have places to be." Kain opened the driver's-side door.

"Do you think you should go after him while you're so weak? Remember you once put him in the hospital." Siren stepped close. "Nearly killed him, didn't you? Take me; drink from me."

"You'd like that, wouldn't you?" Kain shook his head.

Siren sighed, looking exasperated. He reached out and grazed the scarring, swallowing when Kain jerked away. "I'd like to see you the way you looked that night at Manticore. The most beautiful man I'd ever seen."

Kain caught his hand. "Touch me again and you'll regret it."

"Do you really need to carry these now you're with Nick?" Siren pushed.

Kain's jaw tightened as he struggled with himself. "I'm not asking for your help."

Siren reached out, touched Kain's tense shoulder.

And Kain's lips covered the bite Nick had made. Siren gasped as he bit down. Hard.

SIREN was panting, leaning against Kain's car. Kain licked the mark.

Hoarsely, Siren said, "Kain, I wanted to tell you...."

"What?"

"The losing time. It's not normal for us."

Kain looked away, eyes bleak like the late-winter cityscape. "I figured. Nick thinks Finn's involved somehow. Whatever the fuck is going down, I'm going to get to the bottom of it. Fix it. Find Nick and get his bossy little ass back under my roof." His lips quirked. "Let him work with a contractor and renovate my house."

Siren studied Kain. "You love him."

"Yes."

"Does he know?"

"How could he not?" Kain looked faintly annoyed. "I promised to tear out my seventies bathroom for him!"

"THINK about it," Nick continued, counting off fingers. "Kain was changed that night. He and Ross fought. And Aaron, Ross's boyfriend, died."

Luke nodded, sipping the herb tea he'd made for himself.

Nick leaned forward. "Or did he?"

Nick's Blackberry beeped imperiously and he checked it. "Kain! He sounds in a mood. I'll just text him back where he can find me...."

A knock on Luke's apartment door made Luke's eyes widen.

"No one knows you live here?" Nick guessed.

"Not 'til Siren helped me back to my place." Luke shook his head, unlocking the door. "Maybe Kain tracked you down already with his help."

Bang!

Nick dropped his Blackberry.

Luke lay on the floor, bleeding, staring up at the man who had shot him.

Finn smiled coldly at him. "Hello, Luke. Silver. You'll stay down." He pointed the gun at Nick. "And *you,* dear, sweet, interfering little Nick. You just couldn't leave it alone, could you? Kain was isolated, disgraced, ripe to fall for the murders of all those whores." His eyes narrowed. "Silver won't kill you but a bullet will."

CHAPTER 30

"WHERE the fuck is Nick?"

Luke's eyes snapped open.

"I'm not dead?" His voice sounded curious, removed to his own ears.

Scarred face, green glowing eyes. Kain.

Who faded from Luke's vision only to reappear a moment later with a dish towel featuring Quan Yin, Chinese goddess of mercy. Somehow her sorrowful face and Finn's got mixed up in Luke's head so that he whispered, "Please let me heal you, Finn…."

"Siren told me about you; you're a shape-shifter. Tough. So you should be okay. I've called someone to take care of you." Kain had his phone in one ear. "And I called 911."

"Oh, good. If I don't make it, be sure to get the bullet as a memento. Solid silver," Luke mumbled.

"What the hell is going on?" A new voice, shocked.

Kain stood. "I need you to take care of him, Ross. And stay with him tonight; something's going down I don't want you mixed up with."

"Did you…?" Ross swallowed thickly. "I can't believe you'd hurt someone."

"I never have." Kain's voice was flat, certain.

Mask

KAIN'S gaze took in the leather portfolio leaning by the door, the abandoned Blackberry on the floor in front of the couch.

He knelt by Luke, shaking him. "Who took Nick?"

"Finn," Luke whispered. "He shot me and—"

"Do you know *where*?"

"Nick was talking about…." Luke closed his eyes, grimacing as he tried to remember. "About that fire at your apartment. How he was convinced all you'd been through… was connected to that night."

Kain's mouth hardened. "The fire. Someone died." He looked at Ross. "Or did he?"

"What are you saying?" Ross whispered.

"Nick thinks someone's been stalking both of us for months. Someone who maybe wanted to get back at me… and you," Kain said. "You haven't met someone recently, have you?"

"Not that it's any of your business, but yes. He reminded me of—" Ross paled. "Oh, my God! He was so jealous of you! I told Aaron over and over that we'd only ever been friends."

"Stay with him." Kain pushed Luke flat when he tried to struggle to his feet. "You're shot, remember?"

LUKE came around as he was loaded into an ambulance, Ross climbing in with him, looking dazed.

"F-Finn," Luke whispered.

"Shhhhh. I'm sure Kain won't let anything happen to him." Ross's eyes were moist. "He's actually a very good friend."

"The thing behind this… you know him?"

Ross rubbed his jaw, still pale. "I might have been dating him recently. Again."

"I B-BROUGHT him, Aaron! The little troublemaker and his big-fucking-mouth." Finn shoved Nick into the gaping brick ruin of the penthouse.

Nick looked around, taking in sodden furniture, the burned-out kitchen with silver appliances, an Italian hanging fixture nearly at floor level.

The place was only a little worse off than Kain's house, he thought with a touch of graveyard humor.

"Kain's fuck pad," a grave voice informed him. "Once upon a time."

"So I gather." Nick folded his arms, trying not to give away how scared he was. "You're Aaron, aren't you? Ross's boyfriend, Kain's rival. One of the dark fey fed too deeply off you the night of the fire and…." He swallowed, remembering how he'd almost died when Kain had lost control.

He took a deep breath, steadying himself.

Kain. Kain will come for me.

A rough laugh, like a blade scoring wet brick. "Finn's mind is a little broken, like the rest of him, but he's been very useful this evening, bringing you here and disposing of Luke."

Nick's breath left him as Aaron stepped from the shadows. The cold, the driving rain, dissipated the worst of the smell but—

"Oh, fuck!" he whispered.

"This is what your Kain made of me! You think *he's* scarred? The fucker could still hire someone to service him, but those same whores would look at me and—"

Nick panted, hand cupped over his nose to ward off the scent of the revenant. "All those boys. *You* raped them, killed them."

A smile revealed oozing gums. "Mitchell thought he'd done it! I planned to lure Ross into that big pile where Kain had hidden himself and make it look like Kain had done his best friend." The grind of denuded bone as Aaron lurched closer. "But then he found you. How, I don't know, but you weren't one of the little rent boys he used. I couldn't find you."

"In a chat room," Nick clarified, throat tight as he saw Obsidian really had been lost, needing rescue, just as he'd sensed so long ago. "We met on the Internet."

"He became obsessed with you. Watching you at night working at that Pancake House. One night I almost had you when you threw out the trash but…. He wouldn't have liked you so much after I was done!"

Aaron flattened a bony hand against one of the pillars, leaving a smear of congealed blood.

"Even set up your little boyfriend, Miguel, so you would break up and then Kain could touch you, have you. What would be better than if he believed he'd killed *you*, his obsession? But Finn here kept fucking up, so I couldn't get to you."

Nick shuddered and looked to Finn.

Finn stared back, eyes glassy but oozing slow tears, as if he were locked inside himself, locked inside since Aaron had violated his mind, broken it.

"And Mark?" He swallowed thickly, not wanting to know, but driven now. He'd told Kain they had to look in the shadows.

"He was the quintessential victim. Kain already hated him for touching you. Finn kept me apprised of everything that went down at the house. I made him in my image, but taught him enough to trick you on Halloween."

"A revenant," Nick choked. "You played the role of my rescuer, Armand. Was it just a game to you, watching Mark stalk me?"

"Mark fucked up. He lacked my patience."

Aaron yanked Finn close.

Finn made a high, soft sound as teeth sank into his neck, tearing.

"*No!*" Nick lunged for Finn. Aaron shoved Finn aside, so he crumpled to the burned-out hardwood, gasping.

"Leave him alone!" Nick bent down to cradle a shivering Finn, bruises, blood; for months he'd been caught in a nightmare, kind, gentle, trying to be a friend to Kain. Even warning Nick away… to protect him, not from Kain, but from Aaron?

A fist caught Nick's hair, yanking his head back. Aaron loomed over him, so fucking strong, teeth hung with shreds of skin.

"Niiiiicky. Your innocence, I want to put a bruise on it," he said in that same affectionate voice he'd used the night he'd stalked Nick and Kain through Kain's house.

Glass shattered. Nick blinked as water lashed his eyes through the open windows, the tattered curtains shifting like rising ghosts.

Kain.

Hair in his eyes, crouched, glowing green eyes.

He leaped for Aaron, hands wrapped around rotted flesh clinging to exposed bone. Wisps of hair shaking, plastered to a bare gleaming skull. Throwing Aaron across the room to smash into brick.

And then Siren was also there, rolling with the thing, Aaron. Nick fell back, holding Finn, protective, watching Kain and Siren's shadows writhe as lightning illuminated the apartment in a burning second.

In the dark again, the rain striking like piercing needles in flesh, Nick's hand searching, anything, anything…. Groping, hand on the empty wooden block that once had held kitchen knives.

He grabbed the kitchen counter and made it to his feet.

Kain with his arm around Aaron's neck, struggling.

Mask

Siren on the floor, head down, black hair soaked, bleeding—

Nick swung and the heavy wood cracked two of Aaron's ribs. Eyes in open sockets tracked his movement as he struck again and again. Gasping, tears mingling with the rain.

Kain sinking his teeth into Aaron, fingers gripping flesh like webs, tearing—

And then Aaron was down and Kain stared across the space at Nick who was shivering, soaked, splashed by Aaron's blood.

With a choked sound, Nick rested safely in Kain's arms.

Kisses burning his face, his neck. But then Kain was shaking him. "I told you not to play detective!"

Nick leaped higher in Kain's arms, wrapping his legs around him as well as his arms. "Kain. God!"

HIS coat wrapped around Nick, Kain looked over his shoulder at Siren, who was rubbing his shoulder, one eye swelling. He didn't look the smooth entertainer now.

"He's safe." There was relief in the enticing velveteen voice.

Kain gave a curt nod.

"Finn's in my car; I'll take him to his Luke," Siren promised. "Samuel will... dispose of Aaron."

"Siren," Kain sighed. "Maybe one day, if Nick—"

Siren shrugged, lips twisting. "Tempting as your offer is, I don't think Samuel would forgive me."

Kain lifted a brow. "That matters to you?"

Siren didn't answer, already heading back to his vehicle.

IN HIS bed at Kain's house, Nick woke a few days later.

"Finn?" he croaked.

"Shhhh," Kain chided. "You were far too sick. I didn't like it!"

"I'm sorry, Kain. I fucked up and you had to rescue me."

"You did fuck up, but I'd call it even. You rescued us both the other night, remember?" Kain stroked Nick's sweaty hair away from his forehead. "And anyway… you came down with a bad flu bug from getting soaked at the apartment."

"Kind of a comedown for the boyfriend of a superhero," Nick said ruefully.

"Some superhero." Kain played with Nick's fingers. "You were right about everything. It was never me hurting anyone."

"Only yourself."

Kain swallowed, nodding. "You had a visitor while you were sleeping."

"Who?" Nick frowned, drowsy, holding Kain's hand.

"My son wants to meet you when you're conscious."

Nick's lips curved. It would be okay. Kain was healing. He'd pulled off his rescue of the prince in the tower. "I'd like that," he said shyly. "As sizzling as our online conversations were, do you know what really drew me to you?"

Kain shook his head, looking bemused.

"I knew you needed me. And now." He licked his lips. "I want my reward."

"Kitten!" Kain shoved him back onto his pillows. "You're too sick."

"'M a bit feverish," Nick judged. "But getting off helps."

"I doubt the nurse I hired will approve, Nick." Kain swallowed thickly and Nick read his eyes, what he didn't put into words.

I missed you.

"No screwing around now. If you continue to get better, you can consider it your reward." Kain stroked the hair off Nick's forehead. His fingers were trembling slightly.

Noticing that, Nick smiled. He knew where he stood, how Kain felt. He pulled him close and whispered his fantasy.

TWO nights later, since he couldn't entice Kain any sooner while he was still so weak, Nick crouched in the awful seventies bathroom, nude, handcuffed to the towel rail.

He looked over his shoulder at the shadow looming in the doorway, knowing just who it was.

He remembered Obsidian telling him he wanted *to chain you in darkness. You love being so fucking helpless. You'll love taking cock, any cock, but especially mine.*

He made a needy sound as lubed fingers penetrated.

"Shhhhhh."

Kain kneeling behind him, his knees between Nick's, and then the broad head broached him and his head fell back as he made another soft sound.

Oh, yes, this is what he'd been craving.

Fucked like one of Kain's hustlers, eyes heavy lidded as he lived it at last. "I love you," he whispered.

Kain's fingers twisted in his hair. "Mine, Nick."

Kain didn't say the words, but Nick felt them, in the building heat, in the way he licked his neck and then the searing bite that made Nick gasp.

Love against his skin.

JAN IRVING has worked in all kinds of creative fields, from painting silk to making porcelain ceramics, to interior design, but writing was always her passion.

She feels you can't fully understand characters until you follow their journey through a story world. Many kinds of worlds interest her, fantasy, historical, science fiction and suspense—but all have one thing in common, people finding a way to live together—in the most emotional and erotic fashion possible, of course!

http://www.janiceirving.com
http://jan-revealed.livejournal.com

www.ingramcontent.com/pod-product-compliance
Lightning Source LLC
Chambersburg PA
CBHW051541260626
47170CB00003B/1045